DR. FAKE FIANCE

LOUISE BAY

Published by Louise Bay 2023

ISBN – 978-1-80456-015-0

ONE

Beau

Nothing beats the French Alps. Blue skies, white powder snow, sunshine—not to mention the views. It's invigorating. It's life-affirming. It's life-*changing*. That's why I decided last night to ask Coral, the woman I'm here with, whether she wants to move to London and into my apartment. I'm not far off thirty, all my brothers are settling down, and I really enjoy going on trips with Coral. She's fun, up for adventure, gorgeous—we're really compatible.

We stand in place for the chairlift and it scoops us up, heading toward the top of my favorite run in this area. The Sarenne is an infamous ten-mile black run, the longest in the world, and three thousand and thirty meters above sea level. To my mind, it's the jaw-dropping views that make it special, especially the vista just before you start. That's when I'm going to ask Coral to move in with me. I didn't plan this before I came out here, but we're having such a great time, I thought, why not? We both like the same things and it would give us some time to get to know each other more.

"You ready?" I ask from beside her as the end of the lift comes into view.

"I'm going to beat you this time," she replies. She's competitive and knows how to have fun. Every time we take a trip together, I like her a bit more. She's opened up a little this trip about how she wants to move on from yachting and put down roots. It's perfect timing.

I chuckle. "Okay then."

We slide off the chairs and come to a stop by the sign directing people down the mountain.

"Take a picture, will you?" she asks. Coral's Instagram is impressive. It helps that she works on superyachts, where there are plenty of photo opportunities.

I pull out my camera and she poses by the sign. I take a couple of shots and send them to her.

"Okay, let's do this," she says, snapping the visor on her helmet shut.

"Yeah," I say. "Just one thing before we do." I'm grinning. I can't wait to see her face when I ask her.

She stops, slightly ahead of me, turns back and lifts her visor. "What?"

"So I've been thinking about stuff."

She glances at the start of the run and then back at me.

I continue. "We always enjoy our trips together. We're compatible. We enjoy each other's company. I thought it might be nice if you moved to London." I fumble at the Velcro fastening of my pocket and pull out my front door key. "How about we live together?"

She laughs and I grin back, but she just nods to the start of the run. "Are we going or what?"

I bristle at her just ignoring my question. "Yeah, when you've answered me."

"But you're not...serious?" she asks. "You can't *actually* think I'm going to give up my job and move to London."

"You said you were looking to move on from yachting. It's not like I can easily practice medicine in the south of France."

"Right," she replies. "And I'm not asking you to. Because, this—" She gestures to me and then back to her with her ski pole. She laughs again, and this time I can't help hearing a sharp edge to the sound. "You're not the guy I settle down with. You're the guy *before* the guy I settle down with. The warm-up guy."

I can't quite see because of her helmet, but the tone of her voice tells me she's rolling her eyes, like I'm ridiculous for thinking she might want to get serious with me.

"What are you talking about?"

She sighs. "I'm not wasting time talking about this. I want to have fun. Are you coming or not?"

"That's it?"

"That's what?"

"I just asked you to move in with me and you basically were an arsehole about it."

"She sighs. I'm not being an arsehole. I'm being realistic. We're nothing. We never were anything. We're never going to be anything. Buddies, yeah. Friends who go on trips together. But we were never more. And anyway, I was going to tell you—I got engaged last month."

Engaged? Why the fuck is she here with me?

I feel like my head's about to explode. It's not hurt I feel, just anger I've been so foolish.

I try and take a step toward her, and it's not like the scenery and the helmet, the ski gloves and poles don't remind me, but somehow, for a second, I forget I'm wearing skis and I trip over my own legs. I overcorrect and before I know it, I'm falling backward.

I feel the orange mesh fence that cordons off the edge of the mountain against my back, and for a split second, I think, yeah, I'm just going to land on my arse. Then time slows down and the orange mesh gives out. I'm not sure if I've toppled over it or pushed through it, but I'm kicking out my legs, trying to get my balance. I don't even know which way is up at this point. And then I stop feeling the ground. Not on my hands, not on my legs.

I'm free-falling.

TWO

Vivian

Getting my own coffee is a luxury. Sounds weird, but the thing I'm looking forward to most now I'm in London is being able to go to a coffee shop. It's just a flat white, but to me, it's freedom. I used to get my own coffee in New York, until TMZ found out where I lived. I was ambushed, then I was papped coming out of my apartment building and it was plastered all over Page Six. Another resident of the building might have alerted them. New Yorkers don't like celebrities in their buildings. They might have been trying to drive me out. But then again, it could have been my fiancé, determined to twist the knife he'd planted deep in my back.

I've tried to keep my outfit simple, just like in New York before I was outed. I've pulled on my training gear, nothing too attention-grabbing. I like to keep it plain and black—leggings, t-shirt and a zipped hoodie. No patterns, no large brand names that will make me stand out. I grab a Yankees cap, stuff my hair into it, pull my sunglasses on and go.

I've learned my lesson from New York and have rented a house in London. That way, there's no doorman to be bribed for details of my coming and going, and no other residents to chatter about me to anyone who'll listen. Nope, I can just arrive and leave as I please without being gawked at. Not even my manager knows where I am.

I pull my front door closed on the house on Chester Terrace. It's a gorgeous cream stucco house that looks just as pretty as the pictures I saw online that made me want to rent it. Plus, it has a recording studio in the basement—not that I've used it since I arrived two days ago.

Because jet lag.

And heartbreak.

The outside of the house is surrounded by black iron railings, it's a block away from Regent's Park, and just two blocks from the coffee shop I'm about to test out.

I've been practicing a British accent. Vivian Cross definitely doesn't have a British accent, so hopefully if someone does suspect it's me, I'll throw them off.

I put my earbuds in as I walk, but don't turn them on. I need to know if someone is on to me, but I want to look the part. Head down, I turn left, away from the park. There aren't many people about. It's early after all.

A middle-aged man with a small dog—a Pomeranian or something—comes toward me. I keep my head down as we pass. He doesn't seem to suspect anything. I glance over my shoulder, but he's not looking back as if to say—*was that Vivian Cross I just passed?*

My heart inches higher in my chest. I'm doing this! I'm out in public and no one is noticing me.

I pass three more people before I get to Coffee Confidential, and none of them give me a second glance. I have to trap my lip between my teeth to stop myself from grinning like a Muppet.

Now's the real test. I push open the door and it's like the bell is as loud as Big Ben. I freeze at the sound, but no one turns around. One guy on the right looks up from his newspaper, but looks down immediately, like he's waiting for someone and when he registers I'm not that person, he's not interested. Suits me.

I take a breath and head over to the line. There are just two people before me.

The guy in front is tall with mussed light brown hair and a blue t-shirt. From the back, his broad shoulders make me feel like I'm on a yacht and he's a sail. His navy polo shirt clings at his trim waist and he looks like he's right out of a Ralph Lauren ad.

I pull out my phone, just for an excuse to keep my head down. I can't see anything with my glasses on, but no one needs to know that.

As I take the phone out of my hoodie pocket, it's like it's alive—practically launching itself out of my hand and onto the floor at the feet of Ralph Lauren man. We both crouch down and he gets to my phone first. I try not to look at him as he hands it over, but I can feel his stare boring into me as if it's searching for something. I can't avoid glancing at his hand as he passes me my phone. It's large with a tan that suggests he's spent the entire summer outside.

"Thanks," I say and then I mentally chastise myself for not using the British accent. But it was just a syllable, right? How different can one syllable be in the same language.

"My pleasure," he replies as we both stand, me pointedly not looking at him. "What part of the States are you from?"

Apparently a syllable can give far too much away about a person.

"New York," I snap—just like a New Yorker not interested in the guy talking to me would. I look down at my phone, trying not to wince at how rude I just was. I'm just *really* not interested in having a conversation. Especially with an attractive man. Or any kind of man. Yesterday, I looked up whether there is such a thing as an all-female commune I can escape to. For now, London and a snappish attitude will have to do.

"Love New York," he says, ignoring my not-so-subtle signs to stop talking. In New York, I could have sung the entire soundtrack of *Dirty Dancing*—my favorite movie soundtrack—and the guy in front wouldn't have flinched. But not in London. I thought the Brits were meant to be uptight. The line moves and we all step forward. "You go ahead of me. You look like you're in a hurry."

Urgh. If I say no, he'll insist and we'll end up having more of an interaction than I want.

"Thanks," I say and step forward. There's only one person in front now. I need to get out of here before anyone else tries to speak to me.

Another cashier arrives at the counter, which means me and Mr. Ralph Lauren end up ordering at the same time. I can see the cashier grinning up at him as I order my flat white, and she breaks out into a loud laugh at something he says. I haven't seen his face, but Becky—whose name is on her badge—is obviously quite smitten with him. Maybe he's a regular. I pay and move to the pick-up station, happy that none of the staff have taken any notice of me at all. This outing would be perfect if I hadn't dropped my phone.

Of course, my new friend follows me because he's waiting for his drink too.

"I'm Beau," he says as he stands next to me.

I'm fake-engrossed in my phone, but I nod like I've heard what he said. But I don't offer my name in return.

He's not deterred. "What's your name?"

I sigh. Why won't this guy leave me alone? There are plenty of women in London to hit on. "Adele," I say. It's the fake name I usually use when checking into hotels—a little joke I have with myself, since my last album outsold her last album in its first week. Of course, I love Adele. *Everyone* loves Adele. That doesn't mean we don't have a friendly rivalry. But we're adults. It's not about to turn into a Katy-Taylor situation.

"It's a pleasure to meet you, Adele," he says. Before he can ask any more questions, Adele's name is called and I step forward to take my coffee. I don't even say bye to Mr. Ralph Lauren, just scuttle out of the store and head back to the house.

I got my own coffee and no one realized who I was. I'm calling it a win.

THREE

Beau

Not many people have a real understanding of how lucky they are to be alive. I'm not one of those people. And as long as I'm alive, I need coffee every morning.

I head toward Coffee Confidential and spot the woman who was in there yesterday—Adele. She's a New Yorker and not much into chitchat. "Hey!" I say as we both reach the door at the same time.

"Hi," she replies as I hold the door open, trying not to smart as my shoulder burns. She doesn't so much as give me a smile. She was a little frosty yesterday, too.

If I'd let getting rejected by Coral and then falling off a three-thousand-foot glacier get to me, I'd be just as frosty back. But I'm not that guy. Lucky for me, I only fell twenty feet and, even luckier, I only dislocated my shoulder. The cherry on the cake is that Coral didn't check in to make sure I was alive. There's absolutely no ambiguity in regards to our relationship anymore.

The fall cut my skiing holiday short, but I can't really

complain. I didn't want to hang around to say another word to Coral.

"How are you this morning? It's Adele, right?" I ask, following her inside.

She pulls her mouth into a tight smile but she doesn't reply. Silently, she communicates, *Mate, fuck off. I'm not interested.* Fair enough. She probably gets hit on by guys all the time—she looks like she might be cute if you strip off the dark glasses and cap.

The queue is shorter today and Adele goes right up to the counter. She doesn't take long to place her order and move across to the collection station. She clearly doesn't want anyone bothering her. She's fixated on her mobile and is standing right up close to the station, with her front angled toward the wall—like she's put herself in the corner for naughty behavior. I chuckle to myself. She *really* doesn't want anyone bothering her.

"Good morning, beautiful," I say to Kimberly, behind the counter.

"Hi Beau." She beams at me. Is it me or are redheads always gorgeous? "Your usual?"

"I'm honored you remembered." I place my palm on my chest, then hold out my phone to pay.

"How could any of us forget?" she asks, blushing at her own response. "You're always so...happy."

It's nice to think me coming into her coffee shop adds something to her day—a serotonin hit or just an additional smile.

"Have a great day," I say as I move over to the pickup station, making sure I give Adele her space.

They call out her name and without looking, she reaches out for her cup, still focused on her phone. She turns and charges toward the door. Before I can move, she slams into me and her scorching-hot coffee explodes onto my chest.

I react quickly and before I'm aware of the heat, which I know will come, I drop my phone and rucksack and strip off my t-shirt.

"Fuck," I hear her say. "I'm so sorry."

She turns back to the station and picks up some napkins and offers them to me. I take them from her. Not because I really need them—I have a towel in my bag. But I don't want her to feel bad. "Thanks." I smile at her. "I'm fine."

"But your shirt." She's got dark glasses on, but I don't need to see her eyes to know what she's looking at. It's the same thing everyone looking at me—bare-chested in the middle of the coffee shop—is focused on.

My scars.

A long time ago, I wasn't as lucky as I was today when hot liquid came into contact with my body. My skin is long-since healed, but the marks remain. It's like the skin on one side of my chest and my left arm has melted and rearranged itself. It's a different texture to the skin on the rest of my body, and various areas remain numb to this day.

I was very lucky.

Today, the coffee down my front won't require a hospital stay. Or permanent marks that will stay with me for the rest of my life.

I still have seven more lives.

"God, I'm so sorry," she says again, still keeping her sunglasses fixed in place.

"It's not a problem. Just an accident." I dry myself off with the napkins, then wave my drenched t-shirt in front of me.

"Here," she says, unzipping her hoodie. "Take my jacket."

I laugh. "That's very sweet of you, but I don't think it will fit."

"It's oversized."

"Still not quite big enough." I rifle through my backpack and find another t-shirt—the one I was planning to wear on my run home.

"Can I buy you a new shirt?" She pulls out her wallet and starts to take out cash.

I put my hand on her wrist. "Stop. Seriously, I'm fine. My t-shirt will wash. There's no harm done here."

The barista calls my name. I pull on my fresh shirt but before I can grab my americano, Adele grabs it and hands it to me.

"Thanks," I say. "That was nice of you."

"At least let me pay for your coffee," she says.

I laugh again. Why does this woman keep trying to give me money? "I've paid already. It's all fine. Don't worry." I sling my rucksack on my back and make my way to the exit.

"Are you sure you're not hurt?" she asks. "Should you get checked out by a medical professional?"

I hold the door open and she steps through. "I *am* a medical professional. I'm a doctor. And I'm honestly fine. You don't need to worry."

We stand outside on the pavement facing each other. Her dark glasses are huge and hide most of her face, but not her pillowy lips and sharp Cupid's bow. She's completely kissable. Coral might have cured me of any desire to settle down, but I've not turned into a monk. Is that blonde hair under that cap?

"You're a doctor?" she asks. I nod. "That's good. So you're not burned?"

"Not this time," I reply, acknowledging I know she's seen my scars. I'm not embarrassed by them. It was so painful for so many months, but those burns changed my life in all the right ways.

"Right."

"Can I walk you somewhere, Adele?" I offer.

She sucks in a breath, like she's remembered where she is. She shakes her head.

"It's a beautiful day, what about a saunter around the park?"

"Saunter?" she asks. "That's funny."

"It is?"

She shrugs. "Kinda. It's very British."

"Not very New York," I say.

"Is it beautiful?" she asks.

"The park?" I ask. "You've never been? It's lovely. Come on, indulge me in a ten-minute detour. Then you can feel like you've made up for throwing your coffee at me."

She glances around, almost like she's waiting for someone. Then she takes a deep breath like she's about to step off the platform at a bungee jump. "Okay."

We start to walk toward the park. "Here," I say, holding out my coffee. "Take this if you can cope with black coffee."

She folds her arms. "I'm not throwing my coffee at you and then taking yours. That's a step too far."

I smile. It's more words than she's said to me in total in the twice I've seen her. "Share it with me?"

She shakes her head.

We cross the road and head into the park.

FOUR

Vivian

It's like my heart knows this guy is being genuine, but my body has this weird reaction to new people. It's as if someone presses a "reject" button inside me. If I hadn't thrown scorching coffee over this guy, I wouldn't be walking in the park with him, despite how hot he is.

"You live in London, Adele?" he asks.

He's using the Adele name a lot. I can't decide if he's just one of those people who uses names a lot or whether he knows I'm Vivian Cross and he's testing me. Even though he's a stranger to me and I owe him nothing, I can't help but feel bad because I'm not telling him the truth. I don't know if it's me or him making me feel like that.

"No, just staying a few weeks." The park is nice. The canopy of trees makes it feel so much fresher, almost like we're not in the city. It's been months since I've been in Central Park. After the breakup, I didn't want to go out of my apartment. Everywhere felt unsafe. And then after

TMZ found out where I lived, there was no going out even if I wanted to. Even inside didn't feel safe at times.

"Is it your first time in the UK?"

Not if you count my world tour two years ago. Or when I played Glastonbury three years ago. "I've been here a few times before," I say.

He nods like what I'm saying is really interesting. "For work? Or..."

"Mainly for work," I say. I don't want to lie exactly, but he doesn't need to know who I am. "Tell me more about your job. Must be pretty exciting to be a doctor, huh?"

He chuckles next to me. His laugh makes the corners of his eyes wrinkle adorably and it makes me want to smile. His face is just as much of a Ralph Lauren model as the rest of him. He has a strong jaw and perfect sun-kissed skin—the kind of gorgeous that just gets better with age. "Not exciting exactly, but I enjoy it. I like helping people."

I spot something on the side of the path. It looks like a skeleton on a chair. "What the hell is that?"

"I'll protect you!" He holds out his arms and creates a wall of hard body between me and the skeleton. Then he drops them. "It's a sculpture." A skeleton is draped back-wards over a brass chair, which is set on a bowl that's filling with water. "Seasonal, but it's here year round."

"Okay," I say. People want to make art about all sorts of things, I guess. "You think it's real?" I ask.

"The sculpture?"

"The skeleton," I ask.

"It's not."

"How can you be sure?" I ask. "It looks pretty realistic."

"Well," he says, lifting his hand and scratching the back of his neck. I try not to look at the exposed skin on his taut, brown stomach as he speaks. Partly because it's rude to stare and partly because I'm not sure I should be noticing a man's skin. A man's hands. A man's smile. I'm supposed to be nursing a broken heart. And I'm absolutely, definitely, one hundred percent doing my best to ignore the way a breeze tumbles down my spine when he looks at me. "I'm a doctor. But also, my brother knows the artist."

I look around and find the plaque describing the work. "Urs Fischer. Your brother knows him?"

"Yeah, I think he commissioned some stuff from him. I remember my brother telling me about this piece and how it's not a real skeleton."

"Huh," I say. "What does your brother do? Is he an art collector or something?"

"Definitely not an art collector. Honestly, I'm not quite sure what he does. I know it's something to do with finance." He winces as he speaks.

I laugh because it's exactly how I'd describe what my brother does for a living.

"You have a beautiful smile," he says, and I'm suddenly self-conscious under his stare.

"Thanks," I say, a little flustered by the compliment because it feels so genuine. I have plenty of people in my life who blow smoke up my ass, but this guy? He doesn't seem to know me. He's not on my payroll and it feels good to be noticed by him. I feel special—not because of my singing voice or my songwriting, but because I'm me.

"You have any brothers or sisters?" he asks.

I clear my throat. I don't like lying to the guy, but I don't want to give anything away either. He doesn't need to know who I am. I just want to enjoy this walk through the park and get home. "Yeah. I have a brother." It feels nice to be honest, but I don't add that I have a sister too.

A group of young women come toward us and I turn

away, feigning interest in the sculpture again, my heart pounding in my chest. One of them shouts, "Oh. My. God."

Fuck. I knew I should have gone straight home. I can't be more than a hundred meters from the edge of the park. I could probably run and be home in just a few minutes.

"You okay?" Beau asks from beside me.

I dare to glance around and realize the girls have passed me by. They can't have noticed me. The must have been *oh my god*-ing about something else.

"You seem jumpy," he says.

I manage a fake smile. "I'm fine. Let's keep walking. But let's keep to the edge of the park if that's okay?"

"Yeah, okay." He has to run to catch up to me, but I don't want those girls to figure it out and come back to see if it really is who they thought it was.

"You come here a lot?" I ask. I think if I really lived in Chester Terrace, and I wasn't a celebrity, I would come here a lot. In fact, even given I am a celebrity, I would come here if I lived in London. Just not at the moment. I feel like I have a bounty on my head. It will blow over. It has to.

"I'm staying with my brother at the moment. So, I walk through the park to get to work every day. What about you? Where are you staying?"

"Oh, just back there?" I indicate over my right shoulder with my thumb.

"In King's Cross?" he asks.

"Kinda."

"You never said why you were in town. You here for work?"

"A bit of a break between jobs."

He nods. "Nice. It's such a great city, isn't it?"

Unfortunately, I've not seen much of it. There are lots of benefits to being famous. But there are downsides too.

Not being able to just go out wherever you want is one of them. If I'm on a publicity tour or I'm going out for dinner or something, I make sure I take security. I don't want to have to deal with that right now. Not here. I just need some time to myself. I can't arrange security without telling people where I am. At the very least my assistant would have to know. And at the moment, no one knows. Not even this very attractive man I'm walking through the park with.

"It's a great city," I say. "I like that anyone can be anyone here."

He grins, and I look over at him and then away, because I get a warm buzz in my stomach that feels a little...dangerous. "I love that you see that. That's it exactly. There's space for you, whoever you are."

My heart flitters in my chest—not at the sentiment, however great it is to be able to be yourself, but at his compliment, and the way he's so pleased with what I've said. I nod as we go through a particularly shady spot on the path. I can barely see because of my sunglasses. It doesn't help that clouds have filled the sky.

"You know there's no sun here, right?" Beau says. I glance at him and realize he's kind of asking me to take off my sunglasses.

"I know," I say. These sunglasses feel like armor. With these on, it feels like I'm a few feet away from the world and it's the only way I can handle it.

"As long as you're okay," he says.

He probably thinks someone's punched me in the face and I'm trying to hide a black eye.

"I'm fine. I just don't like...bright lights." My ex-fiancé would always accuse me of liking the bright lights a little too much. In the end, I think he enjoyed the fame more than I ever did.

A couple holding hands walks toward us. I see her glance at me and then whisper to her boyfriend, who then looks over at me.

Shit. I knew I couldn't stay lucky for long.

"Hey," I say, "let's follow this trail down here."

I head between some bushes, dipping so I don't hit my head on the low-hanging branches of the trees.

"You know this isn't a trail, right?" he asks from behind me. We get through the bushes and meet another path, parallel to the one we just left.

"Oh," I say. "I thought this was a cut-through."

The corners of his full mouth lift, but his eyebrows are pulled together like he's finding me half-amusing, half-confounding. I can live with that.

"So what's the story, Adele? Why are you diving into bushes and keeping your sunglasses on in the dark. Are you in witness protection or something?"

I sigh. It's hard to stay anonymous when you're engaging with someone for any length of time. I nod side-ways, toward the bushes. He seems like a decent guy and it's not like he knows where I live. And I can't come back to the park again. I'm about to shock the shit out of someone.

"Stand here." I position him so he's facing the path and I'm opposite him, so if anyone was to pass us, they wouldn't see my face.

"Okay." He's acting like I'm a complete lunatic, but he's going to realize I've got everything to hide.

I take off my cap and let my almost white-blonde hair fall out and then I raise my sunglasses to the top of my head.

"You're..." I wait for recognition to register on his face. "Beautiful."

I put my cap back on, but leave my hair out and my sunglasses off, watching for his reaction. "Thanks."

"You're looking at me like you're waiting for my head to explode," he says.

I look away. "No, I just. No, I was—it's fine. No worries." I bite back a grin. It's been a while since I've met anyone who didn't know exactly who they were meeting. Of course, I always introduce myself with my name, but I can tell by their eager smiles and effusive greetings, they know who I am. This guy doesn't have a clue. And it's like I can hear choirs singing *hallelujah*.

He's not just gorgeous. And charming. And British.

He has no clue who I am.

I don't think I've ever found a man hotter.

He pulls his eyebrows together farther. "Did I miss something?"

"I like you, Beau," I say. I pat him on the arm, trying not to shiver as I hit hard muscle, and we start to walk.

He smiles. "I like you too, Adele."

I laugh. I feel bad I'm lying to this guy. "Adele isn't my real name."

"Oh, okay," he says. "You don't like to give your name out to creeps in coffee shops?"

"Something like that."

"So are you going to tell me?" he asks. "Or do you want me to guess?"

I can't stop grinning. I feel like a freak. I can't remember the last time I smiled so much. "You can guess."

"Esmerelda," he says, without skipping a beat. "Or Gertrude. Yes, you look like a Gertrude."

"Stop," I say, almost giddy at his silliness. "You're a terrible guesser."

He puts his hand to his chest like I've cut him to the core. "That hurts."

I roll my eyes. "My real name is Vivian." I watch, to see

if he starts to connect the dots, but there's not so much as a glimmer of recognition in his eyes.

"Oh that's pretty. So much better than Adele."

I grin and we lock eyes as we walk. "Thanks," I say. "I appreciate it."

"But there's something else, isn't there?" he asks. "I don't know what exactly, but I feel maybe your name isn't Vivian. Or maybe it is and—I'm definitely missing something."

I shrug, not quite sure how to tell him, or whether I should.

"Come on!" he says. "It's like I'm not in on the joke. I have four brothers. You're perpetuating childhood trauma here!"

He's adorable and sexy and funny and it's weird I'm thinking a man is even worth speaking to, let alone *adorable* or *sexy* or *funny*. But here I am.

"I'm Vivian Cross," I stage whisper.

He steps back. "The singer?"

My stomach roils and instantly I hate the fact he now knows who I am. I was enjoying our conversation so much when he thought I was just some girl. "As opposed to...the accountant?"

He laughs. "How did you know that's my accountant's name?" We grin at each other, because he's ridiculous and I kinda like it. "And so the glasses and the cap are a disguise." And there it is, all the dots joined into a tidy picture.

"Urm, yeah." Instantly I feel a little awkward. I put my glasses back on and sweep my hair up into my cap, pulling the front down as low as it will go without knocking off my glasses.

"But this isn't America. I'm not saying you're not famous here. Of course you are. But..."

"But in London, humans don't have facial recognition?" I look up and smile at him.

He shoots me a grin. "I'm not saying that. Just...no one's going to bother you."

I let out a half-laugh. "If you say so, but if you don't mind, I'm not going to risk it. Not at the moment. I've been in the news cycle a little too much for my liking recently." It might have been okay pre-breakup but now, there are new stories about me every day. How I'm heartbroken. How I'm a witch who can't keep a man. How I'm in hiding. How I'm having an affair with a married, older producer. How I'm desperate to date a Kennedy. The list is endless.

"Fair enough. So now you've come clean, what are you really doing in London?"

"I'm really taking a break between jobs. I've got a new album out in a few months and I'll have to travel to promote it. I just wanted a break."

"So you've come to London to have a break except you have to wear a disguise and you can't go anywhere without being worried someone's going to recognize you. I don't see how that's any kind of break."

I get that's how it looks. "You'd be surprised. It's a break being hidden. No one knowing where you are."

"Oh, so the break isn't from work, it's from the people in your life."

I consider it. "Maybe."

"That's very sad. You should spend time with people you want to spend time with."

"I do." My tone is a little defensive. "Mainly." The problem is, Matt was always my safe haven—my rock when I wanted to get away. Being with him, just the two of us— that was the vacation I so desperately craved every now and then. Relaxing with him, all the fears and frustrations would disappear and I'd be able to cope with the fact that everyone in my life was someone I paid to be there. Everyone except Matthew.

The fact that all along he's been at the center of my betrayal makes me want to run away from the world and never come back.

"Maybe I don't. I think if you like and trust everyone you spend time with, you must be very lucky."

His expression is disconcerting, almost like he feels sorry for me. No one's looked at me like that for a very long time. "I am very lucky," he says. "I learned that lesson early and hard." He nods down at the scars on his arm.

"How old were you?"

"Twelve. My brothers and I were chasing each other around the house like feral cats. We knew the kitchen was off-limits when we were acting like that. What can I say? I knew I was about to get caught and pummeled, and the kitchen was the only escape. I ran into my mother carrying a pan of boiling water."

I wince. "Shit."

"It was made worse because I was old enough to know I screwed up, so I ran from my mother because I knew she'd be so angry with me. The pain didn't kick in straight away. By the time she caught up with me and the ambulance had arrived...well, the burns were second and third degree. I spent a lot of time in hospital."

"God, I'm so sorry." Without thinking, I reach for his arm and stroke a finger across the marks that peek out from under his t-shirt. I know from the coffee shop that the scars run over at least one half of his chest.

Our eyes lock and he gives me a small smile. I don't know if it's because he thinks it's weird I'm touching him or because he likes it. I drop my hand, suddenly aware that he's a stranger I probably shouldn't be touching.

"I learned a lot. It made me appreciate life. Ever since, I've wanted to squeeze out every moment of every day. I consider myself incredibly lucky."

I nod, trying to fully absorb what he's saying. He's describing the exact opposite of my life at the moment. "And then I go and pour hot coffee all over you. That must be triggering or something."

"Ahh, it didn't touch my skin. Just my shirt. It's fine." The path splits into two and he nods to the left. We continue walking in that direction. We're deeper into the park now and I don't know why, but I feel kind of protected here. People pass us, but they don't seem to glance in our direction. I start to settle a little.

"So what's it like being an international pop star?" Beau asks.

Lonely, I don't say. I shrug. "I love writing music. And I like playing it for people who enjoy it. I'm very lucky to do what I love."

He narrows his eyes. "That sounds rehearsed."

I laugh, because it's my stock answer when people ask me about my job and he's seen right through it. "Yeah. Maybe."

"So what's it really like? I can't imagine you sit down at your desk or at the piano or whatever at nine in the morning and take a lunch break and then clock off at five."

I glance up at him and grin. "No. It's not like that."

"So what does a typical day look like?"

No day feels typical at the moment. Usually when I'm not writing, or preparing for a tour or a performance of some kind, I'd be at the home Matt and I shared. I'd cook for him, work out. But now? "I don't really have a routine here in London."

"Apart from getting coffee," Beau says.

"Yeah. I know it sounds weird, but it's a treat for me to be able to walk out in public and go get myself a coffee."

"And you can't do that in America? Where did you say you live? New York?"

I don't want to think about New York. Matt moved out but I don't think I'll ever be able to go back to my apartment. The memories of the life we had together and the life we were meant to have together and how it was all clearly a lie. He wasn't the man I thought he was. "Yeah. Sometimes I can get away with it in New York." Not since Matt and I split though. The appetite for paparazzi shots of me looking miserable is at a peak.

Beau checks his watch. "Shit, I have to go. I'm sorry. I see my first patient in fifteen minutes and I'm a fourteen-minute walk from here."

"Don't be sorry. Thanks for being so nice about me spilling coffee on you and triggering your childhood trauma."

"Anytime you want to spill coffee on me, go right ahead." He pauses and his lips purse like he's considering something. "You want to do this again tomorrow? Coffee and a walk in the park?"

My stomach swoops. My immediate thought is tomorrow he'll bring the photographers. At the moment, he could make a couple of thousand dollars from tipping off one of them. I don't want this guy to be a jerk, and he doesn't seem like he is, but I was engaged to a man I'd known twelve years and I thought he was a stand-up guy. My good-guy radar is broken. "Maybe," I reply.

He laughs. "I'll take a maybe. It's been a pleasure,

Vivian Cross. I hope to see you tomorrow." He gives me a two-fingered salute and heads off in the other direction.

I stand and watch him head out of the park for a few seconds. Should I trust him? Probably not, because I can't trust myself to figure out which ones are the bad guys. But maybe I need to see him again to test myself—to prove my theory that the men I attract are villains.

FIVE

Beau

I see Jacob coming down the hill to where I'm standing outside Hampstead ponds. He keeps telling me cold-water swimming will feed my need for adventure. I'd get it if we were in Greenland or something, but we're in Hampstead— home of Harry Styles and Sting—a place where you can't live in anything but a shoebox unless you're a millionaire. It's not like we're off the beaten track here. Plus, my need for adventure has been dimmed a little since coming back from skiing. I don't know what it is. My feet are still itchy, it's just I'm not sure another trip is going to help.

"You're early," he says.

I glance down at my phone to see the time. "Yeah, my last patient didn't turn up." I had a couple of no-shows today and used the time to Google Vivian Cross. Images of her from our walk have been playing through my mind on a loop. It's like she's a song I can't stop humming.

"You ready?" he asks, nodding at the ponds.

I sigh. "Yeah—shock the shit out of me."

"It's better than you think it's going to be."

"If you say so."

"And even if it isn't, what else were you doing tonight? Hanging out with Nathan and Madison and a screaming kid."

"Your niece, you mean?"

"How long have you been there now anyway?" he asks.

"A couple of months. The house is so big, it's not like we're bumping into each other. And Nathan's out a lot."

"Any plans to move out?"

"Probably not before I finish this contract. What's the point? I'll be off somewhere after that and I won't need anywhere to stay." *Maybe I'll be off somewhere,* I think to myself. I don't have any definitive plans. "And when I come back, I'll come and stay with you and Sutton."

He rolls his eyes, but he doesn't say no. So I'm taking it as a yes.

"Where are you off to this time?" he asks.

I shrug and we head down to the arrangement of huts by the waterside. "Probably husky mushing. I've always wanted to learn how. You want to come?" The guy who does the mushing emailed me the other day and I haven't gotten back to him. It's not like me. I don't know if it's getting knocked back—quite literally—by Coral. Or maybe it's my thirtieth looming. I just don't have the same desire to get away.

In fact, I can't stop thinking about a business idea I've been turning over in my mind for the last couple of years: adventure travel for disabled children. I was lucky to survive my burn injuries without any lasting impact other than the physical scars. Other kids aren't so lucky. They miss out on so much.

"What?" He looks at me like I've lost my mind. "You'll

disappear for a month or something. I don't want to leave Sutton."

I groan. "Invite her. We can all go."

"I come from a place of authority when I say husky mushing doesn't make Sutton's list of top ten things she wants to do before she hits forty." He pauses. "You thought about maybe getting a girlfriend to go on these adventures with you?"

I shrug. He doesn't know about me asking Coral to move to London.

"I used to go on trips with Coral."

He chuckles. "Yeah, but she wasn't your girlfriend. You two are just fuck buddies who travel together."

Apparently so. "Yeah, well not anymore," I grumble.

"What?" he asks.

"Nothing." He doesn't need to know about Coral. He doesn't even know about my dislocated shoulder. I can't tell him without it getting back to Mum and she'd just worry. It's easier to keep it to myself.

We head to the changing rooms and start to change.

"There's a new doctor in A&E. Australian. He was telling me about a shark attack he worked on in Perth. You could always go swimming with sharks after husky mushing."

"The idea isn't to get killed, or even attacked. I'm not interested in a near-death experience." My brothers just don't get it.

"I'm sure most people *don't* get killed."

"Oh good," I reply, not trying to hide the sarcasm in my voice. "It's still a no from me. It's not danger I'm interested in, Jacob. I just want to make sure I don't miss out."

Jacob shakes his head at me, unbelieving.

I think back to chatting with Vivian earlier today, her

hair stuffed in a cap and sunglasses on, pleased to be getting her own coffee. Is she miserable hiding from life like that? She can't even walk into Marks & Spencer and pick up a prawn sandwich. What must that be like? I suppose I don't know her well enough to understand the flip side—the parts of her life making up for the lack of M&S prawn sandwiches.

"Would you want to be famous?" I ask as we head outside.

"I think it would depend on why you got famous. I imagine Louis Pasteur felt pretty good about it. Or Marie Curie. But if you're Ian Brady? Not so much."

"I'm not suggesting you might want to start murdering people to get your name in the papers. But I don't know... did you ever want to be a pop star?"

Jacob groans. "Fuck me, mate, is that your next project? Have you ever sung a note in your life? And 'Swing Low Sweet Chariot' when you're five pints in doesn't count."

"I'm not saying I want to be a pop star. I'm just thinking it's probably more difficult than we think." I can't imagine a life in which getting myself a coffee is a big deal. A treat even.

"If you say so. But it's not something I've given much thought to. Why are you asking?"

We come out of the changing rooms and head over to the water. It's a balmy sixteen degrees, but not bad for September—not great for swimming in open water. "Where are the inflatables?" I ask. "And the cocktails?"

"Funny," Jacob says.

We climb into the water, Jacob first, and I don't miss his grimace at the cold as he lowers himself in. What did I sign up for?

"So what's got you obsessed with being famous?" He's

holding on to the steps. "You feel like you missed out by being a GP?"

"No, I..." I'm not sure if I should tell Jacob about Vivian. She was clearly guarding her privacy really carefully. But it's not like Jacob is going to alert the press. "I ran into Vivian Cross."

"The singer?"

I nod as I climb in. The cold is barely noticeable—to me. Jacob's lips are practically blue.

"Where?"

"Just getting coffee. Do you know her? Are you a fan of her music?"

"Not particularly. Sutton plays her in the car sometimes. In fact, I think she has tickets to see her live next year. So how come you ran into her? Was she swarmed by fans?" His teeth are chattering. "I'm freezing, let's swim."

We start a gentle breast stroke and continue to talk. "She had a cap and glasses on. She was trying not to be recognized."

"Wow," he says.

I glance at the trees around us, the expanse of sky above us. It's actually beautiful here in London. Surrounded by green and a bright blue sky. Maybe I'm missing out by not being here for longer. It's nice to do this—something I've never done before—with Jacob. Maybe I'm missing out on all sorts of things because I'm always planning the next trip. Who knows, I might have even put together a business plan for the company I've been thinking about for years.

"Did you speak to her?"

"Yeah. She's nice. Guarded obviously. I just think it must be weird to have to hide out all the time."

"She's probably used to it," he replies. "And anyway, the advantages will outweigh the disadvantages, I'm sure." It was such a Jacob reply. Measured. Sensible. Logical. "I'm going to do some crawl or lose my bollocks in the cold."

"Swimming is definitely the most logical choice out of those two options," I reply.

He dives under then starts a forward crawl and I follow him. After I figure out my breathing, I find the swimming, the cold, the fresh air meditative and soothing. It's almost as if I'm sloughing away the stuff that needs to be left behind and polishing the important things to a glimmering shine, so they can't be missed.

I focus in on Vivian and how much she misses out on the everyday stuff because she's famous, and how maybe I've been a bit like that. I've been traveling the globe, searching for the next thing, so I don't miss out. But maybe I'm missing out anyway, just in a way I didn't expect.

SIX

Vivian

For the first time in over a week, I switch on my US phone and sling it on the counter by the mixing desk. I try and ignore the voicemail notifications and the ping of the messages that follow each other relentlessly. I know without looking the vast majority of the messages and voicemails will be from Tommy, my manager. He's managed me since I was sixteen. He saw something in me, even back then, and I know he'll be hurt I've frozen him out.

It's not personal. I just needed some space. Some time.

It's not that I'm done, or that I'm ready to let the world in. It's just...I want to stop running. And down here in the basement recording studio of Chester Terrace, I feel safe. Protected.

I ignore the phone and take a seat at the baby grand in the live room, behind the glass. I've not even thought about writing since the stuff with Matt happened, but the melody I've had circling my brain for the last few days is tugging on my hand and asking for attention. I'm not ready to give it life. Not yet.

I put my fingers on the keys. I take a breath and start to play. Bach. *Prelude Number 1 in C Major*. I've been playing it since I was six years old and it feels like a cozy blanket on a rainy day.

My dad is a singer and a far better piano player than me. Even now, he still has a slot at a hotel bar in Chicago on Friday nights, playing jazz standards. My mom was a piano teacher, and their shared love of music seeped into my soul. They taught me everything I know.

I switch into the start of "Green Dolphin Street". I need to call my dad. My parents know I'm okay, but I haven't told them where I am. Not because I think they'll knowingly betray me, it's just easy for them to get caught out. Before I know it, someone in the grocery store will have asked Mom what I'm up to and within the hour, Page Six will know I'm in London. My mom will feel like hell and I'll have to move on. It's just easier if they don't know.

The messages ping in one after another.

A recording studio in the basement of the Chester Terrace house serves two purposes. First, I can hide from the housekeeper when she comes three times a week to clean and leave food in my refrigerator. She makes the best lasagna. She doesn't know it's me living here and I'm careful not to leave any clues out that would let her guess. I always make sure I'm down here, but today is the first time I haven't just laid on the sofa and watched movies or scrolled my phone. Today is the first time I've used the instruments down here.

I start singing the melody I've come up with and add some chords on the piano. I can't help but smile. It sounds nice. Happy.

My British stranger, my newfound something.
My British stranger, I just need one thing.
From you.
To me.
There's one thing you have to be.

Beau might have inspired the lyrics, but of course I don't need anything from him. I'm not an idiot. But just having a normal conversation with someone who didn't know who I was—and who didn't seem to want anything from me even after I told him—has been like ducking under the shelter of an umbrella in the middle of a thunderstorm. Maybe I'm already soaked to the skin, but at least it's a temporary cessation of the relentless wet. A welcome break. I'm not dry. I probably won't *ever* be dry, but at least I can open my eyes without getting stung by the driving rain.

Be yourself and I'll be me.
Be yourself and I'll heal me.

I freeze when my phone begins to ring. It's only ten, which means it's five in the morning in the US. Who could be calling me?

I get up from the piano and head back into the control room.

Tommy's name and number flashes on the screen. I take a deep breath, pick up my phone and answer.

"You're up early," I say as if we spoke just yesterday.

There's a brief pause before he replies. "I'm trying to get a workout in."

"Then I guess you should go do that. Self-care is important."

"Thanks for picking up," he says.

I nod silently.

"Can I do anything?" he asks.

"Arrange for Matt's murder. Or...mild dismemberment. Torture at the very least."

"I'm going to state for the record that I know you're joking when you ask me to arrange a homicide. And I think the torture will take care of itself. The guy is...a horrible human." He sighs. I know he's hurting because I'm hurting. "I wish I saw it before it got to this. He just came across as one of the good guys."

I let out a hollow laugh. "I thought so too."

"I've hit him with a ton of lawsuits as we discussed. I think it should shut him up for a while. There haven't been any stories in over a week. I don't know if you've been following things."

"I haven't." It's been difficult, but I've really tried to keep away from social media and the tabloids. I've kept my focus on Bravo and Netflix. I haven't even been able to listen to music. Even other people's music that's clearly not about me and Matt brings back memories.

"Good."

"Have you spoken to Lisa?"

Lisa is the therapist Tommy recommended. "No. I just want to keep everything...private. As much as I can, anyway." I'd usually fly private to the UK, but when I left New York, I didn't even want Betty, my assistant, to know where I was heading. I went online and ordered a ticket on a commercial flight. With the private terminal access I found online, I seem to have slipped into London unnoticed.

"It might help to work through things," Tommy suggests.

"I just need some time."

"You got it," he says, and then we're silent. Because what else is there to say?

"Have you spoken to your parents?" he asks.

"A little. They know I'm okay."

"Good. And you know you can always stay at my house in LA."

The thing about LA is, I wouldn't be able to get my own coffee. "You know I hate LA."

"I know but it's easy to hide here."

"No, it's easy not to leave the house there."

More silence twists between us.

"How are you?" he asks.

I don't know how to answer the question. I've been focusing on escaping the press. I haven't thought about very much beyond maintaining a low profile. Every time thoughts of Matt and what he's done creep back into my head, I push them away again. "I'm fine."

He sighs. "I need to talk to you about work. The label's freaking out because you're off grid. They want to know you're going to promo the album."

"Have I said I won't promo the album?"

"No," he replies. "Does it mean you will?"

"Of course I will. Promo doesn't start until mid-October anyway. We're still in early September."

"You think you'll be okay by then?"

I was with Matt twelve years. I found out a few months ago he was leaking information about me to the press. I've had four and a half months to grieve a relationship I thought was going to last the rest of my life. I thought Matt was my soul mate—the only person in the world I could trust completely. The guy who was one hundred percent in my corner—not because I paid him, but because he loved me.

"Did you know anything?" I ask. "Or ever suspect he wasn't the guy I thought he was?"

There's an intake of breath on the other end of the

phone. "Not at the time, but looking back...there were a few things that didn't fit completely."

My heart hammers in my chest, like the sound of impatient feet in a stadium. "Like what?"

"Just once or twice he called me asking questions about release dates and things. I think I told him when I knew. Jesus H. Christ, I've known the kid since he was eighteen. Looking back, I think he was digging."

"Digging?"

"For information that would have been...valuable."

I shake my head. "How could I have been such an idiot?"

"This isn't about you. This is about him."

"It's absolutely about me. It shows what a terrible judge of character I am. He shared my bed for twelve years. You'd have thought I'd have caught a clue along the way." The music industry is full of sharks and I've always prided myself on being pretty savvy.

"There was a fox in the hen house, alrighty. But that ain't the hen's fault. It's all on the fox."

I know Tommy is trying to make me feel better, but it doesn't help. Of course Matt's betrayal showed who he was—a liar and a cheat and a complete asshole. But it also says something about me. That I'm naïve, trusting, gullible.

"The answer is yes, I'll be ready for the middle of October." Matt has taken a lot from me but he hasn't stopping me from working. I won't allow it.

"Good," he says. "But if you're not, you just say the word."

"I'll be ready, Tommy. You don't need to worry about that."

"Okay, if you say so." He pauses and clears his throat.

"You know the label will want the focus on the album," he says. "During the publicity tour."

"I do know that." I brace myself. I have a pretty good idea about what he's going to say, but I'm still hoping he won't.

"They're probably going to want to soften up the ground there a little bit. Your brand has always been all about the girl next door who's been with her high school sweetheart since, well, high school. They're going to want to have a strategy to deal with the Matt situation." He's warming up before the main act. I can tell when Tommy wants to drop bad news. He gets a little tight in the throat, and his little southern twang colors his words.

"I'll take a look at their publicity plan when they come up with it. And obviously I want Felicity to work on this with them." Felicity is my PR rep. The label only cares about selling records, to the exclusion of everything else—including me and my wellbeing. I might have been betrayed by my boyfriend, but even I'm clever enough to know that. "We've been keeping the wheels in motion for you. We're dealing with things. Coming up with plans. You know."

"Plans?"

"Uh-huh."

"Tommy, quit beating round the bush. What is it you don't want to tell me? Because I'm pretty sure I know what's coming and you not saying it is just making me think it's worse than it probably is."

He blows out a breath. "They think the easiest way to spin the Matty story—"

"Matt. He's not Matty. He's Matt." He's Matty to his parents, to his high school friends, and until recently, to me. To people who love him, he's Matty.

To me and my team now, he's Matt.

Or shitbag. They're interchangeable.

"Right. We don't know how he's going to react, but we expect him to speak out. Afterall, he has contacts at the tabloids. I think the idea is to make anything he says seem like it's coming from a place of bitterness. A place of jealousy."

Here we go. The ball is about to drop.

"Everyone agrees the easiest way to do that is to create a new romance between you and...another...star."

I groan. It feels so obvious. So cringey. And Matt will see right through it.

"I knew you wouldn't like the idea, but we've put together some really great names. Sports stars. Music stars. Actors. You'd have your pick of people. Your brand is so—"

"Stop talking about my brand. Talk about *me*. I'm a person. Matt and I—us splitting—it's a *personal* thing."

More silence.

"You're right. Of course it's personal. Of course it's painful. But I'm trying to protect you. If you go out to promote your album and the last thing anyone knows about your personal life is that you and Matt have split, those are the questions you're going to get asked. They're going to ask you whether you channeled your emotions into the record. They're going to ask you if this is a breakup album—"

"How could it be? I was still in love with him! I still thought he was my soul mate when I wrote every track."

"You want *that* to be your answer? You want to have to talk about Matt in every single interview?"

Of course I don't. "I just want to talk about the music."

"But your music reflects your life. You know that. Isn't it better to get people excited about you and Harry Styles or Drake or—"

I groan. "Not another musician," I say.

"Fine. An actor then."

The last thing I want to do is relive the death of my relationship in every interview on the publicity tour. Tommy is right about that. "Could I just be pictured out to dinner with a couple different guys? And then be coy in the interviews and just say I'm dating."

"You could." He says it like he's thought of that and it's an option, but not a good one. "But you know how sexist the media is. If you're spotted out with different guys, the narrative is going to turn quickly into you being a slut."

"I've slept with one guy my entire life, Tommy. I'm not a slut."

"I know that. You know that. And even if that wasn't the case, it shouldn't matter. But like I said, the media is sexist. It's your decision. I'll support that if it's what you want to do. But I don't think it will steer people's attention away from you and Matt sufficiently. The story will be 'Vivian Cross dates x, y and z after breakup with high school sweetheart. What went wrong?' Whereas if you're in love, if you're dating someone seriously and you're writing music about them...that's where the focus will be."

I slump back on the sofa. I can't argue with him. Whether I like it or not, he's right. My options are fake-date a celebrity where we're both using each other or answer incessant questions about my failed relationship. Or don't promote the album, break my contract with the record company and have them sue me. I'm between a rock and a hard place and somewhere really shitty.

"Send me the list of names," I say. "No musicians."

"You'll have it by close of business."

We say our goodbyes and I head back to the piano, but instead of the new melody, I revert back to Bach. I can't write after that conversation. I love to write songs and have people listen to them and connect to them. And to make that happen, I'm going to have to make sacrifices, which is probably going to include dating some hot actor for convenience.

A match made in heaven.

SEVEN

Vivian

It's ridiculous because I'm supposed to be heartbroken about Matt—and I *am* genuinely heartbroken about Matt—but there's a spark in my step as I leave Chester Terrace today. I'm excited to see if Beau will be at Coffee Confidential. I enjoyed his attention yesterday. I liked that when I took my hat off, he didn't know who I was right away and when I told him, he didn't start asking me for concert tickets or to name the famous people in my phone. He seemed...normal. He treated me like *I'm* normal, which ironically made me feel incredibly special.

When I found out about Matt leaking information to the tabloids, it wasn't just the personal betrayal that was devastating. It was the thought that I'd never have anyone treat me like I'm not, well, Vivian Cross. Matt had known me before all that.

As I approach the coffee shop, through the glass front, I scan the heads of the customers to see if he's arrived. The line isn't very long. It wouldn't have taken him long to order his coffee, pick it up and split. I glance at my phone. It's exactly the same time as I got here yesterday. I really hope I haven't missed him.

I glance around and see Beau coming up the street behind me. We maintain eye contact as he approaches and I have to bite back a smile.

I'm almost giddy.

I didn't miss him. He's right here. His smile is wide and I'm momentarily shocked at how handsome he is. I'm not blind—I checked him out yesterday. But today? He seems taller. And broader. His jaw a little more chiseled.

The butterflies in my stomach have added energy to their choreography.

"Hey," he says, bending to place a kiss on my cheek. "You look beautiful." He holds my gaze for a beat and the heat rises in my body. I have to look away. "Ready for coffee and a walk?"

I nod, pretending I'm not flustered at all, and we head into the store. We don't say much as we order our coffees and wait for them to arrive. We exchange glances and smiles. I don't want to speak just in case people overhear or recognize my voice and it feels like he gets it without me having to say anything.

"Ready?" he says as he hands me my drink.

I nod and we head out.

"New cap," he says as we cross the road. This one is plain navy with red trim. "Is it a kind of uniform? Dark colors, no brands, nothing that might stand out."

"You're starting to see all my tricks."

"Things are slotting into place." He grins and I pretend not to feel it between my thighs. "Do you miss not being able to do normal stuff?"

"Sometimes. But it's been so long now and there are... perks to being well-known."

"I don't think I appreciated how well-known you are until I Googled you yesterday."

I nod. It's not unexpected. I would Google me too if I were in his shoes. It is a little disappointing. It would be nice to meet a person who has no idea who I am and no interest in finding out beyond what I have to say for myself.

"I get why you might be excited to get your own coffee."

"Tell me about you," I say, wanting to change the subject. "What do you do for fun?" I don't need to hear about how famous I am or contradict ridiculous stories that I know are online about me. One of the good things about traveling with what some people would consider an entourage, is that your assistant or you manager or your PR rep becomes your gatekeeper. They shield you from questions you don't want to answer or news you don't want to hear.

"I went swimming with my brother in Hamstead ponds last night after work. I'm not sure it falls into the category of fun, but...it was an experience."

"Did you get caught?" I ask.

He laughs. "You're allowed. There's a whole setup for people who want to do freshwater swimming. Jacob does it a lot. I was a freshwater virgin until last night."

"How was it?" I ask. "Other than cold?"

He laughs. "Yeah, it was cold, although I didn't mind that much. It was...better than I expected. More thought-provoking."

Thought-provoking? I want to follow up and ask him to elaborate, but it feels weird to be nosy about someone when I'm not willing to share. "You must be close with your brother if you live together and hang out after work too."

"Oh no, I live with one of my other brothers, Nathan, and his wife and my niece. I rented my place out when I did some trekking in Tanzania a year or so back, and every time I come back, it kind of doesn't coincide with the lease being up. Then when the lease is up, I'm often abroad and so I just renew. I'm in a cycle."

"Two brothers? That's a lot of testosterone when you were a kid."

"I have four brothers altogether. Well, five if you count my cousin who's—yeah, five. There's a lot of us."

I come to a stop on the path. "There are six of you? And no sisters? Your poor mom." I can't even imagine what his brothers look like. I bet there are some very happy women in London right now.

"She loves having five boys. And Vincent." He pauses. "My dad? That's another story." We start to walk again. "You said you had a brother."

"And a sister," I confess, not wanting to mislead him today.

"Are you close?"

"We're not *not* close. But we lead different lives."

"It would be weird if you were all pop stars. Unless of course you were the Jackson Five or something."

"We're not," I say, and we both laugh. "You probably figured, what with me being alive and white and twenty-nine."

"Are they musical?"

"I think my sister could have been, but she was never interested. My brother plays the saxophone and piano, like my dad." Somehow I've slipped into telling him more than I'm used to sharing. I bat the conversation back to him. "You were saying you like to travel?"

"Yeah, like I said to you yesterday, I like to get the most

out of life. I enjoy new experiences and adventures." He pauses like he's going to say more, but then the silence just hangs between us, like we're both holding back.

"What's your next trip? Rappelling off Everest?"

"Definitely not." He shoots me a grin and then shrugs. "Not sure yet. Maybe husky mushing."

"Wow. Husky mushing. I didn't realize that was...a thing. I mean, as in a thing people go off to learn."

"Tourism is everywhere, I guess." He pauses again, and I can't help but wonder what he's holding back. Is it a question about me? Is he going to ask me to sign something for his niece? Or is he hiding himself?

He seems genuine, although I have zero confidence in my ability to tell the liars from the good guys these days. I seem to have lost the ability to know who's telling me the truth and who's kissing my ass. To be honest, most people are kissing my ass most of the time—probably because I'm responsible for their paycheck or because they want something from me.

Beau doesn't seem to want anything but a walk in the park.

"Your trips are about chasing a natural high?" I ask.

"That's always been part of it. I never wanted to go to my grave not having made the most out of life. Otherwise, what's the point?"

"Wow, we got deep real fast," I say on a smile. I'm silent while I think about what he's said. "I'm not sure being here is the same for everyone."

"Okay..." His tone isn't disapproving or frustrated. It just sounds like an invitation for me to say more.

I continue. "For a start, I don't think people generally think about their reasons for being."

He grins and the corners of his eyes do that adorable

crinkle thing again and the butterflies are back, warm and happy and doing loop-the-loops in my stomach.

"And I think that's okay," I add. "I think if we think hard about stuff like that, it's...painful. And triggering. It's much easier to deal with the stuff here and now in our day-to-day lives."

"I don't disagree. But tell me there's more. I can see you have more to say." I'm used to people listening to me—fame and money have bought me attention in that sense. It's not the attention I find unusual; it's how authentic Beau's interest feels. Beau isn't listening to what I have to say because I'm paying him, or because he's trying to get me to write a song with him or guest on his TV show. I can't be useful to him beyond being his companion on a walk through the park. He's just here for me, not what I can be to him or do for him.

It's exactly what I used to think about Matt.

"And then other people do think about that stuff, but what they want is just to be happy."

We stop and Beau faces me, angling us so I'm looking away from any passing members of the public. I don't know if it's deliberate, but something tells me it is. It's thoughtful and kind and I'm grateful to him. "You're right. I've not thought about that. It's probably why Jacob said no to coming to Norway with me. He just wants to be happy, and to him, that's swimming in Hampstead ponds, hanging out with Sutton and working."

"Maybe you just want to be happy too, but for you, that means having all these unique experiences."

He playfully tugs on my cap. "You're a wise woman, Vivian. A very wise woman."

I feel like a proud pupil who's pleased her teacher. Whether or not it's true, I'm used to being called talented.

Also bitchy, demanding, difficult and lucky. But I don't think I've ever been described as wise before.

"You finished?" His hand hovers over my coffee cup and I hand it to him. His fingers brush mine and as they do, our gazes lock.

A beat passes before he takes both our cups to the trash can by the path and drops them in.

"So tell me what makes you happy? Apart from getting your own coffee." We start to walk again and for a moment I expect him to take my hand in his before I remember we're almost strangers.

"I love writing songs. I mean, thank god, because I can't turn the songwriting thing off. Sometimes I feel like a human fishing trawler, forever cruising the ocean. I'm always seeing inspiration, feeling it—I always have a hook or a lyric in my head. It's who I am, I suppose."

He turns his head to me, eyebrows raised. "So you have a song lyric in your head at the moment?"

I laugh. There's no way I'm telling him I've been singing *My British stranger, my newfound something. My British stranger, I just need one thing* in my head since he left me for work yesterday morning. "Always," I say. "But no, I won't tell you any more."

He glances at my lips and then back into my eyes. "I won't make you. Not yet."

My cheeks heat and I look away. "Don't you have to leave for work?" I ask, and we both stop walking.

"Shit." He pulls his phone from his pocket. "I was having too much fun with you. Yup, I should have left five minutes ago." He narrows his eyes. "Same time tomorrow?"

"You work on a Saturday?" I ask.

"Oh yeah, no. What about hanging out? That way I don't have to rush off afterwards. Unless you have plans."

I didn't have plans, but at the same time, I wasn't sure I wanted them.

"Erm, I'm not sure," I say, suddenly uncomfortable. I don't want to start swapping numbers or giving him my address.

"Hang on." He drops his backpack on the ground, unzips it and pulls out a pad of sticky notes and a pen. He kneels down and scribbles something on the pad and then stands. "I don't want to make this weird. I totally understand you're busy and I'm just some guy you spilled coffee over." He pauses and smiles, and I melt a little inside. "But I like you. I'd like to hang out tomorrow. If you feel the same, give me a call or drop me a message."

He peels off the sticky note and presses it onto my hoodie as if it's a name tag. I can feel his fingers on me long after they're gone.

"No pressure. And if not, then maybe I'll see you in the queue for coffee on Monday." He checks his phone again, winces. "Gotta go." He kisses me on the cheek, hooks his bag on his back and starts a gentle jog out of the park.

My fingers covering the cheek he just kissed, I watch him leave, wondering why it feels like I can trust this guy.

I thought the same about Matt, and look where that ended up.

EIGHT

Vivian

I messaged Beau to ask what *hanging out* would look like and he gave me a list of options. First up was lunch at his brother's place—he offered to cook. It felt like too much of a Netflix and chill option, and he's still pretty much a stranger.

Option two was another walk in the park. It's a good option. So far I've managed to remain anonymous and, much like Central Park, people here seem far more focused on themselves than they are on figuring who's behind the dark glasses and cap.

But I was intrigued enough by option three to go with that choice, which is what Beau referred to as a "lucky dip" —a surprise. Partly because it sounded the most fun, and partly because...I'm curious to roll the dice and see if my picture ends up in the papers. I suppose I'm testing Beau, which may or may not be right, but it *is* necessary.

He told me to dress casually, like what I wear to get coffee, even though we're meeting at six in the evening. He insisted he would pick me up. I agreed after some convincing, but I wasn't about to tell him my address. I said I'd meet him outside Coffee Confidential.

I take Beau's advice and sport athleisure wear, although I put on the leggings that make my butt look a little bubblier than the others. As I arrive, the back door of a blacked-out Range Rover opens and Beau gets out. Does that mean someone else is driving? Someone who knows it's me he's collecting? My pulse starts to race and all of a sudden, I wish I hadn't agreed to this. I have no security, and not even Tommy knows where I am or what I'm doing.

Beau doesn't say anything, he just smiles at me. For a second, I wonder if this is all some elaborate setup and I'm about to be kidnapped for ransom. These things happen. I'm worth a lot of money to a lot of people.

I glance around, not quite sure what I'm looking for.

"You look gorgeous." Beau tugs my cap, bringing my focus back to him.

"I look like I'm about to go on a run."

"That too," he says, his eyes crinkling. "But doesn't take away from the gorgeous part."

My pulse softens and I take a breath. Since Matt, I'm in constant fight-or-flight mode.

I look up at Beau, take a breath, climb into the car and push my glasses onto my head. The partition between the driver and the passengers is blacked out, but the driver could have seen who was getting into the car.

Beau follows me inside and closes the door. "Okay, first off, let me tell you that trying to find something to do in London that doesn't involve too many people and isn't out in public and isn't at my brother's place—well, it's not easy. So if this isn't your jam tonight, I apologize in advance."

I smile. It's kind of him to try. "I'm sure it's fine."

"That's the answer of someone who expects the night to be terrible." He laughs. "I guess it's good the bar is low."

It's like his laugh is a sedative. I start to feel much better about being here. I snap on my seat belt and the car pulls out from the curb.

"Does the driver know it's me?"

"I didn't tell him but he may have worked it out. He's under a strict NDA. He's my brother's driver and he knows the score. My brother had some run-ins with the tabloids back in the day—nothing compared to what you go through, but he's always been very careful about who he has around him. There's no need to worry."

This was partly a test of Beau, so let's see where this takes me. It feels good to get out of the house for a bit, and not just for coffee. Maybe tonight will be okay. "Why did your brother get embroiled with the tabloids? Is he famous?"

"Nah. Not really. For a while there he was very successful and single, and his private life ended up in the papers. I think people were interested because he's... I mean, he's easy on the eye, so his wife tells me. And he was connected to a lot of wealthy and famous people."

That sounds intriguing. "What's his name?"

"You won't know him. Nathan Cove."

Of course I knew him. "Nathan Cove is your brother?" He was gorgeous. Suave and sophisticated. He was like the UK version of John Kennedy Junior.

He rolls his eyes. "Don't tell me people know him in America."

"I think he dated a friend of a friend of mine."

He hums a skeptical hum, if such a thing exists. "I doubt it. He was...a philanderer."

I laugh at his use of the old-fashioned word. "When I

say he dated my friend of a friend, I don't think it was serious. Michelle Frankle. You know her?"

He shakes his head. "I love Madison, his wife, don't get
me wrong. But before then? They all blur into one."

I laugh. "I'm sure. He's a very handsome guy."

"Like I say, he's married, so you're stuck with me."

Stuck with him? "You know this isn't a date, right? I'm
one hundred percent not open to dating anyone right now."

"I'm not into dating at the moment either," he replies, a
grin unfurling on his face. "We're just getting coffee, walking, talking. I'm just saying, my brother's taken."

He's so confident. So relaxed, it's hard to not feel the
same. I just don't want to create expectations in him. I'm
absolutely not going to date him. I'm not going to sleep with
him. I'm not even going to k—

Okay, I might kiss him. But only if he...

I need to stop overthinking.

"So as you've been to London before, I'm presuming
you don't need a third-tier tour from the back of a Range
Rover given by a guy who doesn't know that much."

I laugh. "That kind of tour would be perfect," I say,
feeling a little mischievous. I want to see if this guy is going
to step up.

"Okay," he says. "We're crossing over the Euston Road
right now. Not much to say other than it's a busy road."

I snigger. "You've found your calling. Forget husky
mushing, this is the grand adventure you're destined for."

He narrows his eyes at me in mock anger. "We're
turning into Great Portland Street. On your right is the
Portland Hospital."

"Do you work there?"

He shakes his head. "I'm not a hospital doctor. I'm a
GP. But there are lots of private medical facilities and

doctors around here. Harley Street is just a couple of blocks over."

"And Harley Street is..."

"A street famous for its private medicine. Doctors will be referred to as 'a Harley Street doctor'. To the general public, the connotation is an expensive, excellent doctor or medical practice."

"I see. That's what it means for normies like me." I point at myself. "But Harley Street isn't really that big of a deal?"

He shrugs. "It just means a private doctor who's prepared to pay the rent to be on Harley Street." He tilts his head and smiles at me. "Normie. I've never heard someone referred to as a normie because they don't have a medical background."

I laugh. "My manager uses it when he's talking about people who aren't famous. It's stupid really."

"Ahh, so I'm the normie in this car. Not you."

My American phone bleeps and when I pull it out, it's Tommy. I cancel the call.

"If you need to take it," Beau says.

I shake my head. "It's my manager. I don't need to take it."

"What does a manager do?" he asks.

"Tries to run my life?" I smile at him. "I'm kidding. I've known Tommy since I was sixteen. He's steered my career, helped me make decisions, negotiated with my record label, arranged brand endorsements. He does everything, really. It allows me to focus on writing and recording."

"But you don't want to talk to him," Beau says.

The phone rings again and I cancel the call and put the phone on silent. "Not tonight. I'm too excited to hear about what else I need to know about Great Portland Street."

Beau laughs and I grin, happy I've made him laugh.

"I'm not sure I know much about Great Portland Street. But that's nothing to do with my ability as a London tour guide and much more about the fact that Great Portland Street doesn't have a lot going on." He tries to look serious.

"Oh right. Yes, I'm sure that's the reason," I say, shooting him a grin.

"And anyway, we're turning onto Regent's Street now, which is far more interesting in terms of streets anyway."

"I am all ears. Not literally because that would be weird, but consider my breath baited."

He smiles and we lock eyes. A surge of I-don't-know-what trips something in my circuitry; my cheeks heat and my stomach tips. God, he's gorgeous.

I look away first because I'm not supposed to be feeling anything. It's just absurd. I'm in my period of mourning for a relationship that lasted almost half my life. I'm not interested in anyone else. Absolutely not.

"Regent's Street is named after the Prince Regent—I think he turned out to be George IV. Although I wouldn't stake my life on it."

I wince. "I can hear future you sobbing at missing out at Tour Guide of the Year."

He chuckles and pulls out his phone. "Yes, here it is—his father was mad, so he reigned as Prince Regent until his father finally carked it and he became George IV."

"And when you say carked it, you mean he..."

"Died," he adds.

"Today is full of lessons," I say, in a prim, Mary Poppins voice as if I'm mortally offended.

"You're getting the full-on British experience, here."

I laugh. "I appreciate it."

"We're nearly here." He looks at me and his expression turns serious. "Before we get there, I just want to say that if you're uncomfortable and you want to leave at any point, I'm not going to be offended. Just let me know. The car is going to wait for us the entire time, so it's not like you don't have an out if you need one."

I'm touched at how thoughtful he's being. It makes me feel...safe. "Thank you."

"I've pulled in a couple of favors from a few people. I couldn't get the entire place emptied. But only security and one curator will be in the building."

"A curator?" I ask.

The car pulls to a stop and Beau dips his head to look out of the window. "Yes. In case we want information about any of the paintings. This is where we're going. You ready?"

He's dressed in a white shirt and jeans and still has his backpack with him. I slide on my sunglasses and we slip out of the car and into a building opposite the car. I can hear people either side of me, but I keep focused on the ground and following Beau. At some point he offers me his hand, but I pretend I haven't seen it and ignore it. If the paps are out, the last thing I want is to be photographed holding some stranger's hand.

We pass through modern sliding doors and into a huge lobby. I take off my glasses and turn three hundred and sixty degrees. I glance back at Beau.

"Have you guessed where we are yet?"

I shake my head.

"Come on." He lifts his chin in the direction of elevators at the end of the room. "I don't know if you're into art." We ride up the elevators and the door pings open.

"What kind of art? Are we going to be making pottery? I don't want you going all Patrick Swayze on me."

He chuckles. "We'll leave pottery for another day. Here it's more of the painting kind of art."

We step out into another lobby and I glance left and right. We're in an art gallery. "We're here on our own?" I ask.

"Like I said, the security guards are here. But they're trustworthy. Apparently, a number of the royal family like after-hours tours. They use the same setup for them."

"Okay," I say. He's gone to a lot of trouble for me. It's difficult to know what a normal amount of trouble would be, given I don't want to be seen in public, but I'm certain this exceeds normal.

"You like art?" he asks.

"Honestly, I don't know much about it. I've been famous for all my adult life. I don't stop by art galleries much or ever." It's moments like this that I realize how much I miss out on. I wonder how many times Beau has been to an art gallery. I remember visiting the Art Institute of Chicago with school, but I don't think I've ever stepped foot into an art gallery since. "It's just not something that's even ever been on my radar because some things feel impossible."

"Let's do a tour of the really famous stuff, if that works for you?"

I follow him as he leads the way through the maze of corridors. How had a guy around thirty managed to arrange for us to have almost-private access to a gallery like this? "Is this the National Gallery in Trafalgar Square?" I ask.

He grins. "Yeah, you've heard of it?"

"What the actual fuck, Beau?" I ask as he stops in front of a painting. I look up to find Van Gogh's "Sunflowers" in front of me. It's an image I've seen a thousand times but looking at it here, in touching distance, the colors vibrant, the textures so defined, it's wonderful.

"Van Gogh," he says. "That's the actual fuck."

I laugh. "But how did you get us in here?"

"I know people. Believe me, it's not because I'm a frequent visitor." He spins around. "Although maybe I should be. It's wonderful."

It is wonderful and unusual and so thoughtful. I'm no dating expert, but I'm pretty sure doing something like this for a woman you've just met isn't normal. Matt never did anything close in the twelve years we were together, and he could have asked my assistant to arrange it. And I would have paid.

Lyrics run through my mind.

A thousand pretty pictures and I only want to stare at you. Years of misunderstandings and you show me everything that's true.

"What are you thinking?" he asks.

I started off this evening telling myself over and over that tonight wasn't a date and now I'm standing here kinda hoping it is. No one has ever done anything so nice for me.

I feel my heart open its tightly locked door, just an inch, and sunshine billows in. Could it be this easy to be with someone who isn't Matt?

It's only a few months since we split. I shouldn't even be thinking about anything but licking my wounds, but Beau makes it so...straightforward, almost like everything before him was complicated—tangled ropes and string—and he's here, slicing through everything, making everyone around him feel foolish to think life was anything but effortless.

The way he sees the world gives me hope that this is how easy life could be.

"I'm thinking this is wonderful," I say.

His eyes twinkle. "Good."

I slide my gaze around the walls, taking in the canvasses. "Can we walk? I want to see up close."

"Of course. Which way first?"

I'm drawn to a picture of a group of dancers. One ballerina toward the left of the canvas is reaching down to fix her shoe. "This way. This one is so pretty."

"I'm afraid I don't know much about art, as much as I'd like to impress you with my encyclopedic knowledge. But we can have a curator come and talk to us about some paintings if you like?"

Before I can answer, my phone buzzes in the back pocket of my jeans. I pull it out to see Tommy's name on the screen. I roll my eyes and silence the call, then turn it off.

"Your manager again?" Beau asks.

I nod my head, my eyes still fixed on the ballerina.

"He really wants to speak to you."

I groan. He does. He's emailed me twice today as well. He sent me the list of possible fake boyfriends yesterday, and I know he wants me to narrow it down so he can start approaching people. "I split up with my high school boyfriend recently," I say. "We were engaged. Tommy wants me to pick a new boyfriend—a fake boyfriend—so when I do my press tour, people don't fixate on my breakup. He sent me a list."

"He sent you a list of boyfriends?"

I glance up at Beau and he looks confused. It must sound ridiculous to him.

"Tommy and my label think it would be good for me to be dating someone new when I start to promote my new album. He wants to get the ball rolling."

"Wow. I don't know what to say."

Beau must think he's entered some kind of alternate universe. "It's going to be a setup. There'll be a contract, a set period of time where we'll agree to be seen dating each other."

"So an entirely faked relationship?" he asks.

"Yeah." I turn back to the painting. It's like a tour photographer has taken a candid shot backstage. The painting isn't posed at all. The ballerinas are backstage, either midway through a performance or at the end, waiting for their curtain call. They're not focused on the person observing them, painting them. They are in their own heads, thinking about what they just did well, what they should have done better. What they're going to do next—which parts of their bodies hurt. Some look exhausted, others seem bored.

"I love this," I say. "It feels...authentic. Like the artist sees these women as they are, rather than trying to capture an idealized version of a ballet dancer."

Beau follows my gaze. "Yeah, I can see that. It's not the dancers the audience of the ballet see."

I nod. "Which is the person onstage giving a show. These are the women underneath the costumes." I have a lot in common with them.

I can feel the weight of his stare on me and I turn to him. We lock eyes, but he doesn't say anything.

He gets it.

"Do you enjoy performing?" he asks.

"I like smaller shows. Not big tours where it's night after night, you're required to slip on this mask and make the audience feel something. I've only done a couple of huge tours in my life and at the end...this is going to sound stupid..."

I hesitate because Matt didn't like me to complain about...really anything. I understand—my life is incredibly fortunate. I never have to worry about money. Both Matt and I come from families who are comfortable but by no means wealthy. I know I don't ever have to work again in the way my parents *had* to work to keep a roof over our heads and food in our stomachs when I was growing up. But sometimes, even with enormous wealth, I find the life I've chosen for myself challenging.

"I want to hear," he says.

"I don't want to sound like I'm complaining. I'm really not."

"It's okay, Vivian. Tell me how you feel."

I glance at him and can tell he really wants to know what I'm thinking. It feels so unusual that he would be interested, but I don't doubt his authenticity for a second. I take in a deep breath. "It can sometimes feel like you've forgotten who you are. And then when the tour comes to an end, there's a huge...hole, where you've stopped doing something that completely dominated your life. It's easy to feel a sense of loss and relief at the same time."

He nods. "That must be confusing."

Matt would have shut me down before I'd finished my thought. He would have reminded me how much I wanted the life I have now at sixteen. How much I'd sacrificed for it, how much *he'd* sacrificed for it. He would have rolled his eyes and turned on ESPN.

Beau doesn't know me that well, and has never heard these mixed feelings I have about my career, so I shouldn't compare him and Matt. But it's difficult because the difference is so pronounced. I've just told him how I'm feeling and he listened. It sounds simple but it feels like a warm bubble bath and a glass of champagne. I can't remember the last time I was ever able to do that.

With Tommy and Betty, I always have to temper my comments. I don't want to come across like a brat, or someone who's unstable or ungrateful. And Matt...just wasn't interested.

"Where next?" I ask.

"The Bathers," Beau says.

We wander out of the room we're in and through to the next. My phone vibrates as we walk. I ignore it.

"The fake boyfriend thing your manager wants you to do. Is that normal in the music industry?" he asks.

"Very," I say.

"And you don't want to, which is why you're ignoring his calls." He pauses. "It just seems so ridiculous. And don't people know it's fake?"

"You'd be surprised. Sometimes it's an open secret. Other times not so much. It's just that I feel I need to...be single. Do you know what I mean? I need some space. I was with Matt for so long and he betrayed me so badly. I don't want to have to spend time with someone, even if it's fake."

"Here you are, spending time with me," Beau says, his voice soft.

"Right," I pause, because I know it's different, but I'm not sure how. "But it's not like the press knows anything. This feels like a private bubble."

"Right," he says, his voice hardening a little. "And I'm not looking to get into something. Neither are you."

"You had your heart broken too?"

"Nope, but my shoulder got dislocated when I asked a woman I'd been seeing if she wanted to get a little more serious, if that counts?"

I smile but when I turn to face him, he's not smiling. "She dislocated your shoulder?"

"No, I— It doesn't matter. I'm just at a bit of a crossroads in my life. I'm not ready to decide which direction I want to go." He clears his throat like he's given too much away and pushes his hands into his pockets. "I'm just saying that I'm not looking for a relationship."

"Same," I reply. "Maybe I should fake date *you*."

He chuckles. "Maybe you should."

We come to stand in front of a large painting of a group of people sitting on a riverbank.

"You know what I like about this picture?" he asks. "The boots. From here, they look like the least interesting part of the painting—just a pair of brown boots, and then you get closer and they're a thousand colors: blues, whites, greens, browns. It's a boot but it's so much more."

My heart trips in my chest and I have the urge to reach for Beau. What he's saying is not only true, but it's also insightful and profound and completely perfect in the context of our discussion, and it makes me want to know him forever.

"I like that boot too," I reply. "And I like that you like the boot."

He glances across at me, offering me a small smile as we stand side by side in front of the painting. He doesn't take his gaze from me when he says, "I can tell you really don't want to fake date a stranger, but if you want, I'll do it. I'll be your pretend boyfriend."

It's the last thing I'm expecting him to say. I can tell he's completely serious, but he can't know what he's suggesting.

"That's really kind." I take a few steps back and sit down on the large cushioned bench in the middle of the room. "But also impossible. Whoever is agreed on will be a celebrity—probably an actor or a sports star. It will benefit them too. The contract will require so many public appearances and private appearances together that the paparazzi will be informed of. It's all fake."

"Right." He sits down next to me. "So date me, and then you don't have to go through all that. Plus I can be a little bit charming, and we like each other. Imagine if you create this contract with someone and you hate them."

I smile. He *is* charming and I *do* like him, but he's too much of an unknown quantity. If I couldn't trust Matt, then how could I ever trust an almost-stranger? "It's easier if both parties have...equal interest in the agreement."

He narrows his eyes like he's trying to work out what I'm really trying to say.

"I find it hard to trust people," I confess. "I was with my ex since before I was famous. We were together since high school and I found out he was selling stories about me."

"Wow," he says. "For the money?"

"Honestly, he never told me why, and I didn't stick around to grill him, but I don't think it was for the money. It's not like he was short of...anything."

I hadn't thought too much about the *why*. I'd been too busy recovering from the *what*. I don't say any more, and it's like Beau knows I've reached my limit of confessions, because he doesn't ask me anything else.

"My mum always says everything seems better with a full stomach. Let's eat."

"Your mom? Are you close?"

"Yes, and I've learned that ignoring her comes at a price. She's smart and wise and I make a point to follow her advice wherever I can."

I'm not sure many men would be so comfortable admitting as much, but the more I talk to Beau, the more I'm persuaded that he's not like many men.

He unzips his backpack and pulls out packaged Pret A Manger sandwiches. "I couldn't arrange dinner in here without a ton of people being involved. I thought you'd cope with Pret sandwiches rather than that."

I laugh. "You're absolutely right." He's so thoughtful

and has really considered me in all of this. It's not until witnessing it that I realize how it wasn't like that with Matt. We always had dates at fancy restaurants because that's what he liked.

I smile and glance down at the bench picnic he set up. There's a positive array of sandwiches.

"We have a selection because I didn't know which you'd like. Everything from falafel to good old chicken and avocado."

"Looks great," I say, and I mean it. Yes, I'm used to getting dressed up and going out to fancy restaurants. Matt really enjoyed the latest and greatest New York eateries. But right here, nestled in between the Impressionists, sitting opposite a man with eyes that light up a room, and who might be the best listener I've ever met, I'm having the best non-date of my life.

NINE

Beau

We'd not even kissed, but Vivian was my first thought when I woke up this morning. My second thought was she shouldn't have a fake boyfriend unless it was me. I could absolutely guarantee that I wouldn't betray her. She might not be so lucky with a stranger.

I'd texted her a couple of minutes ago to let her know I was close, and she said she was already in the queue at Coffee Confidential. We'd agreed to meet twenty minutes earlier than usual to give us more time in the park.

I push the door open and see her already standing at the pickup station. She waves, beckoning me over.

"I already ordered yours," she whispers.

A slow grin unfurls on my face. "That's very nice of you."

"Least I can do after our non-date on Saturday. I had a really good time."

"Me too," I reply, taking in her blue sparkling eyes that seem to be brighter than usual this morning.

After she told me a number of times that she wasn't ready to date, we weren't dating, and our evening constituted a non-date, I hadn't asked to kiss her. But it didn't stop me wanting to. Even after what had happened with Coral, something about Vivian drew me to her, over and over, even though we were so different and on such different paths. Maybe the built-in end date for anything between us—since she'll eventually return to the US—makes it easier to think about here and now, with her, and nothing else.

"Adele," someone behind the counter calls out, sliding two cups onto the counter.

"I just got why you call yourself Adele."

She glances at me as we turn and head to the exit.

"Because of the singer, right? You're trying to be funny."

"What do you mean, *trying* to be funny? I'm downright hilarious."

I chuckle. "If you say so," I say, holding the door for her.

All of a sudden, she freezes as someone walks by and does a double-take when he sees Vivian. They don't stop and Vivian charges ahead in the other direction. I follow her but glance back at the guy who seemed to recognize her.

I catch up to her at the crossing.

"Is he following us?" she whispers.

"Not at all. He's long gone. He probably just thought you were his ex or something."

"Or he was paparazzi."

"Do they get up this early?"

"Believe me, they'll do *anything* to get a shot they want." There's a tinge of bitterness to her tone that I haven't heard before.

"And does it matter if he photographs you?"

"Usually I would just accept it. It's only, no one knows I'm in London. I'd prefer to keep it that way for now."

"Well you don't need to worry about that guy. I can't even see him, he's so far away."

We walk silently until we get to the park.

"I'm sorry, I'm just tense. That guy freaked me out. Thank you for being so patient with me."

"You don't have to thank me."

"You probably don't want to hear about my ex, but he was the one who was paranoid about being papped or spotted by someone who'd message DeuxMoi. He used to say he was protecting his privacy, so I learned to be wary on his behalf. And now look at me."

"Hang on—I thought he was leaking stuff to the media. You think that's why he didn't want to get spotted? In case they let on they knew him? Or like...he didn't want to dilute the value of the shots he arranged by allowing unplanned photos?"

We get under the canopy of trees in the park where Vivian always seems to relax a little. "I don't know. Maybe. Or maybe he wasn't stressed about getting spotted, but he was hungry for it. You know?"

"Hyped," I say to confirm what she's saying. "If that's the case, he's not going to like being single. No one will want his picture now."

"Right," she replies.

"Has he tried to win you back?" I ask.

She narrows her eyes. "I think he called right after it happened, but everything was such a blur. Oh yes, he wanted my engagement ring back." She laughs—it's a sad sound and doesn't suit her. "I sold it the same day. I paid for the damn thing, after all."

"At least you get to write the breakup album."

Her expression turns serious. "I won't waste another note on him."

She looks so wounded. I want to scoop her up and make it better. The best thing I can do is change the subject.

"Can you write a song when it doesn't feel personal to you?" I'm fascinated by her job. The entire Cove family revolves around medicine—or at least, it did when me and my brothers were growing up. But for Vivian, that passion was music. It was so different from my world.

She taps her finger on the white lid of her coffee cup. "No, but that doesn't mean the song has to be about me and whatever I'm experiencing—although a lot of my songs are. If I read a book or watch a movie that moves me, I can put myself in the main character's shoes and write a song based on that point of view. Does that make sense?"

"Yeah, that's cool. You get to watch films and listen to music and claim it's your job."

She laughs. "I suppose so. But it's possible to find inspiration in all sorts of things."

"What's the weirdest thing you've ever taken inspiration from?" I ask.

She looks away from me. "I was stuck in traffic in LA once and I used it as a metaphor for being stuck in a rut in —" She pauses, and I get the feeling she's putting bits and pieces together in her head. "You know, being stuck in life."

"I like that. Does that mean you're looking for inspiration the entire time or do you have to say to yourself, 'can I take inspiration from my trip to the coffee shop today?'"

She smiles and blushes and she looks lighter than before. Like she's enjoying herself. "Both."

We walk slowly along the path. The leaves have shifted from green to yellow over the weekend and I wonder if that's a metaphor that could be used in a song. Perhaps something about the passing of time, the beginning of the end of a relationship or phase in life.

"Did you ever answer your manager's call?" I ask.

She groans. "Not yet. I'm enjoying the bubble I'm in right now. I'm not ready for it to pop."

"Can I ask who was on the list?" I ask. "Leonardo DiCaprio?"

"Not sure I'm young enough for Leo," she says, and I almost laugh before I realize she's completely serious. *Gross.*

"You know I'd be happy to be your fake boyfriend." I don't want to be pushy, but I don't want her to get hurt again, and the only way I can make sure it doesn't happen is to fill the role myself. Neither of us is looking to start something serious, so it seems the perfect solution: I like spending time with her, but don't actually want to be anyone's boyfriend. I don't think I'll ever want that. Coral made sure of it.

"You're sweet," she says, grinning up at me.

"You're beautiful," I say. She's really breathtakingly gorgeous, but she has a sweetness in her that makes me want more of her.

"You're cute," she says. "It's the dimples."

I pull my eyebrows together. "I don't have dimples."

"You totally do." She prods at my cheek and I revel in her touch. "There, and—" I catch her hand before she can prod me again and slide my fingers through hers.

"Babies have dimples." I clear my throat and drop my voice as low as I can. "Not men."

She laughs and without thinking, I bring our linked hands to my mouth and kiss the back of her palm through my smile.

"Hey Vivian," someone calls from ahead of us. "Who's your new boyfriend?"

"Shit," Vivian hisses under her breath and stops walking. "Shit, shit, shit."

I lift my head, trying to figure out who spoke. A man with a camera comes into focus.

"Don't look at him," she says. Her head is dipped and she turns away. I turn with her. "I've got to get out of here. Where's the nearest exit?"

"Back where we came."

"Vivian!" the voice calls. He's clearly following us. "How are you enjoying being in Britain?" I hear the snap of the shutter as the man points his camera.

"Where are we headed?" I ask.

"I just need to get out of here."

"Come on," I say. "I know what we can do."

We head straight out of the park, not looking behind us, and luckily there's a cab just ahead with its light on. I hold my hand out and it pulls in. I open the door and usher Vivian inside.

I pull the door closed. "Just drive, please," I say to the cabbie, and then I turn to Vivian. "Where are we going? What's your address?"

She glances over her shoulder and I follow her gaze. I can't see the photographer.

"I'll drop you off," she says. "Where do you work?"

"No, I want to see you home safely, Vivian. Where are we headed?"

She folds her arms in front of her chest. "Go to your work," she snaps.

"Oi, where are we going?" the driver asks.

What choice do I have? "Twenty-three Welbeck Street," I say. "You're coming in with me. I'm not leaving you to go home alone."

She doesn't argue and I'm grateful. There's no way I can leave her. Being caught by a paparazzi photographer is her worst-case scenario. I thought she was being paranoid, but I can see how it must be distressing for her. It was like that guy had been lying in wait. Like he was hunting her.

We're at my building in just a few minutes and silently exit the cab. I unlock the large black front door. She goes inside, and I look up and down the street, checking to see if I can see anything unusual before I follow her.

"Just head up the stairs," I say.

She doesn't answer but follows my instructions.

We head into my practicing room and I pull out a chair.

"You okay?" I ask as she takes a seat. She's worrying her bottom lip with her teeth and squeezing her hands together.

She nods her head. "I doubt he followed us here. But now people know I'm in London. And now they've seen me with you."

I want to pull her into my arms, but she's like a spooked animal. I don't want to make her feel more uncomfortable.

"You're safe." I sit on the desk next to her, careful not to touch her.

She presses her fingers against her forehead. "I need to call Tommy. And Felicity. She needs to get in front of this. The pictures might be live within the hour."

I check my watch. I have a patient in ten minutes, but I want to help her. "Do you need to be at home or can you make the calls you need to from here? There's a free office next door—the accounts manager is on holiday."

She stands. "Yeah, is that okay? I can't go back to the house."

"For how long?"

She shrugs. "It's too close the park. I don't think I can go back there ever. It would have been fine six months ago—maybe they would have found me and taken my picture, whatever. But now? Since I split with Matt, the paparazzi attention has just been off the charts. When I was in New

York, my building's doorman said he found someone trying to hide in my car's trunk. I'll move into a hotel."

No wonder's she's scared.

"You can stay with me," I offer. "And my brother and his wife."

She glances up at me. "That's very sweet of you. First an offer to be my fake boyfriend, now you're suggesting we live together. What's next, a ring?" She laughs nervously, and I smile, but I'm serious. She can stay with me; Nathan and Madison wouldn't mind. "Can you show me where the office is?"

I drag my fingers through my hair. "Of course. This way." The office is right next door to mine. "You can use the phone or...if you need anything, message me. You have my number, right? If I'm in with a patient, I won't be able to answer, but I'll come and find you as soon as I'm done."

"Thanks, Beau," she says and slips into the small office.

"Don't leave before you say goodbye."

"Okay," she calls, and I shut the door.

TEN

Vivian

I hate to wake Tommy, but I know he'll be mad if I call Felicity without speaking to him first.

"Vivian?" he shouts into the phone. "Are you okay?"

"Everything's fine," I've raised my voice slightly as I'm not sure if it's a bad line. "But we need to talk to Felicity. I just got jumped by a paparazzi and we need to get ahead of it."

I hear sniffling and snuffling at the other end of the phone. "Vivian?"

"Can you hear me, Tommy?"

"Shit, what time is it, are you okay?"

"We need to get Felicity on the line, I just got papped."

"Right. Give me a second. Move over, Robbie," he says to his husband. "I need to find my—right, I've got my glasses. Let me dial in Felicity."

I wait as Tommy tries to connect the three of us. I can picture him squinting at the screen, punching buttons with his hair standing on end.

"Right, is that the three of us?" he asks. Videos of Tommy and Felicity pop up onto my screen. Tommy's hair *is* standing on end, but he's made it to his office and he's pulled on a shirt. Felicity, on the other hand, looks completely put together in a black round-necked jumper and a string of pearls. It's as if she's been up an hour already despite it being four a.m. in New York.

"How are you, darling?" Felicity asks in her mid-Atlantic drawl.

"I'm fine," I say. "I've been staying in London and keeping it under the radar but I got papped this morning. About thirty minutes ago."

Felicity nods. "What were you doing, what were you wearing, who were you with?"

"Walking in Regent's Park. Athleisure, a cap and sunglasses, just like I am now. And..." I sigh. I really don't want to talk about Beau, but I suppose I have to. "I was with a guy from the coffee shop. We were just taking a stroll through the park."

"A guy from the coffee shop?" Felicity asks, arching one eyebrow.

"You're dating a barista?" Tommy bellows, incredulous.

"I'm not dating anyone, but if I was dating a barista, that would be perfectly fine."

"It's four a.m., I'm in no mood to argue with you, but to be clear, you're not dating the barista?" Tommy asks.

"He's not a barista. He's just a guy I bumped into at the coffee shop. We've taken a walk together a couple of times. And I'm not dating him."

"Are there shots of you kissing?" Felicity asks, making notes as we talk.

"No. We're not kissing—not in the photo, not anywhere."

"Holding hands?" she asks.

I hiss out a breath as I remember what we were doing just before the paparazzi called my name. Did he get pictures of me reaching for Beau's face? Of us holding hands? Beau kissing my hands?

"I was teasing him and I think we might have looked—yeah, we were holding hands at one point."

"What's his name?" Felicity asks.

"Beau Cove," I reply. "He's a doctor."

Felicity groans, and I immediately realize that she's concerned someone's going to think I'm his patient. "He's never been *my* doctor. I just spilled hot coffee all over him one day. We got talking."

"What kind of doctor is he?" she asks. "Please don't tell me he's a fucking obstetrician, because that's a can of worms I don't want to be dealing with."

"He says he's a GP."

"That's something at least," says Felicity. "The last thing we want is headlines about you recovering from...well, you know."

"So, can you deal with it?" I ask.

"Are you serious about this guy?" Tommy asks. "It's very soon since your split from Matty."

"Matt. And no, I'm not serious about Beau. We're not dating. We've been for three walks in a public park after arriving to the same coffee shop separately to get coffee." And he's made me feel safer, more listened to and interesting than Matt ever did. But they don't need to know any of that.

"Vivian is visiting England and catching up with friends as she prepares for the launch of Everlasting Whispers, the hotly anticipated follow-up to her double-platinum album,

Moonlight Whispers." I'm used to Felicity thinking aloud in our calls, testing out her draft statements as we all watch or listen. Usually we all sit in silence until she's worked through a couple of iterations. But I can't sit in silence as she lists out my album names.

"No," I say. "Don't mention the new album. I'm not sure I want to call it *Everlasting Whispers.*" It's the first time I've thought about the name of the album since coming to the UK.

"That's been agreed for months," Tommy said. "It was the one that tested the best in the focus groups."

"I don't like it. It's stupid in light of the breakup." The problem with being famous is everyone thinks they know you. People were invested in mine and Matt's love story. "I can't go out with an album with *everlasting* in the title when I've just split up with my fiancé."

"She's got a point," Felicity says in a low stage whisper.

"Then what?" Tommy asks.

"We don't have to decide now. What about, *"Vivian is visiting England, catching up with friends and working on new music as she prepares for the launch of her next album, the hotly anticipated follow-up to her double platinum album, Moonlight Whispers.* Then sources close to the star can say that she's doing really well after her split with her long-term boyfriend—we won't mention the fiancé bit—and that she's not dating anyone seriously at this time."

"No," Tommy says. "That suggests she's dating all over. I'm not having that. Who is this guy? Does he have a sister? Could he be the brother of a girlfriend?"

"He's practically a stranger," I reply. "I'm not lying when I say I literally bumped into him at a coffee shop. And no, he doesn't have any sisters."

Tommy purses his lips and taps his pen on his laptop, which I know will irritate Felicity.

"Strictly between us, are you dating? Are you attracted to each other? Level with us, Vivian, we're here to help."

I pause, not sure what to say. I exhale. "I'm attracted to him. He's asked me out, so I suppose he's attracted to me. I've said no, because it's too soon after Matt. We've been for a couple of walks and we had a private tour around an art gallery the other evening."

"So you *have* been on a date with him," Tommy says.

I inwardly cringe. I've been refusing to accept that I've been on a date with Beau, but of course, that's what happened. "I made it pretty clear I'm not going to date him. He didn't try to kiss me or even hold my hand, but I suppose, from the outside looking in, it could look like a date."

"Yes," Felicity says. "That fulfils all the requirements of a date. And now you've been caught together."

"We weren't naked."

"It causes an issue if we start talking about you being in a relationship with Leo or—"

"I'm not dating anyone thirty years older than me."

"Then give me another name, sweet cheeks," Tommy says.

"I haven't looked at the list," I lie.

"Liar." He's known me far too long. "I know you don't want to do this, but believe me, it will save a lot of awkward questions about Matt if you just grit your teeth and choose someone."

"It's true," Felicity adds. "And it might even turn into something. You know half the couples in Hollywood started off as fake."

I groan again. I can't think of anything worse than managing another person's ego. Most celebrities act like spoiled brats as far as I can see—surrounded by people who pamper and fawn over them. I don't want any part of that version of showbusiness. The fact that Matt is a lawyer—a man who, I thought, shunned the limelight—was core to who I was. It kept my feet on the ground. "I'm not going to end up with a celebrity. It's just...not who I am."

"We need to talk about this Beau. Do you have his contact details? I need to brief him, send him an NDA and such."

I suddenly feel defensive of Beau. "What does he need to be briefed on?"

"How to deal with press questions if he gets them."

"I can tell him to say 'no comment.'"

"You know it's easy to get tricked into giving a response. He should also know how paps can goad a reaction out of people. He needs to understand what he could come up against. You've seen the pictures of Bieber looking like the Hulk or even Sean Penn back in the day. None of us need the fallout of your new boyfriend beating up some photographer."

"Jeez, he's not my new boyfriend. How many times do I have to tell you?"

"That's not what the papers will say," Felicity says. "Especially if they have other sources—people at the gallery. Drivers. You know how these things work."

"Things will die down when they can't get any more pictures of us." My stomach sinks a little at the thought that I won't be able to see Beau again. But it's too risky.

"You know, it's just a thought, but maybe we could kill two birds with one stone," Tommy says. "Why don't we get this Beau guy to sign up to be your new boyfriend? This pap shot can be the start of his introduction to the world. Because he's a normie, and a doctor, people won't expect him to travel alongside you all the time. He's got a job to do after all. You think he'd be up for it?"

Has Tommy planted a listening device on me? It's almost like he's heard Beau's suggestion.

"He can't possibly know what opening himself up to being my boyfriend could mean. It's not fair to ask him."

"It wouldn't work anyway, Tommy," Felicity says. "It's not like Vivian is moving to England anytime soon. It would be challenging to spin the story that they're together when they're on separate continents..."

I release the tension in my shoulders at Felicity's dismissal of Beau being my fake boyfriend. I wouldn't do that to him. If I hadn't become successful, I'm pretty sure Matt and I would still be together. Fame can change people. Distort who they are at their core. It's like the flashbulbs have DNA-altering qualities or something. As much as I hate Matt for betraying me, I blame my fame for turning him into the man who would do that. That's not the man he was before I got famous. I won't ruin Beau like I ruined Matt.

"Unless..." Felicity says. "Unless you've fallen hard and it's a whirlwind romance that you've been keeping under wraps since you flew to England after the break up. What if you were to get married?"

"Married?" I realize I've stood up at the desk and can no longer seen the screen of my phone properly. I sit back down. "I'm not marrying a near-stranger just because some guy with a camera jumped out of a bush and took a picture of me!"

"But it's not just that. It's to help with the fallout from Matt. It will be good publicity generally around the album. And it will be good for Beau, too. Obviously there'll be an iron-clad pre-nup in place, but he'll be compensated. He'll be very comfortable. Doctors don't earn much in the UK, you know? You'll be doing him a favor."

"I'm not marrying Beau, and I really don't want to talk about this anymore." This conversation has gone from ridiculous to completely unhinged.

"Just ask him," Tommy says. "Like Felicity says, this could change the man's life with what we'd be prepared to pay him."

I press the heels of my hands over my eyes. Why is life so darn complicated? Why didn't I just invite Beau for coffee at my place? Why didn't I skip Coffee Confidential this morning?

"Just give me his number, Viv. I'll sound him out about it. If he doesn't want to do it, then at least we know. We can rule it out. But if he does...it could work really well for you."

I already know Beau will say yes to fake dating me. He's offered twice now.

I can see how this would work for me. It would look authentic and Beau is a nice guy. I'd enjoy the time we're together, which isn't a foregone conclusion with most of the people on Tommy's list. Being in another serious relationship—at least, *appearing* to be in another serious relationship—would take the heat off me when it comes to promoting the album.

It just isn't fair on Beau.

"He's a nice guy," I say. "He doesn't know how damaging fame can be."

Felicity purses her lips. "Don't you start thinking all

men are like Matt. Matt was a child when you got famous— he grew up in your shadow, and I say 'grew up' only for lack of a better term. This Beau sounds like a *man*. He's got his own career, his own identity. He's not going to be consumed by the attention. After I talk to him, if I think he's that kind of man, I'll tell you and we'll pull the plug."

I groan. "No you won't. Beau fixes your problem. If he says yes, you're not going to blackball him."

"Yes, I will," Felicity says, her accent growing clipped like it always does when she wants me to know she's serious. "As much as I care about your fortune and your career, I care about your heart more." She blows me a kiss through the screen. "We've all been worried sick about you, Viv. It's good to see your sweet face, my darling. Even if it is in the midst of an emergency."

"Okay," I say. "I'll ask him. But not about the marriage thing. That's ridiculous."

I see them both go to speak—I know they want me to hand his number over, but I won't do that. I want to gauge Beau's reaction for myself. And I want to list every potential downside of a fake relationship with me.

"If he says no, he says no and that's the case closed," I say. "I'll let you know what he says. And now that I've turned my phone back on, do me a favor? I want to know if Matt's side starts planting stories. I want to know if I've got leaks in the team. I want to hear about suspicions you have about the people I'm working with or spending time with. You two are the people I trust to give me the information I need. Tommy, you've known me since I was a kid, but I'm not sixteen anymore. I don't want you curating what you tell me. I need to know everything." Looking back, I'd been going around with blinders on while I was with Matt. Now they're firmly off and I'm determined to see everything with fresh eyes.

"Okay," he says. "You got it. Let us know how it goes with Beau."

"I'll give you a call later." Before they start trying to convince me of either handing over his number or asking him to be my fake husband, I hang up.

ELEVEN

Beau

This view of London from the sofa in Vivian's hotel suite is spectacular. If the woman in front of me wasn't trying to convince me of the perils of becoming her fake boyfriend, I don't think I'd be able to concentrate on anything else.

"How many times would you like me to say 'yes' before you believe that I'm completely up for fake dating you?" I take a swig of the beer Vivian got me from the in-suite bar. Apparently, she moved into the hotel this morning after she left my office. I get it—she'll be safer here. Though I would feel better if she had a personal security team.

I can't remember ever being concerned about a woman's safety before. But I suppose most women I've known haven't been in imminent danger.

"I'm not talking about real dating," Vivian says. "There's no sex on the table if that's what you're thinking."

"Vivian, I ended up with a dislocated shoulder the last time I thought about a relationship with a woman. I understand this is just me doing you a favor and we wouldn't really be dating. To be honest, if you needed a real boyfriend, I wouldn't... That's not what I'm looking for. I like you, we get on. I'm happy to step in and help you out."

"Right," she says.

"And anyway, it won't be for long. You'll be through your publicity tour and life will move on." Part of me wants to help her out, but part of me thinks this will be good for me too. I've been in a cycle of being in London and looking forward to going on my next trip and then being on the trip and thinking about being in London. It feels like I need to step off the hamster wheel and reassess. Maybe doing something a little different will help me look at my life and what I want in a different way.

"It will pay well," she says. "Tommy will talk to you about that side of things."

I choke and lean forward as beer drips out of the bottle.

"You're not going to pay me," I say. "Like I'm going to accept money for taking a friend out to dinner."

"You see, I don't think you're getting it. This isn't just a couple dinners at Nobu. This will require sacrifices on your part. When you're off work, I might need you to fly to New York for a photo-op."

Not doing what I normally do is exactly what I want: an excuse to press pause on the next trip, a reason to change the patterns that are starting to feel constricting. Maybe this is the chance I've been waiting for, an opportunity to sit still long enough to put together a business plan—or even learn what exactly a business plan entails. My brother Nathan is the businessman in the family. I have no idea where to start with setting up a new venture, but I bet he does.

"Sounds terrible," I say, sitting back on the sofa,

watching her crossed-legged in the chair opposite me, trying to convince me how awful jet-setting around the world will be. She's beautiful and smart and talented...if I wanted to date someone, she might just be my type.

"I mean it, I will take up all your free time. From what we've talked about, there's lots of things you like to do. Cold-water swimming for instance. Didn't you rappel down a building the other month? And then there's the press attention you'll get. If you've got any skeletons in your closet, prepare for them to come tumbling out."

I laugh. "Well, as long as they stick to me and don't focus on my dodgy brothers, I think we'll be okay."

"They might dig up stuff on your brothers." She stops herself. "It's unlikely—but given your brother is Nathan Cove, they might take that angle."

"They're big boys. They can handle it."

"And there's no sex."

I look her dead in the eye. "Vivian, believe me when I say I don't want to get into anything."

Silence settles between us and I feel the need to tell her more.

"I haven't told anyone this." I slide my beer bottle onto the table and sit back. "But I've been thinking that maybe I need to shift direction." I pause. Have I been heading in a direction or just...living life, directionless? Definitely the latter. "I have a business idea that I've been turning over in my brain for the last ten years and never done anything about. Lately, I've been thinking about it a lot more. The dislocated shoulder could have been a lot worse and...it made me realize that if I had been injured more severely, or worse...I'd have one regret, and it wouldn't be not climbing Everest or making it to the South Pole. It would be not giving this idea a go."

She doesn't say anything, and I go on, filling the silence. "It would be easy to go back to my routine of locuming and traveling, but I think if I start doing something different, I might find momentum and I'd be more likely to put more time and effort into..."

"Your business idea?"

"Exactly."

"So this would push you out of your old habits and allow new ones to form?" she asks, articulating my thoughts way more eloquently than I did.

"Maybe," I say. "My locum job is almost up, and I'd usually start booking flights and planning my next adventure. But my gut tells me it's not the right thing to do. But it is the *easy* thing to do—bury the business idea until after the trip or until next year or until the year after that. I want to force myself out of my normal. I don't want to wake up with regrets. Fake-dating you until you've finished your album promotion suits me almost as much as it suits you."

I reach for her phone on the coffee table in front of us. "Come on. Phone this Tommy bloke and let's do this."

"I think you should sleep on it."

"I think you should stop worrying. What's the worst that can happen?"

She laughs, and it's filled with exuberance and freedom. It's not a laugh I've heard from her before but it suits her.

I grin, keeping my gaze locked on hers. "We both know this is a short-term thing. No love. No commitment." I like Vivian. I like that she's independent and ambitious and comes to London on her own without telling anyone because she wants some time by herself. It's ballsy, and I *really* like that. Also, she's done so much with her life. She's seen so much, traveled the world, met presidents and prime misters. She's squeezed out so much for someone so young and that's kind of intoxicating.

Neither of us wants to date anyone, but I'm not ready to let her sail off into the world without knowing her a little better.

And if anyone was to ask Coral, being a fake boyfriend is about all I have qualifications for anyway.

TWELVE

Vivian

Beau chuckles and I can tell he's taking Tommy's very American welcome in his stride. "Very nice to see you," he says. "I'm Beau Cove."

"Delicious, darling. Very excited about this. Especially now that I've seen you, Beau. You're gorgeous. Let's get Felicity on."

I turn to Beau and give him an *are-you-sure-about-this* look. He smiles at me and slides his hand under mine.

"Really?" I ask.

He shrugs but he doesn't let go.

"You guys are so cute," Felicity practically screams as she comes online. "Where have you been hiding this guy?"

"Okay, calm down everyone. Beau is British and you're going to freak him out if you keep going like this."

"I'm British, darling," Felicity says. "Just haven't been back to the old country in thirty years."

Beau chuckles and sweeps his thumb over mine. "Good to meet you, Felicity."

"We're both very grateful that you've agreed to do this," Tommy says. "I suggest we take the negotiations around the contract offline. If you have a lawyer, you can put me in touch. Really, today is just to say hi and for Felicity to give us some ideas of how we take you public."

"Thanks, Tommy," Felicity says. "Good news is that I've had the paper who bought the pap shot of the two of you in the park hold off publishing tonight on the basis that we'll give them a little something before either of you is spotted together again. So I'm going to go with... *People close to Vivian say she's enjoying some downtime in London with close friends.*"

I look at Beau. Does he think this is completely ludicrous? Because if he does, I totally get it. From a non-celebrity's perspective, this must look beyond weird.

"Are you happy with that?" Felicity asks.

I glance across at Beau. It's partly because I want to make sure he *is* happy, but also because it's habit. Usually, Matt would have taken the lead in these kinds of conversations. I look back at the screen, because Matt's not here and Beau isn't going to be steering my career like Matt did. That's never going to happen again. "That sounds fine."

"And then we'll tell the same publication about the two of you going to dinner. Are you happy to do that tomorrow night?" Felicity asks.

"Beau?" I ask. "This is all happening very quickly. Does that work for you? Do you have plans tomorrow night?"

He turns to speak directly at me, ignoring Tommy and Felicity. "Nothing but a bowl of soup with my brother. I'd much prefer going to dinner with you."

I try not to smile, but it's hard. He's just so focused on me—or it seems that way. It's refreshing. Matt and I were together so long that I can't remember if he ever flirted with me or whether we'd kind of left flirting to slowly drift off, discarded during the course of our relationship. It feels good to be so...*noticed* by Beau. To feel like right here, next to me, is the only place he wants to be. Even if we're both committed to remaining single.

I turn back to the screen. "Tomorrow night works."

"Okay," Felicity says. "I'll speak to Betty and get her to arrange glam and a stylist." I haven't spoken to my assistant for weeks. She's likely been going out of her mind.

"Beau, do you need help with anything?" Tommy asks.

Beau shrugs. "Do you have a preference for where I book a table?"

He's so adorable.

Felicity hoots with laughter and I can see, rather than hear, Tommy chuckling. "Dear boy, all that will be taken care of. We'll book the table. We can send a car for you if you want to let us have an address?"

Beau shakes his head. "I can get here, to the Dorchester, myself. That's not a problem. So you don't even want me to book the restaurant?"

"Absolutely not," Tommy says. "We'll take care of everything. We'll have your car take the two of you to the restaurant and I'll also send some security."

I'm past the point of complaining about Tommy insisting on security. It took me a long time to get used to, but at this point, I've given up. "Please make it discreet."

"Of course, baby girl."

"We'll leak your arrival time and location to a couple of publications. So tomorrow night will be the start of... We need a couple name for you," Felicity says. "B-Viv—god I'm so good at my job."

I glance at Beau and his eyes are narrowed. He's staring at the screen like he can't quite believe what he's a witness to.

Me too, my friend. Me too.

THIRTEEN

Beau

Tonight is one of the few times in my life that I've ever felt self-conscious. I wasn't quite sure what to wear to dinner, given I was going to be photographed by the international media. So I opted for what I would have worn if I was trying to impress a girl I was taking out on a date: white shirt, my favorite jeans and, for good measure, a blazer. Maybe I'm turning into Jacob.

As I take a seat in the cab, I pat down my pockets: phone, keys, wallet. On the seat beside me lay the flowers I picked up during a break between clients this afternoon. I know we're not in a real relationship, but she deserves a man who's nice to her, even if I'm not her boyfriend. I saw them and they reminded me of her—pinks and whites and greens. I can pick out which of the small bouquet are roses. As much as I don't have floral qualifications, I'm not an idiot. I think the florist said the other flowers were snap-dragons and freesias. Whatever they are, they're light and pretty and look like Vivian when she doesn't know I'm looking at her—light and pretty and delicate.

I'm about three minutes from the Dorchester when my phone goes. It's Tommy again. He's been calling me all afternoon, but I've been working. I only don't dismiss it because it's Vivian's manager and I don't want to upset him. Or her.

"Hey, Beautiful Beau," he says as I answer.

"Tommy," I reply. "How are you?" This guy is over the top, even for an American. I'm going to have to ask Vivian if he's always like this or if he's just being particularly...effervescent for my sake.

"We were going to talk about the contract," he says. "You were going to call me."

"Yeah, sorry, I had to squeeze in an emergency patient and now I'm on my way to the hotel." To be honest, I'd completely forgotten to call him back because I was busy Googling how to write a business plan between patients. There were a lot more steps than I'd expected, but now I have a place to start—market research. Most of it I can do online.

"So you're still on for tonight then? You haven't got cold feet?"

I only agreed to this yesterday. What would have changed my mind since then? "No, Tommy. I'm pulling up any minute now."

"Can you sign the contract right now then? I can have someone bring it up to the suite."

I wince because I absolutely don't want that to happen. "There were just a few things that I wasn't that happy with when I skimmed the document you sent over. Like, I don't want to get paid. It feels too weird to me."

"What do you mean, you don't want to get paid?" He sounds like he's spent his entire life believing the world is flat and I'd just proved it's round.

"I'm taking a friend to dinner. I'm not accepting payment for that. Spending time with Vivian is payment enough."

"Think of it as compensation for having to put up with the press scrutiny."

"I don't read the press—or certainly not the kind that talks about me and Vivian going out to dinner."

"They might go through your bins, talk to your friends, all trying to get information about you. These people know no bounds."

We pull up outside the hotel, so I pay and get out. "Yeah, well, I have nothing to hide." What do I care if people go digging around after me? I put most of it on Instagram anyway. I know my parents aren't famous like Vivian is famous, but in the world of medicine, they're as close to celebrities as a person can be. Everyone knows me because of them; it was the same when I started to practice. I'm used to scrutiny.

"But the NDA is part of that contract. We want to make sure that what goes on between you and Vivian stays between you and Vivian."

"Who am I going to tell?"

I head into the lobby and turn left as Vivian's assistant—who messaged me this afternoon—instructed, even though I was here last night. I guess she didn't know that. I head to the lifts.

"I'm going to have to go, Tommy. I'm in the hotel now."

I press cancel and step into the lift.

I turn left when I get out of the lift, but I don't need to

remind myself of the room numbers on the doors to tell where Vivian is. There's a guy who's about as tall as me when I'm on Jacob's shoulders and three times as wide, standing at the end of the corridor in a black suit, looking like he wants to kill me.

He's new.

I shake my head. So many people are involved in tonight. It's certainly not the low-key dinner I'd envisaged when I suggested this. I don't mind. It's just...not how I usually roll.

"I'm Beau Cove," I say as I get to the door.

"You got ID?" the security guy asks.

ID? I chuckle but slide my driving license out of my wallet. I want to offer him a blood sample, but at the same time, I don't want my head pushed through a wall.

As soon as I show it to him, the door behind him opens. "Beau?" A small woman with very short, dark hair pops her head out.

"That's me," I reply.

She tips her head back toward the room behind her and we go inside. "Oh how sweet," she says as she glances down at the flowers. I follow her down the long corridor toward the living room. "You got her flowers. You really didn't need to." She's acting like I'm giving them to her. "I hear you're new to these kinds of arrangements—you know, the fake relationships stuff. Things like flowers—you don't need to do it. You're not really dating." I presume this is Betty, Vivian's assistant, although she hasn't introduced herself and I'm not sure if she's trying to be protective or just rude. "If you let me have them, I'll put them in a vase," she says.

"Erm, if it's okay by you, I'd like to give them to Vivian first."

"Oh, okay. If you like," she says from in front of me, not

bothering to turn around. "My name is Betty, by the way. I'm Vivian's assistant."

"Hi, Betty."

The corridor opens into the same sitting room I sat in yesterday, except everything looks different. For a start, there's at least half a dozen people in the room and the furniture has been changed around so there's a dressing table and mirrors along the wall and a high chair facing the view of the city. Vivian is sitting in the chair, staring straight ahead while one person brushes something on her face and another does something to her hair. A third person paints her nails and another...it looks like she's putting moisturizer on Vivian's legs. I'd like to see the job description for that position.

Jesus, maybe I should have put a little more thought into my outfit today. To be fair, the fact that I put any thought into it at all is a first.

"Hey," I say, meeting her gaze in the mirror.

She bursts into a smile. "Hey," she replies.

"I bought these for you. Do you want me to go find a vase?"

"That's so nice," she replies. "Betty, please can you get some water for the flowers Beau brought?"

Before I can turn around, someone has scooped them out of my hands.

"We're running a bit late," she says. "Sorry to keep you waiting."

"It's not a problem. I feel a little weird not knowing where we're going tonight." I lean against the window and watch as people flit around her, tweaking and puffing and brushing and generally pawing at her. She looks beautiful, but I can't help thinking she looks a little less like herself.

"Oh, Betty, where did Felicity book us for dinner?" she

calls out. It's weird having a conversation about dinner when there are so many people around.

"Sexy Fish," Betty calls from over by the small kitchen.

I nod. "Not far to go then."

"Guys, are we done yet?" Vivian asks. "I thought we were going for a casual look."

"It takes a lot to do a good casual look," the guy who's doing her makeup says.

I squint, trying to make what he's said make sense. "You look great in a cap and some leggings."

Vivian laughs. "This is what it takes to move from coffee run to casual supper." Her phone rings and she picks up, holding the phone ahead of her so I know it's a video call.

"Hey Felicity." She glances at me as if we both know Felicity calling again is annoying, except I have no real idea what's going on. Maybe Felicity needs to call her.

"Darling, you look completely gorgeous. Is Beau there yet?"

"Yes, and he brought me beautiful flowers. You want to see?" Vivian turns in her chair and the makeup and hair people step back so they don't block Vivian's view. The move is so seamless, it could be choreographed.

Betty holds up the vase, and Felicity says, "Lovely, darling. Can you ask Beau if he wouldn't mind signing the e-doc I sent through to him? It's just the NDA. The rest of it we can talk through tomorrow, but we need that NDA signed."

Vivian practically curdles at the request. She's clearly feeling awkward, but I can't tell if it's because I've not signed the NDA yet or she doesn't want to talk to me about anything like that. Awkward is the last thing I want her to feel.

"No problem." I pull out my phone and see the link in my inbox. I pull up the contract and scroll through. I skim the thing and press all the right buttons to make sure I've signed it. "Done," I say.

Vivian's smile is back. "He's done it," she says to Felicity. She mouths *thank you* to me.

"Okay everyone, we're going to have to make a move now. Let's finish up."

It's like everyone steps away at once when Vivian slides off her chair. I'm not sure they would have ever finished if she didn't start her exit.

She takes off her pink satin robe—exactly the same color as the roses in the bouquet I just bought her—and picks up her bag.

"Wow," I say as she comes toward me and I bend to kiss her on the cheek. "You look incredible."

She's wearing a pink top the same color as the robe and it's got big sleeves, though it seems to have a corset-type thing that shows off her breasts in a way I almost can't look away from. Gradually my gaze travels down to her jeans, and I try not to look as blown away as I feel. She really is gorgeous.

"Thanks. So do you. But then you always do."

I smile at her in a way that I hope says, *That was a super-nice thing to say. It feels really genuine and I really like you.*

"Are you ready?" I ask.

"As I'll ever be."

I scoop up her hand and lead her out of the hotel room, leaving the entourage of people behind us. "Let's forget about everything and just have a nice dinner and good conversation."

She wrinkles up her nose like she's trying not to smile. "I think most of that's almost guaranteed." And then she looks at me in a way that I think says, *I really like you too.*

And to think Tommy wanted to pay me.

FOURTEEN

Vivian

The waitress leaves us with our menus and at the same time, Beau and I both say, "How are you?"

We grin at each other. He always seems so relaxed. So happy.

"Are you okay?" he asks again, his blue eyes sparkling at me in the most mischievous way.

"Yes, but I'm used to this kind of thing," I say. There were just two cameras taking shots as we got out of the car and went into the restaurant. They shouted questions at us, but I didn't reply and it was just seconds before we were through the restaurant door.

"But it's not my name they're calling. It's not me they want a picture of."

I laugh. "It absolutely is. Granted, they may want that picture to be with me, but they got their wish. You're going to be named tomorrow. They're going to know who you are, what you do for a living. It won't be long before they know where you live." I still don't feel completely comfortable with Beau doing this when he can't possibly know what he's gotten himself into. But it's too late now.

"It will be fine," he says, like it's no big deal.

But it is a big deal. Matt used to complain about it all the time. Was all that just an act? Given he was leaking details about me and our relationship, maybe he didn't have such a hard time dealing with the scrutiny.

"Do you normally have a private room when you go out to dinner like this?" he asks.

I pause, digesting what he's asked. "You mean, for just two people?" I've done private dining for a group of people, but it's never occurred to me to get a private room for just two people. "I don't think so."

"Because you like the atmosphere of being among people?" he asks.

I'm never in charge of making dinner reservations. Betty always does it without being asked—or at least, without me asking. Matt liked to arrange our dinners out, and I always assumed it was because he liked to feel like he was taking me out—which he was, except I always paid. But maybe his interest in making our plans had less to do with taking me on dates and more to do with ensuring his media contacts would know where to find us. Maybe I'm being paranoid.

Maybe not.

"Can I be honest with you?" I ask.

"I wouldn't want anything else."

I glance away, so I don't see him slide his hand over mine—but I feel the shiver that races down my spine when he does. I look back at him and he adds, "I'm serious. I don't want you ever saying anything to me that isn't true. I don't even want you to sugarcoat it."

I smile, partly because I want to believe him and also

because I wonder what it would be like to get things uncoated in sugar. I've tried to tell Tommy the same thing, but he always wants to wrap even the worst news in a bow with pink confetti.

"I don't think I've been smart enough to think about it. And now I *am* thinking about it, I wonder why I haven't."

"Probably because you have someone else making the reservations."

"I guess. Maybe I will next time. Tonight is all about being seen rather than being private, so I guess it makes sense why a private room wouldn't be a good idea."

"Next time, maybe we should try that—come in the back door, go into a private room and still get great food and better conversation."

I smile, but I'm tense.

"What did I say?" He's grinning at me as he asks. "I can tell something in there was something you didn't want to hear. You don't need to sugarcoat it for me."

I shrug. Here goes nothing. "The next time we go out, we'll have to be seen again. That's the whole reason for us being...public." I pause, but power through to the hard thing. "You know this isn't real, right?"

His grin doesn't falter. He leans back in his chair, his hand sliding down mine, making every hair on my arm stand to attention. "Right. Doesn't mean we can't enjoy our evening though, does it?"

I shrug.

The vibration of his laugh runs down my spine in a way that feels...inappropriate. There's no doubt Beau is attractive, but his confidence and openness is unbelievably sexy.

I shake my head like I can shake those feelings away. *You're still heartbroken,* I remind myself.

"Right. What I want to do while I'm in London is enjoy

each moment. It's such a busy city and I'm always so frantic when I'm here that sometimes I forget. I'm too busy with my patients, or planning my next trip, to see the beauty in the present moment. That's all I'm saying we should do. Let's not worry about what will be in the papers tomorrow —Tommy and Felicity can do that. Let's just enjoy ourselves."

My shoulders droop with relief. "I like that idea."

"Good. Let's order. I'm hungry." We pick up our menus. "Do you know what you want? Shall I order for you?"

I narrow my eyes. "Actually, why don't you order for me without me telling you what I want."

"Really?" He draws his eyebrows together. "Isn't it a safer bet to just tell me?"

"But not as fun."

"And if you don't like it?" he asks.

"Then you can eat it and I can eat what you order for yourself."

He grins at me and buries his head in the menu. Every now and then he looks up as if he's trying to work out from my face whether I have a seafood allergy.

He places the order with the waitress by pointing at the items on the menu so I don't know what he's ordered.

"This feels crazy," I say.

"You need to get out more," he replies with a smirk.

"I'm Miss Apple Pie. Tell me the craziest thing you've ever done."

"Crazy? Probably BASE jumping in Norway. I don't think I was ever in any danger, but on balance, I think I'd rather do something other than jumping off a cliff, even if there is a parachute attached to my back."

"I didn't realize that was an actual thing. I thought... I don't know what I thought, but I didn't expect ordinary people to be jumping off cliffs."

"Ordinary people like us normies?" he asks, laughing.

"I guess I just thought it was something people only did in movies."

"Yeah, well I'm not planning on doing another jump."

"What about out of a plane?"

"Oh I'd do that again. Because there's a bigger drop and you have a secondary chute, it's much safer. I've done a few jumps and it's great. I did the training so I can do them on my own and it's...so beautiful and peaceful. In those moments, I really appreciate how wonderful the world is. And it's not just the views—it's the engineering that has created the parachutes, the scientific endeavor that went into creating the plane I flew up in, the camaraderie of the other people on the jump. There's nothing but a huge smile on my face for a week after an experience like that."

"So, it's like a high?" I ask. It sounds like he's a drug addict chasing his next fix.

"I've never done drugs—got no interest in drugs doing anything other than healing and preventing pain."

I feel my shoulders relax, even though I didn't consciously tense. I never considered Beau could potentially be one of those hangers-on I've seen around bands, just in it for the hand-me-down freebies. The alcohol, the drugs, the sex.

"I've said this before, but it's more that I don't want to miss out. It's a short time we're here."

They bring our food and Beau reveals he ordered everything to share. "This way neither of us has to miss out."

I laugh. "Oh, so the FOMO extends to food too. Do you

think having so many brothers makes you covet things that others have?" I ask, popping an olive from the sharing platter into my mouth.

"Are you trying to solve me? Work me out?" He doesn't wait for a response, like it doesn't bother him whether that's the case or not. "I don't think so. I'm four of five. My cousin Vincent is older, too. He used to spend summers with us. Of course Zach, Nathan and Jacob could do things before I could—go off to football camp, have sleepovers. But I was young at the time. It wasn't until I had the accident that this desire not to leave anything on the field kicked in. At that point, my older brothers were going off to medical school one after another."

"And you chose medicine because they did, and you didn't want to get left out?"

"Fair assumption, but no. I love and admire my parents utterly. I saw what a difference they made to people's lives. I wanted to do that too."

"And you still like medicine?"

He nods. "I really do. But unlike my parents, it's not my entire life, you know?"

"Because you like experiencing the variety life has to offer you."

"Exactly."

"And I bet that applies to women as well."

He's taking a sip of his drink, and he has to pause to make sure he remembers to swallow before he laughs.

I shrug as if to absolve myself from responsibility for the statement.

"It's not exactly the same. I don't seek out variety..." He pauses. "I enjoy flirting with women." I shoot him a look that says *duh*. "But I'm not out to add to a list of conquests. I enjoy female company, but I'm never in one place for any length of time. I do six months in London and then I fly to wherever. Then I'm back and... My lifestyle is not conducive to anything long-term."

"What about the woman who gave you the dislocated shoulder?"

He sighs and puts a forkful of food in his mouth, possibly buying time to answer the question.

"For legal reasons, I need to be clear that she didn't give me the dislocated shoulder. I don't want to misrepresent her." He shoots me a grin. "I was a little taken aback by her response—*literally* taken aback. I toppled over backwards, down a drop. I was lucky it wasn't a bigger fall."

"You said you were taken aback by her response. Her response to what? Did you propose or something?"

He hits his chest with his fist, like he's trying to prevent himself from choking, then grins at me. "Absolutely not." He laughs. "I think I was just looking for something more... not necessarily from her, but from life. She had a job where she got a lot of free time, so we'd traveled together a few times. I'd just suggested she base herself in London at my place for a bit so we could get to know each other better."

"Right." I understand. My life is similar, which is one of the reasons Matt had been on my payroll for about five years before he went back to practicing law. We didn't want to be apart during my first world tour. "And she said no?"

"From what I remember, she laughed in my face and *then* said no."

I wince, a little taken aback that he so openly confessed having his ass handed to him. But that's also one of the things I like about Beau—his confidence means he has no need for ego or pride. He's unashamedly who he is.

"But thank god," he continues. "Like I said, I was

looking for something. Coral saying no has set me on the right path."

Our entrees arrive and it's another sharing platter. "We came to the perfect place for you when it comes to this food. You can eat what you like and skirt over the stuff you don't."

"It's the opposite actually—it's the worst possible place because I like it all, which means I'll eat too much and have to get a treadmill brought up to my suite tomorrow."

"It's worth it. I'll come and work out with you in the hotel gym, if you like?" he asks.

I start to laugh, and it's like I've inhaled some kind of laughing gas or something because I just can't stop.

"Wow, you okay there?" he asks, his eyes widening.

I put my hands over my face, trying to get myself together. I take a breath. "No. Hard pass. First, I am a terrible workout buddy—any distraction available, I'm all over it. Plus, I get really hot and sweaty—it's not a good look."

He narrows his eyes, and it's like a world class tennis player on the baseline, lining up to smash an ace over the net. "Oh, I can cope with you hot and sweaty."

It's like he's set fire to my face.

I tilt my head in faux admonishment. "It's disgusting."

"I can cope with disgustingly hot and sweaty. In fact, I think we should try it. The hotter and sweatier, the better."

A deep, hot throb pulses between my legs. All I can picture is Beau, naked, his hard, hot body over mine, his hair messy because of my fingers, the tendons in his neck straining because he's holding himself back. Him looking at me like I'm the only woman he ever wants to look at from now until the end of time.

"I don't make a good workout buddy," I mutter, and help myself to something crispy on the platter.

"We'll see about that," he says. And then he changes the subject and we start talking about the food.

That's safer. That will stop the heat between us, the enveloping tension that always seems to circle us when we're together.

I hope.

FIFTEEN

Beau

I sit up with a start and come face-to-face with my sister-in-law, who is holding out her phone.

"This is you," she says as if we're sitting around the table in Norfolk, passing each other roast potatoes. Her tone doesn't betray that it's five in the morning and I was deep asleep until she barged into my bedroom.

I slump back onto my bed and groan. "What are you showing me?" I ask, eyes closed.

"You. You're on the interweb. It's definitely you because you're wearing Nathan's shirt. His bloody initials are on your cuffs."

"Initials on his cuffs? What a wanker."

"Are you dating Vivian Cross?" It sounds like she's furious with me but I'm not quite sure why.

"No comment," I reply and pull the duvet over my head.

"Nathan!" she calls, despite the fact that she runs a real risk of waking the baby.

I pull the duvet off my head. "Madison! Stop shouting. Why are you angry?"

A sleepy Nathan appears in the doorway, in boxers. "What's the matter?" he asks through a yawn. "She's sleeping. I just checked on her."

"Your brother is sleeping with Vivian Cross and he's in our spare bedroom and hasn't told us."

"I'm not sleeping with Vivian Cross," I say.

"Not right at this second, no, but you have been."

"No I haven't." I glance over at Nathan, hoping he might help me out and wondering whether I should tell him about my business idea. Will he tease me mercilessly for thinking I could do anything other than be a doctor?

He holds up his hand. "She's a journalist, mate. Just tell her everything. It's the easiest way. Believe me."

"I have no comment. I'm under an NDA, and I don't even think I'm meant to tell you *that*."

Madison's eyes light up and she plonks herself at the bottom of my bed. "What's she like?"

I sit up and scoot back against the headboard. There's absolutely no point in thinking I'm getting back to sleep at this point. "I'm helping her out. We're just going out to dinner a couple times. That's all."

Madison narrows her eyes at me. "You're helping her out by taking her out to dinner. She's Vivian Cross. She's not some poor, shy little bookkeeper who can't get a date." She glances back at Nathan. "You Cove men."

I can't help but laugh, partly because Nathan's laughing, so I figure it's safe and Madison isn't going to hand me my balls on a plate.

"So how do you think you're doing her a favor? Showing her how restaurants work in the UK?"

I sigh. "No. But seriously, I'm not meant to talk about it with anyone."

Madison pats me on the leg. "We're family, Beau. We have to talk about *everything*. Anyway, you can trust me, I'm a journalist."

"That's exactly why I can't trust you. You're a journalist. Vivian has enough written about her in the papers without me feeding the beast."

Madison holds up a finger. "First of all, I'm not a beast, take it back."

I roll my eyes. "I take it back," I say in a singsong voice.

"Second, I'm not that kind of journalist. I write about important, newsworthy things, not who my brother-in-law is shagging."

I go to speak and she raises her finger in the air. "Plus we're family, and even if you told me you'd stolen details of Russia's nuclear capability, I wouldn't write about it. I just love Vivian Cross. I want this to be true."

"You should work in hostage interrogation."

Madison breaks into a huge smile. "I know. Tell me everything."

"If I do, I'm going to make *you* sign an NDA as soon as I can get hold of one. Anyway," I continue, stifling a yawn, "I ran into Vivian and we got chatting. She needs a fake boyfriend and I was happy to oblige. It's as simple as that."

"So you're not actually dating?" Madison asks.

"What do you mean, fake boyfriend?" Nathan asks. "Why would she need a fake boyfriend?"

"Is it because of that shit-head Matt?" Madison asks.

"Yeah. She's about to promote her next album and she doesn't want all the press questions to be about her ex."

"She wants all the questions to be about you instead." Madison squeals, which is the first time I've ever heard an

adult human woman make that sound. It's a little disconcerting. "This is so exciting."

"Why?" I ask.

"Because you're dating Vivian bloody Cross. She's...a
queen. Like we should topple Charles and have her on the
throne immediately. In fact, I might create one of those
survey things...you know that if you get more than four
hundred signatures on a petition, you can have a proposal
debated in Parliament. Can you imagine? Vivian Cross
could be our *actual* queen—"

"Exactly how much sleep have you had in the last
week?" I ask as Madison starts tapping away on her phone.

"Yes, here it is, it's on Wikipedia. The UK Parliament
petitions website allows members of the public to create and
support petitions for consideration by the Parliament of the
United Kingdom. Although...blah blah...considers all petitions which receive 100,000 signatures or more, there is no
automatic parliamentary debate." Her shoulders slouch. "So
there's no guarantee." She looks deflated, like she thought
crowning Queen Vivian was in touching distance.

"Yes, no matter your ambition, I don't think the British
government are about to disrupt the Mountbatten-Windsor
line to let an American on the throne. We'll be a republic
before that happens."

"It would be more likely if she married a Brit," Madison
said, seeming to regain her footing.

"If that Brit was Prince William, maybe."

She sighs and turns back. "So back to reality."

"Oh good," I say. "I like it there."

"Do you like her? Could it turn into something? I mean
you must fancy her. She's gorgeous."

"Am I thinking about the right woman?" Nathan asks.
"Emo, blue hair and nose piercing?"

"No." Madison and I groan. Then she holds her phone up at Nathan, who steps closer to have a look.

"Right, I know the one," Nathan says. "She's beautiful."

"Yeah, I think she's gorgeous," I say. "I'd have something seriously wrong with me if I didn't. And I like spending time with beautiful women, so why wouldn't I agree to be her fake boyfriend?"

"Have you kissed her?"

"No, and can you get out of my room so I can get up and get to work? Nathan?"

"Why don't you bring her over for dinner?" she asks.

"Oh," I tap my fingers on the duvet, "let me think, why wouldn't I bring her over to meet my sister-in-law who just woke me up in the middle of the night to pepper me with questions about her?"

Madison shrugs. "If you'd told us in the first place, I wouldn't have had to, so really, this is your own doing." She stands and leaves, pausing to kiss Nathan on her way.

"Nathan, do you have time this morning to chat about something?" I ask.

"I have to go. I have a call with Dubai in ten minutes. Tonight?"

"Yeah, that would be good."

"She'd be welcome," Madison continues. "I'll pretend I'm not bothered having her over, if it would make things easier."

"I actually wouldn't be bothered having her over, if that makes things easier," Nathan adds. "Just make sure it's not *just* her that you're helping in this situation. I know what you're like."

I wave my hands at them both, trying to hurry them out of my bedroom. They are perfect for each other. It's like watching an old-fashioned scale that's got exactly the same amount of weight on each plate, only one's feather and one's lead.

It must be nice to have someone balance you out like that. Someone who knows all your good bits, but all your bad bits too, and loves you because of all of it.

"Will you be home for seven?" I call as Nathan heaves Madison out of the room.

"Should be."

I look at the bedside clock. Fourteen hours until I confess my plans to Nathan, making my business plan that much more real. I've always thought of the travel business idea as something I might do in the distant future. After all, it's impossible to start a business and live the life I do, traveling regularly, away for weeks and months at a time—sometimes in remote areas without reliable telephone service, let alone internet access.

I'm not convinced the *distant* future is here, right now, but maybe it's not so distant anymore. It feels like the right time to take a few steps toward a project I'm still thinking about ten years later. Given I know nothing about business, talking to Nathan is a shuffle forward.

SIXTEEN

Vivian

For once, I'm alone in my hotel room—sort of. Tommy and Felicity are on my laptop on a video call, but there are no people present who I can't make disappear with the touch of a button. I'll take it.

"The press coverage has been excellent," Felicity says. "Obviously all the main players covered it. TMZ, Daily Mail, Page Six, and it's all over Instagram and Twitter. During the course of the day, we'll leak Beau's name. Probably tell one of the big fan sites who he is. Or we might Anon Please at DeuxMoi."

"Okay then, if there's nothing else, I'm going to grab a shower." I need to distract myself from the fact that I haven't heard from Beau. I received what has become a usual *good morning* text from him this morning, and he suggested we go to the zoo. I'd taken a couple of hours to respond, but in the end, I said no.

Partly because I'm not in the mood for a big outing—all that attention and security and stuff. I don't think Beau realizes what a trip to the zoo would involve. At least I hope he doesn't. That's another reason I said no. I've asked Beau a few times about his thirst for adventure—and his answers are consistent, about making the most out of life. But something in my gut tells me he might be drawn to being with me because of the adventure of it—the adrenaline of being chased by paparazzi, or the thrill of being discovered somewhere we shouldn't be.

I don't know why I'm so bothered if Beau likes the attention. It's not like this is going to turn into something. We aren't *really* dating. If Beau was an actor, I wouldn't think anything about it if he got some kind of kick out of the attention—because I wouldn't care.

But for some reason, I care about Beau. He's referred to us as friends, which feels...good, if slightly aspirational. I want him to be the man he seems to be. It would mean my instincts aren't as fatally flawed as I thought they were.

"There's just one thing I'd like to mention," Tommy says.

My phone buzzes with an incoming message from Beau.

"Yup?" I say, distracted now, wanting to read the message but not wanting to read the message.

"You know I always want to be honest with you," he says. His words capture my attention and I stare at the screen. "I'd forgotten about it until..."

"We've been notified about a story running in Celebrity Express tomorrow," Felicity says.

I sighed. Celebrity Express has never liked me, but they seem to like Matt an awful lot. Most of the things he leaked about me had been through them.

"Is it from Matt?" I ask.

The fact that they don't respond right away is all the answer I need.

"We don't know for certain," Felicity says.

I pause, trying to steel myself for what comes next. Did he plant a hidden camera to record us having sex? He always accused me of not trusting him when I said no to putting ourselves on film—"just for us," Matt claimed— same when he asked for nudes when we were apart. And to think, it was never *him* I didn't trust. I just didn't want to be hacked or burgled. I never considered *he* would be the source of any leak.

"I don't think it will catch on with other news outlets, but it's pictures of him looking downcast." Felicity rolls her eyes as she speaks. "It adds to the narrative that he was a maligned, put-down man who did everything you wanted and you were never happy, yada, yada, yada."

I look away from the screen and try to blink away the tears. It's so ludicrous. I did everything I could so he wouldn't feel secondary to me or the celebrity that both is and isn't me. I take a deep breath and look up at Felicity. From her expression, there's something else. "And?"

"The photos are accompanied by 'confirmed sources' saying you had him on an allowance."

I push out an incredulous laugh. Tommy used to beg me to do that and I always refused. Matt had access to all my accounts, same as I do. Thankfully, most of my money is invested through my financial advisor, and I was able to lock everything down when we broke up. Anyone who knows me—anyone who knew *us*—knows the idea of me keeping him on an allowance is absurd.

"They're trying to portray you as a man-hating career woman," Tommy says.

"Because obviously you can't have a successful career without hating men," Felicity deadpans.

"They're also going to say he tried to get a reality show off the ground, but you said no, because you couldn't bear to share the limelight," Tommy says.

"What?" I pull the laptop onto my knees to get closer to the screen. I can't have heard him properly.

Tommy winces. "There's half a truth there."

"No there isn't," I reply. "We never discussed a reality show."

Silence emanates from the computer screen. I'm beginning to think the connection has frozen when Tommy clears his throat. "I should have told you at the time, but Matt asked me not to." He blows out a breath like this confession has been weighing heavy on him.

"Should have told me what?" I ask.

"He pitched me a reality show. Two, actually. One idea was to document the tour for the upcoming album, and the other was...a series built around when and if you got pregnant."

I push the laptop back onto the coffee table and stand. A reality show? Matt was absolutely venomous about reality shows. I'd get nothing but snide comments when I indulged in a Bravo binge. "Are you sure?" I ask. "Was Matt going to appear too or—"

"Yes. Obviously the show was built around you, but he was keen to be in front of the camera."

I slide my fingers into my hair. "How? Why? He hated the attention."

"Unless he didn't," Felicity said. "Honestly, darling, I think he hated *you* getting the attention. Otherwise, why would he still be feeding stories to the press?"

I sit back down. "Tell me more about this reality show. Was it just me and him? What was it called?"

"*Just One of The Family*, or something equally cringe. It was meant to show me, too," Tommy says. "And his sister."

"Liz?" But of course it would have been Liz—Matt only has one sister. "She's only eighteen."

"He had the idea that she could be your assistant. He would be there as your fiancé-slash-advisor. The idea was to reveal how it takes an army to create a star."

He wanted the credit.

I wonder when it started—when Matt decided he just didn't like me very much. Because he definitely loved me at some point. Hadn't he? When had things changed?

"It gets worse," Felicity says.

I swallow.

"He pitched two titles. The other one was *The Browns*."

Brown is Matt's surname.

"He wanted to kick off the show with your wedding. So you'd be Mr. and Mrs. Brown."

Matt pushed back the wedding several times. Surely it wasn't because he was trying to sell a reality show?

"Obviously, I said no," Tommy says. He sucks in a breath. "But I know he approached a couple of production companies."

"Why didn't you tell me all of this?" I ask. If I'd have known, at least I would have had a heads-up that Matt wasn't the man I thought he was.

"I'm sorry," Tommy says. "Looking back, it's all really suspicious—like he was trying to maneuver himself into the limelight. At the time I just thought he was misguidedly trying to help your career."

"I would never have done a reality show," I said. "I'm way too boring. If you'd have pitched it to me, I would have said hell no and never even mentioned it to Matt. I would have definitely assumed he would hate it."

"We all had him wrong, my darling," Felicity says.

"We weren't all sleeping with him and planning a future with him. Why didn't I see it?"

"You loved him," she says. "You weren't looking for it."

That sums it up. I wasn't looking for it. Well, I won't make that mistake again.

My phone buzzes with another text from Beau, asking about my day. A swell of relief and hopefulness combine in my stomach. Maybe he's not disappointed about the zoo, because he's the man I think he is.

Butterflies swoop and rise in my chest as I think about him.

I like spending time with him.

I light up when he flirts with me.

I look forward to seeing him.

But I refuse to be blindsided again. I text out a reply that will test him. Did he really want to go somewhere public—like, to the zoo. Or is it me that he wants to see?

If you want to, I can arrange security to bring you through the back entrance to the hotel and we can hang out.

Beau doesn't strike me as a man who wastes time. If it's fame he's after, he'll say no.

I get an instant reply.

I can be there at 8. Just tell me where to go.

My heart inches a little higher in my chest. Not even Matt's betrayal can pull it down.

SEVENTEEN

Beau

She freezes when I press a kiss to her cheek.

"You okay?"

She nods, but I'm not convinced. Especially as she hasn't even let me cross the threshold to her hotel room.

"Rough day?" I glance at the security guard standing beside me. I don't expect her to open up in front of him, but I have to ask all the same.

"I guess."

For a moment, I wonder if coming here tonight was a mistake. She's been clear she doesn't want to be anything more the friends. And I feel the same. Except I like her company. I'm enthralled by the way she keeps so level-headed when she's being hounded by the press. And I want to know more about how she sees the world. She's experienced so much, but in ways totally opposite to my own considerable experiences.

She makes me look at things differently.

"I'm here to cheer you up. You look gorgeous," I say.

Her short, platinum-blonde bob is scraped back from her face and she's wearing a jumper and trousers in the same soft, peachy-colored material.

She rolls her eyes and I laugh. She's behaving like a moody teenager. But she stands aside and I follow her into the hotel suite.

"I'm serious. You look super comfy and soft and actually, that probably gives you an advantage tonight."

She narrows her eyes, her gaze flitting from me to the large sports bag I'm carrying.

"This is what I use to carry dead bodies," I say, deadpan. "I'm kidding. I brought some stuff for us."

"What kind of stuff?"

"Let's have a look, shall we?"

I take a seat on the sofa and pull the bag in front of me. "Twister," I say, pulling the game from my bag. I made an emergency dash to Hamleys during my break at lunch and picked up a few games I thought would be fun.

"Twister?" She doesn't sound as excited as I hoped she would.

"And a Cove family favorite, Operation." I pull it from the bag and slide it onto the table. "Connect Four and Cluedo. There we go. Shall we order some food and then start with Operation? It's important for me to assert my dominance straightaway."

"This is...different." Her tone has softened slightly and she comes to sit next to me, picking up Operation. "I didn't have this as a kid, but I wanted it. My best friend had it. We weren't really a board game family."

"We definitely were," I say. "What did you do instead?"

"Sing around the piano."

"Your entire family is musical?" I ask, pulling the lid off the game.

"I guess. My dad is the only one who makes a living out of it, apart from me. My mom was a piano teacher, but she gave it up as soon as she could."

I glance over at her, wanting to know more.

She continues. "You know, as soon as the mortgage was paid off." I assume Vivian is the one who paid off the house, but I don't ask. "But my dad? He won't ever give it up. He loves it too much. Still works twice a week at a hotel bar playing jazz standards. He's a great piano player. And a good singer too."

"Do the people he's singing to know he's your dad?"

"I'm not sure the clientele at the Chicago Four Seasons is my audience."

I set the game up in front of us and open a bottle of wine from the bar. We order room service.

"May the best player win." I raise my glass. She smiles, more relaxed than she was before. "There's just one rule with Operation," I say, shuffling the doctor cards.

"You don't touch the sides or the machine will buzz?" she suggests.

"Two rules. The buzzing rule and one more: no touching." I deal out the specialist cards.

"What do you mean? I gotta touch the tweezers."

We both start dropping the plastic parts into the patient in front of us. "I mean if you're playing, I can't touch you and vice versa."

She narrows her eyes. "Weird rule, but okay."

I chuckle to myself. "You go first."

She picks up a card. "Butterflies in the stomach." She glances at me then quickly looks away.

"Embarrassed, Ms. Cross?" I ask. "Do you have butter-flies in your stomach?" I'm flirting and I just can't help it. I may be gun-shy about relationships, but that doesn't mean I don't enjoy the energy coursing between me and Vivian every time we're together.

Vivian ignores me and picks up the tweezers, so I continue. "Maybe you're just shy when you think about me kissing you," I say. I'm pushing things a little, but...I suppose that's who I am. She pauses but doesn't look up. I bide my time, waiting for her to get closer to that metal edge. "Maybe when you think about my mouth on your pussy."

Buzz. Buzz. Buzz.

She turns to me and I can't conceal my grin. It's a game, right?

"It's just a game," I say, trying to look innocent. I'm doing what I need to do to win. That's all. Right?

"You cheated!" she says.

I shrug. "There's only one rule, remember. My turn." I pick up the tweezers and gently get hold of the butterfly. "My favorite and the easiest piece, in my humble, medical opinion." I pull it out and toss it onto the table. "As I said, easy."

"I only messed up because you interfered."

I raise my eyebrows. "If you're not going to play the game to the best of your ability, you have to deal with the consequences."

"You want me to dirty talk to win? That's *playing* dirty."

"Did I mention I have four brothers? If you're following the rules, it's not playing dirty. Your turn."

She sighs and turns over the card. "Spare ribs."

She takes the tweezers and fixes me with a stare, as if warning me not to make a sound.

"And after I've made you come with my mouth—"

"Beau!" She drops the tweezers onto poor old Sam.

I hold up my hands. "I'm not touching you, not even a little nudge."

She rolls her eyes and picks up the tweezers. I let her settle back into the game, narrowing her eyes in concentration as she inches toward the ribs.

"I'm going to strip you naked and bend you over this sofa," I whisper. The visual makes my dick twitch in approval. I know she doesn't want anything romantic to happen between us and neither do I...but... "You're going to be so wet because you'll already have come so hard, but I'm going to reach between your legs, just to make sure. Maybe I'll play with you a little while, tease you for a bit because I like to hear you beg for my cock—"

"There." She drops the ribs on the table and turns to me, triumphant. "And for the record, you're never going to hear me beg for anything."

I hold her gaze. "We'll see."

"It's your turn," she says. "I'm on a winning streak."

"Not for long," I say.

She lifts her jumper and takes it over her head.

I realize she means business. I laugh. "Oh, you've come over to the dark side now, have you?" Underneath her cashmere top, she's braless in a tight cotton tank top, her nipples pressing against the fabric. I can feel myself lengthen against the denim of my jeans.

"I don't know what you mean."

I turn my attention back to the game, but really all I want to do is reach over and touch her. I turn the next card over. "Wishbone." Fuck, I've never been good at this one.

She grabs a cube of ice from the wine bucket. "It's so hot in here, isn't it?"

I glance up to find her running an ice cube down her neck and along her collarbone.

I look away and pick up the tweezers. I can't lose this

game. I spent at least a decade of my life playing this with four brothers. I'm prepared for anything.

I dip my tweezers when Vivian lets out a contented groan, like she's about four seconds away from the best orgasm of her life. The sound vibrates in my balls.

Buzz. Buzz. Buzz.

I look across at her, her teeth buried in her bottom lip, a gleam in her eyes.

"Outrageous," I say.

She shrugs. "I don't know what you mean. Rules are rules. My turn."

She shifts to pick up the card and I know I'm a goner. Her breasts are like perfectly round, over-sized peaches, and I just want to sink my teeth into her and feel the juice drip off my chin. Fuck, she's gorgeous.

She goes for the wishbone and part of me wants to let her have it so we can skip the games and get naked. I need to control myself.

"How many times do you think you'll come? Three? Four."

She smiles but keeps her hands steady.

"When they ask about me in interviews, you'll get wet just thinking about what I can do with your body. You'll be sitting there, a hundred people looking at you, lights beating down, and all you'll be able to think about is me and how good I make you feel."

Her breathing is shallow. She's a step away from panting. She pulls out the wishbone and looks at me like she wants me. And I know because I'm looking at her the exact same way.

All I can think about is kissing her. All I want to feel is her lips on mine, her arse in my hands, her legs wrapped around my waist.

"Vivian, I'm going to—"

I don't get to finish my sentence because there's a knock at the door.

She glances at me, a sheen of panic in her expression. She grabs her jumper and pulls it over her head as she goes to the door.

Fuck.

I try and will my hard-on away as a waiter appears, pushing a trolley, and sets up the dining table for us.

I manage to stand and tip him before he leaves.

"I can do that," she says. "Tip him, I mean."

"Okay, but I did it."

She doesn't say anything and I follow her over to the dining table. We take our seats—her at the head of the table and me next to her, opposite the window. Our knees touch and neither of us moves away.

"We need to eat or—" She stops what she's saying and dishes me up some of the pasta we ordered.

"Yeah," I agree. "We're both..."

"Hungry?" she suggests on a laugh.

"Yeah. I'm starving," I say, laughing back.

"So you used to play Operation with your brothers and you'd do anything to win?"

"Yeah." I pause. "Not like *that* obviously. I mean, we'd say there was a spider about to fall on their head or we'd shoot each other with water pistols."

"Is it super competitive among you?" she asks.

I think about it. "Back then, for sure. Now, if you get us round a table and we're playing a game, we're going to want to bury each other. But generally in life, we're at such different stages and...we're competitive but we're also rooting for each other. Does that make sense?"

She takes a mouthful of pasta and nods.

"Like my brothers Zach and Dax got really into trading Bitcoin back in the day. They made a lot of money, but they didn't keep it to themselves. They got me into it a little bit, although I was never as dedicated as they were."

"They wanted all of you to win."

"Right," I say. "But if we're pitched against each other, we're going to want to bring each other down." I laugh as I say it. It sounds brutal because it *is* brutal. "What about you? You said you have a brother and a sister. How do they feel about your success?"

"They're both supportive. I think it helps that they're both really happy in their own worlds."

"Right," I said. "That's key, isn't it? If you're happy, you don't resent other people's happiness."

She turns pale in front of me.

"Are you okay?" I ask.

She lifts one shoulder. "Yeah. So my sister is a home-maker. Her husband has his own financial consulting business and they live in the Chicago suburbs. They have a happy life from what I can see. My sister, Sarah, is pregnant, so I'll be an auntie in a couple of months."

"Being an uncle is the best. My niece is still a baby, but I can't wait until she can walk and I can start to play football with her."

"You're living with her, right? Does she keep you up at night?"

I laugh. "No. I'm a heavy sleeper and I'm on a different floor to her."

"Is it weird living with your brother and his wife? I know you want to save money and—"

"Me living with them has nothing to do with money."

"But I get it, it's a waste if you're away so much."

I smirk. "You don't believe me."

"I'm not saying I don't believe you, I'm just saying, it's a waste. I get it."

"It's not about the money. I don't like my flat being empty for months at a time. I also like to reconnect with my family if I haven't seen them. Believe me, it's not about the money."

"Okay," she says, but I can tell she doesn't quite believe me. I can't talk her into trusting me. She's got to find the evidence for herself. "I've eaten enough," she says. "I'm ready to beat you at Clue now." She sets down her napkin and goes to collect the new game from my bag. "I'm definitely Miss Scarlett."

"Really?" I said in my best whiney voice. "I want to be Miss Scarlett."

She laughs. "You can be Professor Plum."

"Can I tell you a secret?" I ask as she's setting out the board and taking the pieces out of the box.

She looks up. Our eyes lock and I just can't look away.

"Professor Plum has a crush on Miss Scarlett," I confess. How could anyone not have a crush on Miss Scarlett? On Vivian? She's a perfect mix of sweet and open and sexy and enigmatic.

A blush crawls up her neck and she breaks into a wide grin. "He does?"

"He absolutely does."

"Good to know," she says.

I take a final mouthful of pasta and then clear the table of our half-eaten room service as Vivian hums to herself while setting up the game.

"What are you humming—one of yours? Do you listen to your own music?"

"Just a melody that has ear-wormed into my brain.

That's how a new song is often born. A hook, part of a melody."

"So you're just going about your day, having a bath, making your bed, walking and bam, that's it, it just pops in your ear?" I ask.

"It's not as sudden as that. I usually don't notice for a while. Even when I'm humming, I don't notice. And then I do. And then I usually find a piano and work it into something."

"Is that why you have a piano here? In case creativity strikes." I sit opposite her and move the board so it's central between us.

"Sure, and I like to play for funsies too. Not my stuff, but other things." She turns the box around. "You know we call this Clue in America. Where does the 'do' come from?"

I shrug, wondering if she'll play for me but also wondering if asking her would be overstepping. I don't want to put her on the spot or make her think I think she's here for my entertainment. But I'd like to hear her.

Casually, as if her actions don't short-circuit my brain, she pulls the jumper off again and drapes it over the chair beside her.

"For the record, for as long as you're wearing that top, you're going to win every game we play." I stand and grab our wineglasses from the coffee table.

She glances down at herself and then back at me. "Oh yeah?"

I place the glasses down by the board, cup her face in my hands, sweep my thumb over her lips and close my eyes, trying to summon every ounce of strength I have not to kiss her into next week. I press my lips to her forehead and release her.

"Right. Time for me to lose."

She laughs. "Well it's no fun if you give up before we've begun."

"It's all the fun. I get to sit here and look at you and try to make you laugh."

After enjoying her beating me at Cluedo, we set out the Twister mat.

"Were you saving the best 'til last with this?" she asks. "If you can turn Operation into... Well, god only knows how you play Twister."

"Worried you're going to lose?" I ask.

She gives a small shake of her head.

I hand her the dial and turn so I'm facing her. "You're worried about my thigh between your legs, my mouth at your neck?" I lean into her and whisper in her ear. "You're worried you're going to start begging me to touch you, just like I know you will."

I circle my hands around her waist and she gasps.

"I don't need a game as an excuse to touch you, Vivian." I press a kiss under her ear and slide my hands up, up, up, until my thumbs skirt the outline of her breasts. "I don't need a game to get close to you." I slide my lips against hers —lightly, in a half-kiss.

I'm close enough to hear her breath falter and feel her body sag against mine. It feels like a victory. I know she's nursing a broken heart—but Matt was dick and she needs to get over him, and I'm more than happy to be the rebound guy. Maybe a rebound is exactly what I need, too.

"I don't need a game to talk dirty to you and get you wet."

"Beau," she whispers.

"You're not used to it." I can tell by the heat in her cheeks that the idiot who let her go never realized how much she likes dirty talk. "But you like it. You like things to get a little dirty." She twists under my hands. I'm not sure if she does it on purpose, but she shifts against my cock, which twitches even with the slightest bit of attention from her.

I reach up and cup her face again, and I stare into her eyes. I see conflict and excitement, but I also see fear.

"I'm going to kiss you now," I say. "Okay?"

She nods and I press my lips against hers once, then again and deeper. I sink into her pillowy softness and slide my tongue between her lips. It's a promise of more.

But not now.

I pull back and she opens her eyes.

"You're beautiful, and I want to do that again. And again. So, I'm going to go," I say.

A vertical line appears just above the bridge of her nose. "Go?"

I press a kiss to her forehead. "I like you. I know neither of us is looking for anything serious. I think we both need to take a beat before we decide if this," I gesture between us, "can or should include...sex."

I don't exactly enjoy the disappointment in her eyes, but I'm not sad about it. Something's shifted. There was a clear line between us when the evening started out and I can barely see it now.

"If I don't step away, things are going to get blurry," I say. "No, they're already blurry. I just think we both need to think about whether this is a good idea." I pull her toward me, our gazes locked. "Sleep well." I press my lips against hers and pull away.

When I get to the door, I turn for one last look. Maybe I'm an idiot leaving like this, but she's been hurt badly. And if there's one thing I refuse to do, it's make her heartbreak worse.

EIGHTEEN

Vivian

I barely slept. When the alarm goes off at seven, I'm sorely tempted to cancel it, roll over, and try to get some sleep.

But there's too much going on in my brain.

I can't stop thinking about Beau.

There's all the good stuff: The way he manages to make a pair of jeans look like the sexiest thing I've ever seen. The way he smells like grass after a thunderstorm. Our kiss. His dirty mouth.

And then there's the bad: The way I've checked TMZ three thousand times since he left to see if he's said anything to anyone. The weird conversation we had about his financial status. He was pretty convincing when he said he didn't have to worry about money—but why? Because he was lying, or because he was telling the truth? Everything he says and does seems to match up, and if I was still the person I was before I found out my fiancé was selling my secrets to the press, I wouldn't be questioning everything.

But then again, I wouldn't be playing Operation with Beau had I still been with Matt.

I call Felicity. Maybe she'll have heard.

"Hey," she says. "You okay?"

"Yeah, I was just checking in. Do you ever sleep?"

"I can sleep when I'm dead. What's going on, darling?"

"Beau came round last night."

I'm met by silence on the other end of the line. And then, "Do you like him? I know there'd been some coffee dates before he signed up as Mr. Vivian Cross."

"Don't say that." My stomach churns. Every now and then Matt would get called that—by his guy friends, his colleagues, sometimes even members of my team. He always pretended he wasn't bothered, and I assumed he took it all in his stride. Maybe he didn't. Maybe it ground him down over time.

"You know what I mean," Felicity says. "So tell me why you're calling. You're wondering whether you should have let him come over? You slept with him and you think he might talk?"

"I didn't sleep with him." I was close to wanting to, but Felicity doesn't need to know that. "But I'm attracted to him. It feels...odd to be thinking about anyone in that way. I was with Matt for so long."

"I know. But a rebound fling might be the best thing for you."

I sigh. I'm not sure I'm the kind of woman who has rebound flings. But who knows? I only ever dated Matt.

"The whole Matt thing is making me question everything. I suppose a part of me is a little concerned that what happened last night has been, or will be, leaked to the tabloids."

"Nothing yet, darling. I've just done a sweep. Even

checked Reddit. There's lots of pieces about the two of you, but it's only stuff we've put out there. I'm a little surprised there isn't more from his camp. Not from a malicious perspective, but he's young, he has friends and colleagues and even brothers. No one seems to be saying anything. Usually the paps or the journos can get something out of someone. But I suppose it's early days."

"Promise me something?" I ask.

"If you promise *me* something," she replies.

"What?" I ask.

"You go first."

"Make sure you tell me everything?" I ask. "I need to know it all, even if you think it's insignificant. Even when Beau's side starts slipping up because they're being hounded or because someone's been through his trash can. Tell me everything. I want to know."

"I've promised I will. You'll know everything I know, as soon as I know it. But you must promise me that you won't let Matt make you bitter or suspicious." She pauses. "Okay, you can be a bit suspicious—most people have an agenda with you—but don't let him stop you picking out the good ones and sharing your heart with them."

I sigh. Easier said than done.

"Try and put the past in the past," she says.

I laugh a little cynically. "How am I supposed to do that when I've got this album to promote? I'm going to fly all over the world and sing songs about the man who betrayed me. Worse, they're songs about how much I love him."

She sighs. "God, I wish you could trash the entire album."

"Yeah, me too." I'd just finished recording it when I found out about Matt.

"Have you been writing any music since?"

"A few bits." The last few days, I've been getting more and more ideas. I've been playing the piano more, but I haven't put pen to paper on anything. "Nothing about the breakup. It's so humiliating, I don't want people hearing about it. It would be like filming myself in therapy or something. No one wants to see that."

More silence on the other end of the phone. "Felicity? Did you fall asleep on me?"

"I'm just thinking. Does the label care about the songs released on the album? Do you have songs you've not previously used that you could supplement so you don't have to sing about Matt?"

"But almost everything I wrote was about him, whether it's been released or not. Two or three songs on every album were more general, but most of my music has always been about him. About us."

Still, her question starts me thinking. "What do you think the label would say if I demanded we trash the album and start again?"

"I think they'd shit their pants," Felicity says.

"But if I had new music. Better music. Like, that would be exciting from a publicity standpoint, wouldn't it? If a boyfriend did me wrong so I dumped an entire album about him, and I met someone else and he inspired me to write an album in just...ten days."

Adrenaline starts to pump through my veins and I swing my legs off my bed. "I could do that. If we got Bobby and Judo to fly over. I wouldn't want to do it without them." They'd been my producers for the last three albums. We're practically telepathic with one another when it comes to music. "I could do a collab. Maybe even two. Wasn't Katy's team asking for a collab and I didn't have time in the schedule?"

"But you're in London."

"Yeah. Exactly. Different continent. Different man. Different music. We can call it *London* or *The London Album*. It's fresh. And new. I like it."

"You're serious about this?" Felicity asks. She doesn't wait for a response before she says, "We need to wake up Tommy."

Talking about this change in direction is like putting on the dress you know makes you look fantastic and someone gives you a shot of tequila at the same time. It feels so good. So right. So exactly what I'm meant to be doing.

I'm sitting around here in my hotel room dreading going out to talk to people about my music. That's not how it's supposed to be. I've always been excited about my music. Felicity hangs up for precisely three seconds and returns with Tommy on video. I can't help but grin at him like it's Christmas morning.

For the first time in weeks, I feel good about what my day has in store for me.

"What's going on?" he asks.

"I'm going to need a studio," I say. "Worst-case scenario, we can use Chester Terrace. I still have a few weeks on the lease there."

"You're feeling inspired?" he asks. "That's wonderful. I'll see what I can arrange for you."

"So inspired that we're trashing *Everlasting Whispers*. I'm going to write an entirely new album."

The phone vibrates with Tommy's howls.

I don't care, because I'm about to record the most important album of my life.

NINETEEN

Vivian

I look up from the piano in the live room to see Beau standing over the mixing desk, watching me through the glass. The door's open and I beckon him forward.

"Hey," I say, standing up to greet him.

His grin is as wide as Texas.

It's early. Beau offered to stop by and deliver coffee when I told him I was at Chester Terrace. I haven't seen him since Operation and our kiss, but I've exchanged messages with him every day since. I'm feeling so inspired, I don't want to be far from a piano.

"Your flat white." He raises the cup and then steps a little too close before pressing a kiss to my lips.

I can feel my blush light up my face. "Thanks. You on your way to work?" I ask.

He glances around. "Absolutely. And you're already at work."

The last few days have been some of the most creative of my entire career. I just can't stop the melodies, the words.

I have four complete songs. They're not recorded yet, but they're ready. "This is my favorite bit—burrowing down and just writing and playing music. There's not much work to it —at least, that's how it feels."

He grins. "I like that. It's good to enjoy what you do. What are you working on? You're singing about me, I hope."

I laugh. "Of course." More than he knows. "I just wrote a song called 'Freedom'. You wanna hear it?"

"Absolutely," he says.

I hand him my coffee, sit down at the piano and start to play.

You used to be my shadow, my rock-solid stone.

And now here I am, out here on my own.

I waited for the loneliness to come and get me in the night.

Instead I found a freedom, an escape from the fight.

Free-dom. I'm flying, high into the air.

Free-dom. Oh baby I'm me without a care.

Free-dom. Life's for living, don't you know.

For far too long I hid my light and now I'm ready to be free.

The melody reminds me of something I wrote before I became successful. My fingers slip over the keys as if they've known this song for years rather than twenty-four hours. It's going to be the first song on the new album and I think it has single potential. It's the only song that remotely references Matt, and it feels like the perfect transition from the old me to the new me—from my old music, so much of which was about him, to new music, which is about me and what's next.

I play the final note and look up at him. His expression is pure joy.

"It's incredible," he says. "Pretty and powerful at the same time. Is that possible?"

I feel like a flower, unfurling under his attention. "You couldn't have paid me a greater compliment."

"It's beautiful watching you play," he says. His attention is so focused on me, it makes me shiver.

I shift on the piano stool and pat the space beside me.

He takes a seat and hands me my coffee.

"Thanks for coming," I say. "I've missed this coffee."

He laughs. "I'll be your delivery boy anytime."

I laugh and rest my head on his shoulder. "I didn't mean it like that."

"I know. It's fine."

It's nice to be around someone who's so comfortable in who he is. Beau doesn't get pissed off at the slightest misunderstanding or wrong word. He's relaxed and clearly pleased to be here. With me.

"Hey," I sit upright and look at him. "I really want to watch that new Reese Witherspoon movie. I know it's dropping on Netflix, but I thought I'd throwback to the olden days and hire a screening room on Saturday. Get popcorn and a hotdog. Want to join me?"

"This weekend?" he asks, and I nod.

His wince tells me everything I need to know and my heart sinks into my shoes. "I'm going to Norfolk this weekend to stay with my parents. But...come with me. There's a few of us going."

"I don't even know where Norfolk is."

"It's by the sea, in the most easterly part of the UK. You should get out of London, get a break from things here."

I smile because I can see the offer is genuine, but there's no way I can go and stay with Beau's parents. "That's really sweet, but I think I'll stay here."

"No," he says. "Come with me. You can meet everyone and—I mean, Madison I think is a fan, and from what Jacob says, Sutton has concert tickets for you next year, but really they'll get over themselves in a hot minute and I promise you won't be uncomfortable."

I sigh. "I should stay. I need to work."

"My mum makes the best roast dinner ever. We can go for a walk up to Blakeney Point. It's so beautiful and no one will bother you, I promise. It's not that kind of place. It's low-key and relaxed. I swear, Tom Cruise filmed a movie around there and no one blinked an eye. You won't be bothered."

The idea of getting out of London appeals to me. I've never seen the country outside of London, save the backstage area of an arena. It might be nice to see some of the English countryside I've heard so much about. But the paps —would they follow me? And the security implications... It would be a lot to organize in just a couple of days.

"How far away is it?"

"Just over three hours in the car. If my cousin Vincent's in town, he'll be going up by helicopter, so we can hitch a lift with him. Or a road trip, just the two of us might be fun."

"I can't—" Just before I'm about to give him a list of reasons why I can't possibly travel up to Norfolk, my phone goes and it's Felicity.

"I need to take this," I say.

"You want me to go?"

I shake my head and swipe up. She and Tommy are on the phone. My stomach dips.

"Beau's here," I say in warning.

"Hey, Beau."

He waves then stands, wandering over to the acoustic

guitar leaning on the wall behind the drums. He is a guy, after all.

"It's 3am Eastern, which means it must be bad," I say. "Just tell me."

"Matt has been pictured having dinner with a woman from his office," Felicity says flatly.

A little under two years ago, Matt decided to go back to work. He got a job at a law firm as an associate. It meant he wasn't as flexible when it came to coming with me on trips, but we made it work. I knew it was important for him to have something for himself. And his mood seemed to lift. I think he enjoyed being away from me and the people I employed, and I completely understood that. I was happy for him.

She doesn't have to tell me who it is. I know already. "Amanda," I say.

He used to tell me about people in the office—his boss, who he said was terrible at his job but a gold-star kiss-ass. The senior partner, who he seemed to have a great relationship with. There were other members of his team: Chip, Alison and his assistant, Janine. And then there was Amanda. I always suspected he was attracted to her, but I told myself it was normal to be attracted to people outside of a long-term relationship.

"You know her?" Tommy asks.

"I know of her. They worked on the same team. Matt used to talk about her." I remember being a little jealous, and when I confessed to him, Matt told me I was being paranoid. Amanda was just a colleague. I felt uneasy because I hadn't accused him of anything—I'd just said I was jealous. He'd made the extra connection in his mind and created something for me to be jealous of.

"We have a quote from Matt's PR. He's enjoying the

company of friends and family as he rebuilds his life after his split, blah blah blah."

"He's hitting back after the pictures with Beau," I say. I can't be angry. We're not together and we're not getting back together. In the words of the wise and wonderful Taylor Swift, *We are never ever getting back together.* Shouldn't I be happy for him that he's moving on? Or that I'm rid of him at least.

"There's just one more thing," Felicity says. It's always Felicity who delivers the bad news. Tommy has my back one thousand percent, but he absolutely doesn't like to upset me. "They're also pictured going back to her apartment building. Holding hands."

My stomach swoops, and I press my palm to my belly button. "Okay. Thanks for letting me know." What else is there to say? Yes, I want to know how long it's been going on for. Yes, a masochistic part of me wants to know if he was planning to leave me for her. Yes, I want to know if they've had sex or if they're serious, or if he's just trying to make me jealous.

But neither Tommy nor Felicity have the answers to those questions. And wanting to know is more about the habit of caring about Matt than anything else.

Matt and I are done. I'm never getting the answers to those questions, and I have to be okay with that.

"You okay?" Tommy says.

I shrug. "I'm happy I didn't find out another way. Thank you for telling me."

"He's a shitbag, straight up," Felicity says.

I shake my head. I don't want to go into a Matt-bashing session. Not now. Maybe when I've had a chance to digest what they've said. Maybe when I've sneaked a look at the pictures online. But not here. Not with Beau in the room, not in this place where I've managed to carve out a little bit of the world that's not about Matt. "You should both sleep. I'm in the middle of writing. We can talk when you wake up at normal human hours."

"Are you sure you're okay?" Tommy asks.

"She's better off without that horror-story of a man," Felicity says, and I can't help but smile.

"I'm fine. You go off and get your beauty sleep. I love you both."

I cancel the call before they can make any more fuss.

Taking a breath, I spin around on the stool. Beau is sitting behind the drums with sticks in his hands, looking like he's just landed on Mars. "I'm sorry about that. I had to take it."

"Don't worry about it. Are you okay?"

I nod. It's half true. I know I *will* be okay. "It was bound to happen. And leaving him was my choice."

"You can be angry about it, though."

"I suppose I can, but not now."

Beau lifts his arms and cracks the drumsticks over his head.

One, two, three, four.

And then brings them down again without playing a note and laughs at himself. "That's the extent of my drumming capability."

"It's good you know your limits." I can't stop smiling, despite the news about Matt. "You always make me feel so good," I say before I've had a chance to think about what's coming out of my mouth.

He fixes me with a stare. "You don't even know how good I can make you feel."

I roll my eyes in an effort to cover up my blush. "Can I ask you something?"

"Anything," he says, and I know it's true.

"Is it rude to belatedly accept your invitation to Norfolk?"

"You mean, because you've gotten that news about Matt, you think you might offend me because joining me for the weekend is clearly an effort to take your mind off your ex?" He's beaming at me as he stands and crosses the room. "I don't care why you say yes, so long as you do."

"Then I guess I'm coming to Norfolk."

TWENTY

Vivian

As we get out of the helicopter and head toward Beau's parents, who are standing in front of their house, I suddenly think I should have booked a hotel. When was the last time I stayed at someone's house? I haven't thought about logistics, but maybe I should have. I don't even know if Beau and I are going to be in separate rooms. It's not like we're having sex, but why should his parents assume that?

"Dad's the one shouting," Beau says on a laugh. He's carrying my weekend bag along with his own. I glance around, taking in the fields and the trees and big, blue sky above us. We really are in the middle of nowhere. His family probably thinks I'm being a diva bringing a security guy with me, but I didn't want to walk into a situation and feel vulnerable.

"You want me to check out the house?" Jim asks from behind.

I turn, hoping to keep my voice from carrying to Beau's parents. "No thanks. I'll only need you if we go somewhere." Betty has arranged for him to stay nearby, and Jed is coming to cover the night shift. But now we're here, it seems a bit overboard to have two guys on security.

"Don't stress about it," Beau says. "And ignore whatever my dad says."

"What do you mean? What's he going to say?"

"You know, he might just tease you about the body-guards. He was a father to five boys and my cousin. He can't exist without giving people shit."

What have I gotten myself into?

"Beau!" his mother calls and steps forward, toward the gate Beau holds open for me with his foot.

"And you must be Vivian." She pulls me into a hug. "So lovely to meet you."

"Lovely to meet you, Mrs. Cove."

"Call me Carole."

"Vivian," Beau's dad says, holding out his hand for me to shake. "How do you do? My name is John. I do not answer to any other name. Just Dad or John." His grip is firm, like an old-school dad, and there's something comforting about it, even though it's not the warm hug Carole offered me.

"Not true, Dad," Beau says. "I've called you a lot worse."

"Yes, but I haven't answered to it. Dog," he shouts at nothing in particular.

"Sometimes you answer to Grumpy Knickers," Carole says.

"Carole," he mumbles under his breath.

"Come in, come in," Carole says. "I hope you don't mind, but I'm going to set you to work. I'm really behind cooking dinner. I've been on Zooms all day."

"Have you been working, Mum?" Beau asks.

"Not really. Just meetings and things. You know how it is."

"She doesn't think it's work because she hasn't got her scalpel out," John says. "But it's work, just the same. Dog!"

Just then a Labrador comes tearing around the corner heading for the four of us.

"Here he is."

"This is Dog," Beau says. "Very creative name, I'm sure you can agree. Dad named him."

"I never claimed to be creative," John said. "I'm a scientist. I leave artistry to the people who are good at it."

"Creativity gets better the more you use it. Just like anything else," I say. "And anyway, I think Dog is the funniest name I could ever imagine for a dog. It's very creative."

"I like her," John says, tipping his head at me as he talks to his wife. "Even if she is American."

I laugh. "I like you too, John."

As we go in, Beau has to bend so he doesn't bang his head on the lintel.

"This is so charming," I say, taking in the terracotta tile on the floor, the low, beamed ceilings and the tiny windows. "It's like how I imagined England would be before I came here and stayed at the Dorchester."

Carole chuckled. "She's funny. Thank god. I did worry when you said you were bringing an American, but then Vincent makes me laugh all the time. You need a sense of humor in this family."

Carole's acting like we're getting married or something. I glance at Beau but it doesn't seem to have registered with him.

"You're laughing at him, not with him, Mum," Beau says. Carole rolls her eyes.

"Come through to the kitchen, get yourself settled, we'll get you a cup of tea and then I'm going to set you to work. You're the first to arrive but we have a cast of thousands descending."

"Bloody children. Someone told me," John points animatedly at his wife, "that because we had boys, we'd never see them again once they'd gone off to university. Can't get bloody rid of them. Are you going to take this one back to America? Get him off our hands?"

He pulls out a pine chair from the kitchen table and I take a seat, watching the whirlwind of activity in front of me.

"Ignore him," Carole says. "We need pinnies. Which one do you want? Did I tell you Vincent got me an apron, just like Jacob's?" she asks Beau. "I'm going to wear that one, because Jacob's face will be a picture—if you pardon the pun." She pulls some things out of a drawer. "Look at this, Vivian. My son, Jacob, got me an apron with his face all over it. He likes to wind up his brothers and say that he's my favorite. He is of course, and he's by far the most handsome out of all my boys, but I don't tell them."

"Hey," Beau says. "You're not supposed to have favorites."

Carole looks at me and rolls her eyes as if the two of us are in on the joke. "I can't help it. Vincent's my favorite now. She hooks an apron over her head and as it unfurls, about twenty different images of a very handsome man's face stare back at me.

"You wear Jacob." She flings another apron at Beau. "Vivian, you can have one with dragonflies on it or a blue-and white-striped chef's apron."

"I'm having that one," says John, and I can't help but laugh.

No one's standing on ceremony, treading on eggshells or fawning over me.

And I love it.

I FIND a hair tie in my jeans pocket and pull my hair back. My shirt sleeves are rolled up and I make a start on peeling the apples.

"You okay there?" Carole asks me. Beau and his dad have been sent out to collect mint and a bay leaf from the garden.

"Happy as a pig in shit," I reply and then wince. "Excuse my language." I toss the newly peeled apple in my hand into a bowl of water and then move on to the next.

"If you haven't already heard far worse than *shit* out of John's mouth about his own sons, I'll be surprised. We don't get offended by swearing around here."

She's so warm and joyful, it's easy to feel comfortable around her.

"You're very close. And loving with each other. It's wonderful," I say.

"I'm very lucky," Carole replies. "Are you close with your family?"

"We're not *not* close," I reply. "But we all have very different lives. My brother and sister are older and married —not to each other, you'll be pleased to know. They live twenty minutes from my parents and thirty minutes from each other. I see them a few times a year and I speak to my mom most weeks."

"Beau says you're a famous singer. I'm sorry but I don't listen to music much. A bit of Chopin here and there and even a bit of Sibelius, but that's about as modern as it gets for me."

"I'm a piano player first and foremost, so I love Chopin. My dad taught me starting when I was four. I always warm up with a bit of Bach."

She turns to me, grinning. "Oh gosh, I'm a sucker for Bach. *Partita number* 2 during a rainstorm."

"Oh that's a favorite of my mom's. I love it too. So...kind of heart-wrenching," I say.

"That's a good description." She comes to sit opposite me with another peeler in her hand. "You always wanted to sing pop music?" she asks.

"I like to play all kinds, but yeah, I suppose I never considered being a jazz pianist like my dad."

"Oh, he's a musician too?"

I smile up at her as I dunk another apple into the water. "Yeah. He loves it. He doesn't have to work anymore, but... it's not work to him."

"That's the best kind of work—the kind that doesn't feel like it. I tell my boys that all the time."

"Beau says you're an incredible surgeon."

"I'm retired now. I do some speaking engagements. John and I spent so much of our boys' childhoods working, we wanted some time to enjoy them as adults and watch their careers. Working in a hospital—it's not conducive to family life. Now, we have at least one of them up most weekends and sometimes it's three or four or all of them. I absolutely love it, as you can probably tell. And I'm building an extension so we can have their wives and girlfriends to stay. And the grandchildren when they come. We have one so far, and another one on the way with Vincent and Kate's little one."

"Do you miss it?" I ask her. "Surgery, I mean."

"Sometimes. But I gave it up under my own terms—not

because I had an uncooperative husband or a man who demanded the limelight for himself." I freeze at her words. Is she sending me a message? "So many of the women I trained with took a less challenging route to either accommodate family—no judgement—or their partners' careers. Excruciatingly frustrating. John never asked me to make a choice. Not by his words or actions. So our careers with a growing family were tiring and life at home was chaos, but it meant we both wrung out all our careers had to offer. We left nothing on the field. When we retired, we were ready."

I smile. "I like that. You always felt like your husband was supportive?"

"It was one of the reasons I married him. John is a very clever man—there's no doubt about that. But I was cleverer and it never bothered him. More than not bothering him, it was one of the reasons he loved me. There's nothing more attractive than a man with confidence enough not to be intimidated by a clever woman."

I laugh. "You're so right."

"I like to think the pair of us were good role models in that way for our sons. The ones who are settled have chosen very clever women. Independent women who don't *need* to rely on their husbands for anything, but choose to. That's what the boys saw at home."

Before I can ask more about her other sons, John and Beau appear followed by a couple. I can tell just by looking at the man that he's a Cove. This family is just too darned good-looking.

"Vivian, this is my older brother, Jacob, and the woman who's far too good for him, Sutton."

I drop my apple, wipe my hands on my apron, and stand.

Jacob gives me a sharp nod and reaches out his hand,

but a whirlwind of a woman pushes through the throng of people. "Vivian," she says. "Christ on a bike. You are gorgeous. Even better in real life." She takes my hands in hers. "Give me thirty seconds and I'll get over it all, but I just need to say that I'm a huge, huge fan. I mean, I bought your first album way back in the day."

"I started young," I say to everyone, and they laugh.

"Come on, Sutton," Beau says. "She's off the clock."

"It's fine," I say. "I never get tired of hearing that people like my music."

"Well, I do. And so does Madison—that's Nathan's wife. We're coming to see you in concert next year. Are you still going ahead with the album release?"

I suck in a breath. "I am, although it might look a bit different to what people were expecting. Me included."

"That sounds...exciting. Tell me everything."

I laugh, but give nothing away. I want the whole world to find out about the album at the same time.

"Give Sutton a glass of wine and an apple to peel," Carole says. "I've never seen you so excited."

"Carole, this is *Vivian Cross*."

"She's our guest and no matter who she is, she deserves a little space," Carole says. "Jacob, can you do everyone a round of teas and coffees and wine if people wish?"

"I would love a glass of wine," I say. Usually, when I'm around new people, I don't drink. But here, with these people, there's no need to be on my guard. They are kind and loving and despite Sutton's fangirling, not here to document my misdeeds or record my mistakes.

"Good afternoon!" a fellow American voice booms in the kitchen. I turn to see a huge, handsome man filling the door.

"Vincent, love, where's Kate?"

He points in front of him and through the throng of people, a shorter, gorgeous lady comes toward us, circling her hand on her stomach. There's a cacophony of hugging and back-slapping. Amid the chaos, I greet Kate and then Vincent.

"Where in the States are you from?" I ask Vincent.

"I live in the UK now. But the last place I lived was New York."

"You miss it?" I ask as he hands me a glass of wine.

"This Malbec is fantastic. Better be—I own the vineyard. And no, I don't miss New York. You won't either. There are differences, sure, but why would you want to be too far from this?" He circles his finger in the air.

"Oh, I'm not moving to the UK permanently," I say. "I just came for a bit of a break from the tabloids."

He chuckles. "And you met Beau." Beau joins us in the increasingly full kitchen and Vincent slaps him in the back. "You look happy."

"I'm always happy," Beau says, but there's something in his smile that doesn't quite reach his eyes.

"It's true," Carole interrupts. "Beau is the most positive person you'll ever meet. He always cheers me up. He just sees the good in everything."

"In too bloody much," John mutters as he holds up his wineglass, full of red. "He needs to focus a bit more."

"Who says?" Carole says. "Beau is happy going between practicing and experiencing what the world has to offer. Just because it wouldn't be our choice, doesn't mean it's the wrong choice."

"You're the one who bleats on about grandchildren. Beau never stays still long enough to impregnate anyone."

Carole holds up a hand. "It will happen when it happens." She glances at me. "It just takes the right woman. If Vincent is about to be a father, anything is possible."

They both laugh conspiratorially, and I exhale as Carole skillfully shifts the attention away from me. I'm not quite sure what Beau has told his parents about us, but I'm pretty sure it's not that we're about to start a family together.

Sutton's focus has also shifted. As promised, after her initial excitement, she's now fully immersed in a conversation with Kate, who's smelling Sutton's wine with a look of longing.

"You okay?" Beau snakes his arm around my waist, and I nod.

"I'm happy I came."

He booms with laughter. "Don't speak too soon. The rate we're going, we're not even going to get apple pie, and that's the only reason I'm here."

But that's not true. He's here for the same reason all of us are—to feel a sense of belonging. To revel in what looks like unshakeable bonds of trust and friendship, where no one's a star yet everyone feels special.

Beau's wrong—no matter what else happens, I'll be pleased I saw all this.

TWENTY-ONE

Beau

Sitting across from me at the dining table, Vivian laughs at one of my dad's terrible stories and I can't help but smile. I can tell by the way she grabs his arm and tips her head back, she isn't simply being polite. He must have said something that really amused her.

I knew that the Cove family wouldn't stand on ceremony, but I had a sliver of concern that Vivian might be so used to being on show or at the center of everything that she might not feel comfortable.

I didn't need to be worried.

Our gazes meet and I don't—can't—look away. She's beautiful. There's no glam team here, no designer dresses, and she looks as gorgeous as she ever has.

"Right," Dad says. "I'm off to bed. Dog will be up at six no doubt." He slaps his thighs and stands. Vincent and Kate have already gone to bed because Kate's constantly tired, and Nathan and Madison have gone back to their place.

"You two up for a game of Codenames?" Jacob asks.

"I'm not," Sutton says. "It's time for me to turn into a pumpkin." She turns to Vivian. "It's a gruesome process and I don't want you to have to witness it. Growing the stalk is the worst part."

"You're weird," Vivian says. "But I like you."

"You should be weirder than you are, given you're Vivian Cross, but it's nice that you're not."

"I'm going to take that as a compliment," Vivian says. They exchange hugs like they've known each other for years.

Jacob leans down to where I'm sitting. "She's great," he says.

She really is. All I can do is nod. Anything else and Jacob will know more than I want to give away. Jacob slings an arm around Sutton and they head upstairs to bed.

I pull Vivian down onto my lap and she circles her arms around my neck.

"It's been such a lovely evening," she says. "I don't want it to end."

"We can stay up a little longer," I say, not wanting the evening to end either.

Her fingers stroke the back of my neck. "Wanna show me your room?"

Our gazes lock and I try to figure out if she's saying what I think she's saying.

"I can," I reply, in the most neutral tone I can manage. I've been consigned to Mum's sewing room, which used to be an office, which originally was a barn across the driveway from the house. I stand and instantly miss her warmth as she slides off me. "Yeah, I really want to show you my room." I take her hand in mine. I pat my jeans pockets to make sure I have my keys and we head out into the rain. It's not heavy, and she doesn't ask for an umbrella or even try and cover her hair with a hat. She's exactly the opposite of who people would think a global singing star would be, and it's like I'm in on the secret—the real Vivian.

Vivian has her own room in the house, but I'm really hoping her tour of mine will last the night.

"Is this where y'all toast the marshmallows?" She nods over at the firepit.

"Yeah. When it's not raining. And given we're in Norfolk, that's about three days a year."

"I like the rain," she says as she squeezes my hand.

I open the door to my bedroom, revealing the made-up sofa bed and Mum's sewing equipment.

"There's not much to see," I say, closing the door.

She laughs. "At least it's dry." She tilts her head as she gazes up at me. I circle her waist with my arms as she slides her palms up my chest, making my entire body shudder on the inside.

"Did you bring me in here on false pretenses?" I ask. "I thought you wanted to see my room, but it looks like you're planning to seduce me."

"Maybe. Or maybe I'm hoping you'll seduce me?" She runs a finger over my lips and I close my eyes to try and control the urge I have to strip her naked and lick her from the inside of her ankle to behind her ear.

My voice drops at least an octave. "Are you sure that's what you want?"

She nods and my skin tightens all over.

"But when we met, you were adamant—"

"Before I knew *you.*"

She knows exactly what to say.

"Are *you* sure?" she asks. "I know that before—"

I lean and press a kiss against her lips, sliding my tongue

through to her soft, wet mouth. My entire body sags with relief. It's like I've arrived home.

I don't care what came before, what pledges I made about maintaining my singledom for eternity, about the fact that Vivian might change her mind tomorrow and fly back to America and break my heart in the process. Right now. Here. I just want us to be as close to each other as we can be, mentally and physically.

I smooth my hands up her back, as if I'm trying to reassure myself she's here. With me.

As she pushes her fingers through my hair, I let out a groan. It feels so good. *She* feels so good. I want to stretch out these moments we're about to have so they don't end, so they just loop around and start again like some time-based mobius strip. There, we'd spend the rest of time together, interlocking across the driveway at my parents' house.

"Don't overthink this," she whispers.

"I can't think about anything at the moment."

She steps back and out of my arms and strips off her shirt.

I close my eyes in a slow blink, trying to get hold of myself. It just feels like the stakes are so high and she's so beautiful and...and I don't want to be the good-time guy. The guy before the one she gets serious with.

"You're overthinking," she says.

She's right. I'm thinking about everything.

She dips her fingers under my shirt, skating her fingertips over my scars before pushing at the fabric. I strip it off, then watch as she familiarizes herself with my uneven skin.

She leans forward and presses kisses on my torso over and over again. Something in the way she touches me clears my mind and makes me shift gear.

She's beautiful. And half naked. And standing right in front of me.

She stands after peeling off her jeans and it's like someone renewed my batteries. I step toward her, cupping her face, and turn us so her back is against the wall.

"I'm thinking about all the ways I'm going to fuck you," I say, and her cheeks instantly redden. "How many times I'm going to watch you come, how much you're going to beg for more, how good I'm going to make you feel."

She looks at me with a combination of trepidation and desire and it fires something up in my gut. There are skeletons in both our closets we need to free, boundaries we need to cross, new ground we need to tread. Tonight will be about resurrection for both of us.

As we kiss, my fingers find the lace of her underwear and delve inside. She squeaks and I pull back to look at her for permission.

"I haven't waxed," she says. "I didn't realize... I mean, I should have—I'm sorry, I—"

I work my fingers lower. "Please don't tell me you're apologizing to me for not removing hair on your body that's entirely natural and healthy. I want your pussy however it's served."

She frowns at me as if she's trying to process what I'm telling her, then I find her clit and her jaw slackens.

"For the record," I continue, as I circle and press. "I don't give a fuck if you wax or not. Frankly, at this precise moment, you could be wearing a Spiderman costume and it wouldn't affect how much I want you."

A smile nudges at the corner of her mouth and then her head falls back and she gasps as I reach her wetness. God she feels good on my hand. Hot and wet and sweet.

She grips onto my shoulders and I bury my head in her

neck, kissing and sucking, almost like I'm trying to consume as much of her as I can. I pull down her bra straps, freeing her breasts, and feel myself thicken as they tumble out.

How have I waited this long? Why have I been holding back?

"We've wasted so much time," I force out through shortened breaths.

"Just what I was thinking."

Well, no more.

I sink to my knees and pull down her underwear. "I'm going to make you come so hard."

"Beau!" she half-heartedly chastises.

I catch her hips and hold her still as I bury my face into her pussy. She smells like ripe peaches and I want to eat every last morsel of her. Slowly, I trail my tongue around her clit, circling, dragging, teasing and tasting.

"Beau!" she cries again, more urgently.

She bucks against me, almost like she doesn't want to give into the pleasure of it. Her fingers in my hair freeze. Without removing my tongue from its new favorite place, I look up at her.

"You don't have to," she says.

I'm so dazed with lust, my dick is so full and heavy at the taste of her, it takes me a beat to realize what she's said.

I don't want her to ever think that anything I do for her is performed out of a sense of obligation. Slowly, I stand, pick her up, and place her on the bed. I kneel between her thighs.

"Look at me when I tell you this," I say.

Her lips are red and swollen, her hair deliciously rumpled. She looks so fucking sexy I can barely breathe.

"Tonight you're going to be appreciated by a man. We're going to make each other feel good, but no one is going to do anything they don't want to do. I want to taste you. I want to make you come. I don't know what you're used to and frankly, I don't care. I want you. I want your clit on my tongue and your breasts in my mouth. I want you on my fingers and on my cock, I want you covered in my come, and I want to taste nothing but you for days. That's how tonight is going to go." I pause and take a breath. "You good with that?"

She smiles almost shyly and then gives a small nod.

And I get to...play, because this could never be work.

I watch her as I circle her clit with my thumb and then slide a finger through her folds to her tight, wet cunt. She groans and pants and part of me wants pull out my phone and record this so I can watch her every expression on repeat forever.

But I don't even ask. I get the impression that Vivian is used to being the one providing pleasure in the bedroom, rather than being lavished with pleasure the way she deserves. I wouldn't want her to say yes to me filming her just to make me happy, when that's not what she wants.

Instead, I try and commit her blissed-out expression to memory. As my thumb continues to circle and tease, I flick my tongue over her clit, lapping and licking.

My desire rachets up with hers as she climbs higher and higher toward the summit of her orgasm, her back arching off the bed, her hands fisting the sheets.

"Oh god, Beau," she says. "I think I'm—" Her entire body shudders and she contracts around my thumb as she comes.

Fuck, the critics are right: this woman is a phenomenon.

"Beau," she calls out, and I realize I've just been gazing at her.

"I'm here," I say as I slide up beside her.

She reaches for me, clamoring for me, like if she doesn't cling onto me, she's going to fall off the world.

"You okay?"

"More than," she says, her voice breathy. "More than you can ever know."

There's a dull pang in my heart that this woman clearly hasn't been worshipped as she ought to have been.

She fumbles at the buttons of my jeans and I strip awkwardly, without getting up. "I think you might be right about something." She trails her fingers over my chest and along the dips and peaks of my abdomen. "I think you might make me beg."

With that, I flip her onto her back. "Oh I'm not leaving here until it's happened."

"All the more reason to try and hold back." She shoots me a small smile.

I groan and steal a kiss as I nestle between her thighs, my erection pressing against her warm clit. If I stay here, I'm going to explode all over her. I take a breath and kneel.

My entire body is throbbing with need to be inside her as I reach for the condom I have in my wallet.

"You're fucking gorgeous, you know that, right?" I ask.

"*You're* fucking gorgeous," she says. It's not like I've never had the compliment before, but hearing it from her, it hits differently. Maybe it's because we've spent so long getting to know each other before we've landed here, naked together. Maybe it's because it feels like she knows me. Like better than...a lot of people who've known me longer.

"I'll take it," I say.

She grins at me. "I'll take it too. From you it feels...nice."

Everything about tonight is a thousand times better than nice, but it's the perfect word because I know in my gut how she feels—because I feel it too.

She's nice. And she's entirely perfect.

I grab a condom, tear open the packet and slide it on. I catch her watching me, taking in how hard I am. Because of her.

We lock eyes and I crawl over her. My heart is beating in my chest like it's trying to escape and my skin's so tight, it feels like the blood is going to burst out of my veins.

"Fuck, Vivian," I say as I brace my arms either side of her head, just taking in this moment.

She slides her hands over my lower back, lightly encouraging me closer, as if she knows I'm trying to hold it together.

I press against her entrance, my heartbeat pounding in my ears. Is this how Formula One drivers feel before a race? Or racehorses behind a starting gate? We're not in a rush, but it feels like we've been waiting for this for so long.

Our gazes still locked, I push into her. Her fingernails on my shoulders bite into my skin, and thank god, because it takes the edge off the perfect fucking feel of her all around me. She's so tight and warm and so fucking *right*.

I push in as deep as I can go and try to steady my breath. Her chest is heaving in a staccato rhythm as if she's at the end of a race, not the starting line.

I get it. I'm right there with her.

I press my forehead to hers and pull out, trying to think of something else, anything but the delicious drag of her around my cock.

"Beau," she breathes out. All I can do is nod. I calm myself, taking a few deep breaths, and try and switch my focus to her, how she's feeling rather than her grip around me, her perfect breasts, her nipples sharp and attention-seeking, her skin soft and smooth.

"Does it feel good?" I ask, pushing back inside. I manage a slow rhythm.

"Too good. Like you might split me in two."

I groan at her words. "Fuck, Vivian."

"But it's so deep, Beau."

I knew I was right. She likes dirty talk.

I push her knees wide and thrust in as deep as I can.

She gasps.

"Like this?"

She nods. "So deep."

"That's right. I'm so deep in your pussy and I'm covered in your come and I love it."

She whimpers, and I have to look away or I'm going to explode inside her. She grabs at my waist, trying to bring me closer.

"Beau!" Her tone is concerned and my gaze flits back. "I think. Oh god. I'm—" Her head tips back and she arches her back as she climaxes again.

I can't help but smile. At least it's not just me.

It feels fucking great to make her feel good.

I press a kiss between her breasts and keep up my rhythm, pushing us both closer and closer. I won't stop, won't let myself come, until she's there again with me.

"Oh god," she says, when she realizes I'm not going to let her recover this time. "Oh god," she calls, louder this time.

I nod. "That's right. Give in." Somehow I know she needs permission to feel everything she's feeling right now.

Her fingers slide up the sides of my torso, making me shiver, and I can feel sweat sheeting my body as I keep pressing and pushing, pounding over and over.

I recognize her expression of incomprehension this time. Orgasms seem to be something unusual to her. But it sets something off in me and this time, I know I'm not going to be able to hold back.

"Again," I say, as if I'm demanding it from her.

She closes her eyes in a long blink and my entire body tightens. We both fall together off a cliff of bliss.

I regain consciousness, lying on my back with Vivian in my arms, the condom discarded on the floor.

"I think you're wonderful," she says. "Like, *phenomenal* in bed." She sighs. "But also an awesome human."

I chuckle. "Thanks. The feeling's mutual."

"But," she says, pulling out of my arms and sitting. "I need to verify my initial findings about the phenomenal thing." I realize she's playing with a condom wrapper, trying to get it open.

"Oh yes, the verification process is important," I reply.

She nods as she manages to rip open the wrapper. "It might go on for a while."

"All night even," I say.

"And that's just stage one," she says, examining the condom. "There's the second stage. That can last...even longer." She places it on the tip of my erection. It's clear she's rusty or maybe even entirely new to condoms, but I'm happy to let her self-teach at this point. I need to save my energy. Clumsily, she sheathes me and then glances around before swinging a leg over my hips.

"We'll just have to do what it takes," I say, watching as her breasts sway as she moves.

"It will require commitment," she says.

I nod, as if I understand the sacrifice.

She lifts up on her knees and places the crown of my cock underneath her, then leans forward.

Fuck, this woman might just end me. But what a way to go.

I cup her breasts, and she groans as she slides onto my cock.

The sound reverberates across my limbs.

I'm done.

Completely done.

It's like I've passed through some kind of threshold in my existence and I know that whatever happens from here on out will be different to everything that's gone before.

She circles her hips and I count in my head, one, two three, wondering how high I can get before I have to take over. Because she feels too good and I'm not sure I can handle it.

I slide one hand around her waist, wanting to regain some semblance of control. Because right now, I'm totally at Vivian's mercy.

The way her hands seem to absentmindedly skim her stomach.

The way her breasts sway and shift, the way she manages to take me so fucking deep.

The way her head tilts back when I'm buried in her like she can

Only.

Just.

Take.

It.

Her rhythm slows and she starts to whimper.

I take her by the waist and lift her up and down on my cock. It's like she's overcome by sensation, unable to operate her body on her own.

I thrust my hips up to meet her over and over and over, trying to get more, get closer, get deeper. Her body convulses under my touch, her orgasm stretching out for longer this time. Just when I think she's done, she seems to come again, and it's too much for me. The sight of this woman coming over and over on my cock, the feel of her— it's over.

I thrust up one final time, emptying myself into her, wishing for the first time in my fucking life that I wasn't wearing a condom and she was completely full of every-thing I can give her.

TWENTY-TWO

Beau

We look out into the ocean, wind whipping around our faces, the salt from the ocean thick in our hair, and I pull Vivian toward me. "It's gorgeous, isn't it?"

"It really is. But not just the view. You're right, no one is looking at me." She tugs on the navy-blue bobble hat that my mum loaned her. "But not just because of this. Because they're all the stars of their own lives. They don't come here to celebrity-spot. They come here to fill their souls with this view. They come here for this feeling: that we might get swept up by the wind at any moment and join the seals in the sea. They come for the knowledge that we'll go home tonight and sleep like huge redwoods. It's a special place, Beau Cove."

God, *she's* special. Doesn't she know it? I cup her face, her nose red with cold, her cheeks warm under my fingertips. I press my lips to hers. "I like listening to you talk."

"I like you kissing me," she replies.

I press my lips to hers again and our tongues slide

together, the sensation something like the feeling I had when I summitted Kilimanjaro or saw my first blue whale. I want to capture this moment in time and relive it my entire life.

We pull apart but our gazes stay locked. Neither of us needs to speak. It's like we both know that something between us has shifted here in Norfolk. I'm not sure if she's dropped her guard since being out of London or if I'm slightly different when I'm with my family, but things have turned from fun to...kinda beautiful.

"I'm so glad you're here," I say.

"I'm so glad you invited me."

"Let's walk back to Blakeney."

"Can I confess something?"

Excitement swirls in my gut. I'm not quite sure why.

"When we passed in the car, I spotted a shop I'd like to stop in."

I laugh. "Okay, let's go and find it."

Vivian knows exactly where the shop is. As I follow her inside, she pulls off her gloves and starts browsing the glass cabinets full of jewelry. "Is it too much if I buy your mom and the girls something?"

"I don't know. What did you have in mind?"

"This necklace," she says, pointing at a gold necklace with a sycamore leaf pendant hanging from it. "Can I take a closer look at this?" she asks the shopkeeper, whose hair is piled on top of her head so abundantly, I think there's an eighty percent possibility there's a bird nesting in there.

"Of course." She pushes her red-framed glasses to the top of her head and grins like we're her favorite people. She takes the necklace from the cabinet and places it on a flat blue cloth on the counter.

"It's lovely. Heavy. I love the detail." Vivian turns her head to me and I nod in agreement. "And it's gold?"

"A solid nine carats."

"Is it your only one?" she asks.

"Let me check." The shopkeeper crouches and starts rummaging in the drawers beneath the cabinet. "I have more." She stands and puts a small box on the counter.

"I was actually hoping you had...four." Vivian slides her eyes to mine. "That's right, isn't it? Your mom, Madison, Sutton and Kate."

"It's very generous," I say. "And completely unnecessary."

"But they're so lovely. The women and the necklaces... and I'd really like to treat them. You think it will look too flashy?"

My reply sticks in my throat. I'm so moved that she sees what I see in my family and that she's considering them. She's generous, but not just in monetary terms. Her care for them is a gift. I shake my head in reply. "They'll love it."

She beams back at me and turns her attention back to the jewelry. "Do you have four?"

"I think I do." She disappears again as she crouches. "Yes. Four and the one on display, so that's good luck."

"Fantastic." Vivian gasps. "This. *This*. It's *so* beautiful." She points at a ring under the glass that looks like a thin leaf of a weeping willow has been dipped in gold and wound in a spiral. Glancing back at me, she says. "Do you like it?"

I nod. "Yeah, it's pretty. But anything would look pretty on you." I drop a kiss on her temple and the shopkeeper lets out a quiet *awww*.

"You two on honeymoon?"

"Not quite yet," I answer, and Vivian laughs.

"Can I try it on?" Vivian asks.

"You can, but I need to warn you that it's the only one I have. I only got one in."

She hands it to Vivian, who tries it on her middle finger, but it's too small.

"I think it would look prettier on your ring finger," the shopkeeper says.

Vivian tries it on her right finger and then pauses before she tries it on her left.

"Does it fit?" I ask.

"On my left ring finger," she replies.

I nod. "Then I should buy it for you."

A grin unfurls on her face. "Really?"

I shrug. "Absolutely."

"Can I wear it right away?"

I chuckle. "If you want to."

She slides it onto her left ring finger, then holds her finger out, looking at it admiringly. "I love it." She stands on tiptoes and presses a kiss to my cheek. "Thank you."

I pay for her ring and she pays for the necklaces for my mother and sisters-in-law, and we head back to the car.

"You know, people might start to think I'm more than just your boyfriend, what with you sporting a ring on that particular finger. You okay with that?"

She narrows her eyes. "I'm okay with that. Are you okay with that?"

Sensation blooms in my chest and I'm not quite sure what it is. Pleasure? Happiness? Contentment?

Maybe it's all those things mixed together.

I shrug. "I'm okay with that."

Vivian grins. Her rosy cheeks get a tiny bit rosier.

"You did such good peeling yesterday, you're bound to be put on potato duty today, fair warning." I scoop up her hand while we walk.

"I like to help. It makes me feel like I'm...part of things."

We're gazing at each other when our attention is pulled by someone calling Vivian's name. We haven't brought security, but for a flash, I feel like we should have.

"Vivian! Can I get a picture?"

I put my body between Vivian and whoever is speaking, then I see that it's a girl around fifteen, coming toward us in wellies and a puffa jacket. She's definitely not paparazzi.

Vivian approaches the girl. "Of course."

She asks the girl questions about her favorite songs and I take a picture on the girl's phone, then hand it back.

"Thank you," the girl's mum mouths at me.

We wave and I can hear the girl squealing as we head back to the car.

"Are you okay?" I ask.

"I'm fine. It's nice that people like my music. She was respectful and I just made her day. How can I be anything but happy about that?"

I chuckle as I unlock the car. "That's a lovely way to look at it."

"It's the only way to look at it. I've been in hiding a few weeks now, but I can feel the old me emerging. The one that appreciated every privilege, every sunset, every note I can sing."

God I love listening to her. I love watching her. I love touching her.

There's nothing about the way I'm feeling about her that's fake.

TWENTY-THREE

Vivian

As I carry the last of the dishes into the kitchen, I'm singing.

I'm blue.

You're you.

There's something that's just so true.

Speak out.

Speak up.

I wonder if I'll fall, but...

"That's a pretty tune," Carole says as she slides the dishes on the counter. "Is it one of yours?"

"Just something I'm working on," I say. "But I'm always working on something." Or at least I have been recently. The period after the split from Matt was probably the longest I'd ever been without writing. There were days immediately in the aftermath when I wondered whether I'd ever write again. But the words, the music, the desire to write again came back, first as a slow trickle. Now the ideas are flowing like it's Niagara Falls inside my head.

"Just like I said, work shouldn't feel like work. Go join

the others around the firepit. I'm going to head up to bed just as soon as I've finished loading the dishwasher."

"I can help," I say.

"You'd help me by going out there and enjoying the rest of your night." She touches the necklace I gave her at dinner, which she insisted on wearing immediately. They all did. "Thank you again for the necklace. It was so thoughtful of you."

"Thank you for a lovely evening," I say.

"I'm so pleased you came," she says. "You obviously make my Beau so happy."

I smile at her, wondering what I should say. Then I figure I should just speak from my heart. "He makes me very happy, too."

I give her a hug and then head out to the firepit, where Jacob and Sutton, Vincent and Kate, and Nathan and Madison are. There's a spare seat next to Beau. Smiling, he watches me come out of the house and doesn't take his eyes off me as the others continue to chatter.

"You okay?" he asks.

"Vivian," Sutton says. "Look what Jacob found." She gets up and turns three hundred and sixty degrees, then grabs something from behind her chair. "A guitar. Do you play?"

"Sutton," Beau says. "Stop."

I smooth my hand over his knee. I whisper, "It's fine. But thank you." I reach for the guitar as she hands it to me. "I'm not a big guitar player. Let's see."

A hush twists around the fire and I place my fingers and strum. "I might need a bit of help here, so make sure you join in."

I strum the opening chord for "The Long and Winding Road". It's my favorite Beatles song and it seems fitting as

I'm sitting here, among these people who I met because I spilled coffee on a guy. To be sitting in front of a man who seems to have my happiness at the front of his mind, despite the fact I didn't know him a couple weeks ago.

Maybe that's why I feel like the best version of myself with him.

Maybe that's why I feel so safe with him.

Maybe that's why I was led to his door.

I turn to Beau and we lock eyes, him looking at me, me looking at him, me singing to him, him singing to me.

When the song's finished, I pass the guitar to Vincent, who knows a few chords. After swapping seats with Beau, Vincent starts messing about with Jacob.

"Hey," Beau says. "That was beautiful."

I grin up at him. "Thanks. It's my favorite Beatles song."

"It's my favorite now too."

I laugh. "How did you get so charming?"

"I mean it. It's great having you here." He slides his hand into mine and I shift closer to him on the bench so there's no space between us. His warmth seeps through my jeans and my shirt, and I can feel him all over.

"It's great being here. With you. I don't think I ever want to go home."

He holds my stare and neither of us says anything, because we both know our lives are supposed to take us in opposite directions. But just now, there's something in me gathering speed to change course. Does he feel it too?

"Take me to bed, Beau Cove," I whisper.

"Thank god Mum's got me sleeping outside," he says, "because Vivian Cross, I'm going to make you sing all night."

Again, I think.

TWENTY-FOUR

Beau

We get back into my bedroom, and Vivian is tugging at my shirt before the door's closed. I spin her around and press my body against hers, cupping her chin and sliding my tongue between her lips.

I pull back. "Watching you play that guitar." I shake my head because it's difficult to describe how much I loved watching her play. She looked so comfortable and at home, and the fact that she looked like that, in a place *I* call home, surrounded by my family... I've never felt anything like it. "It was wonderful. I can tell how much you love it."

She beams up at me and sweeps her fingers over my cheekbones. "I had a really good time tonight. Your family..." She shrugs.

"What?" I ask, my eyebrows pinching together.

"You make sense, now I've spent some time with them."

"I do?" I ask.

"You do. They're...really quite something."

"You're really quite something." I hook my fingers

under her t-shirt and sweep it up over her head, then smooth my hands down her back. Her skin is like her voice, creamy and soft as velvet.

We undress between kisses. There's less speed, less need to take everything all at once. There's an unspoken agreement between us: We want to take our time. Linger in all the right places.

Once we're both entirely naked, I lay her down on the bed and lie beside her, on my side, my head propped up on my hand. My view is spectacular. I smooth my hand over her stomach, cupping her breasts, pinching her nipples between my thumb and forefinger.

"Did you always know you wanted to be a singer?" I ask.

"Pretty much," she replies. "Or involved in music in some way. I grew up around it. It's in my blood."

"Like me and medicine, I suppose. We both found our calling early." I'm talking to myself but to her as well. It's like the barrier between my words and thoughts has completely broken down. I don't have to filter anything for her.

"You said you were at a crossroads. You think medicine is your future?"

I roll on top of her and press a kiss to her neck. "I enjoy being a doctor so I can't imagine medicine not being in my life. I've just got to figure out how."

"Well, I can confirm you have a good grasp of female anatomy," she says on a laugh, and I can't help but enjoy her happiness. It's like I can feel everything she feels and I want her to feel nothing but joy.

"Oh yeah?" I ask. "Maybe I need to brush up on one or two things." I crawl down her body, pressing my lips against her warm, soft skin, stroking, licking, claiming her for myself.

She's mine. She's mine. She's mine.

I've never felt like a woman belonged to me the way I do with Vivian. Is it some kind of Neanderthal instinct that gets released after the kind of sexual connection we have?

Vivian's fingers in my hair make me groan against her skin and she writhes underneath me. "Beau," she whispers. "Beau, please. I need you."

"You need me?" I crawl up her body and reach for a condom, our gazes still locked. "Tell me again."

"I need you...inside me. Please."

I groan at the longing in her tone. The begging she said she would never do.

We don't look away as I plunge into her. I'm not sure how it's possible, but somehow it feels even better than last night. It's like the connection we created then has strengthened and somehow magnified. I feel so close to her—not just physically but mentally.

I piston my hips and she wraps her legs around me, like she wants to get closer. I dip my head, trying to block out as many sensations as I can. I've never felt so much all at once.

The idea that she might be feeling a fraction toward me as I'm feeling toward her is mind-blowing to me.

"Vivian," I mutter against her skin. "Vivian, Vivian, Vivian."

She shifts underneath me and I lean back slightly, lifting her leg and draping her ankle against my shoulder. We both groan at the change in angle.

I keep pushing into her, wondering if anything will feel this good again.

"There," she gasps. "Oh god."

"You feel so fucking good, Vivian. So fucking tight."

The start of my orgasm bellows in the distance and I can barely think, my blood pounding in my ears. "You. Are. So. Fucking. Special."

She cries out over and over and over, like she just can't keep the sounds in.

My heart is pounding on my rib cage, trying to escape, and my orgasm is thundering in the background, threatening like the warning swell of a tsunami.

She contracts around me, her back arching, her body pressing into me. I can't hold back.

Flashes of white light fill my head, a guttural roar breaks out of my throat and pleasure thrusts up my spine as I explode up, up, up into her.

"Shit," I say, pressing my forehead against hers and then rolling to her side, bringing her with me so we're facing each other. "I...love making love with you."

A small smile lifts the corners of her mouth and she cups my face. "I love making love with you too."

We lie, limbs intertwined, exhausted in contented silence for what seems like the longest time.

"Thank you for inviting me here," she says. "I..." She stops herself, but I want to hear what she's thinking.

"What?" I ask. "You can tell me anything."

There's a beat before she speaks again. "I feel free when I'm with you," she says. "Like...you like me for whoever I am. I don't have to worry about being me. You know?"

I nod and pull her closer. "You should never worry about being you. You're amazing."

She sweeps her fingers down my side and I shiver at her touch. Then she slides her hand between us and wraps it around my thickening cock. She looks at me, her eyes dark, and bites down on lip. Her expression—a little bit bashful, tinged with pure lust—elicits a low grunt.

Tentatively, she starts to move her hand up my shaft. "It feels..." I jerk and twitch in her hand and she smiles, her movements growing more confident. She leans in to kiss me, her tongue pushing against mine.

I like this side of her. The side that knows what she wants and takes it.

"I don't want to use a condom," she says. "Are you...tested?"

I nod. "Are you..."

"I have an IUD fitted."

I suck in a breath in an effort to calm my heartbeat that feels like hooves on concrete. I shift to my back and pull her on top of me. I slide her onto my cock as if she was made for me.

She feels like instant bliss.

She moans as I push her hips down, taking her as deep as I can go.

"You want me to come inside you?" I ask. "You're greedy for it, aren't you?"

"Beau," she calls out, her limbs going limp.

I shift so she's lying on her back and I'm standing on the floor. I need the leverage to get as deep as I can.

"I've got as much as you can handle. I'm going to come so much, it's going to cover you. All down your thighs. All over your stomach."

She convulses around me, but I don't stop. I keep plowing into her, because I can't get enough and I don't know if I ever will.

"But you're the one that will come the most, isn't that right?" I ask. "Because you can't get enough." I thrust into her. Again. And again. And again.

Sweat sheets my body and gathers at my forehead. My

heart rate is about to hit one ninety before it rips out of my chest.

"Fuck," I hiss.

Vivian twists, her body going rigid. I feel her throb around me, almost milking me, and I can't stop myself now. As much as I want her to come again before I surrender, there's no turning back. My climax is charging toward me like an invading army.

I feel her come undone underneath me and it's as if her orgasm engulfs me. I push into her a final time and we come apart together.

TWENTY-FIVE

Vivian

The alarm on my phone is so loud it feels like it's actually buried under my skull.

"What the fuck is that?" Beau says from beside me.

"There's only one number that can get through when my phone's on silent. It's Tommy." I leap out of bed and pull on my jeans and shirt. I'm dressed before the third ring and swipe up to see Tommy and Felicity.

"Good morning," I say. I glance round to see if I can see the time. The dawn has arrived, but it definitely hasn't had its coffee yet.

"Maybe for you," snips Felicity. "But here it's still the middle of the night. We wanted to make sure you were well rested for what we've got to tell you."

My stomach drops and I glance over at Beau, who's headed to the bathroom.

"I presume you don't have anything to tell us?" Felicity asks.

My brain scans to think what she's trying to get at. "I made an apple pie?"

"Are you engaged?" Tommy asks.

I feel the gold wrapped around my finger. "Oh, engaged? No." I hold up my hand to face the screen. "But Beau did buy me a ring."

Felicity and Tommy both groan. "Does that mean you *are* engaged or you're not engaged?"

"It means I saw a ring in a shop that I liked, Beau bought it for me and this is the only finger it fits on."

Felicity clears her throat.

"I presume a picture got out," I say.

"Someone posted something on their Instagram and it got picked up by a fan account and things have...escalated."

"Are you really in Norfolk?" Felicity asked. "The far east?"

I laugh. "It's beautiful."

"So, we need to know how you want to play this. Do you want us to put it out there that after a whirlwind romance, you and Beau are engaged?"

My stomach clenches at the word *engaged*. All the press Matt and me did about the engagement, all the stories that were written. The fake ring replica I had to get made because I was so paranoid about the real one getting taken from me.

"Yes," Beau calls. "That's fine with me."

"It is?" I call back.

"I don't care. We're already fake dating. What does it matter if we're fake engaged?"

"True, but..." We weren't actually *fake* dating anymore. And if our relationship had turned real, why complicate things and make them fake again? "You don't think it's better if...we keep it authentic?"

He appears in the doorway to the bathroom, his chest hard and defined. My fingers itch to press against his hot skin just like they had done last night. He doesn't say anything, just tips his head, beckoning me over to him.

"Give me a second," I say to Tommy and Felicity.

Beau disappears into the bathroom and I follow him.

"First," he says and presses a chaste but lingering kiss on my lips. "Good morning."

I try and fight the smile that's bursting through to jazz dance over my face.

"Second, I really don't mind what you decide here. I'll support you however you need. You don't need to worry about me or my feelings or whatever it is that's going on with us. Because..." He slides his hands over my ass and pushes me against him. I curl my fingers around his neck. "Whatever is between us is between *us*. Whatever's in the press is in the press. There's no confusing the two. We are who we are, no matter what anyone is talking about."

He pauses and I think I'm meant to say something, but I'm just thinking about how much I like this guy. Really like him. Everything he says feels like the best thing anyone has ever said to me. Everything he does is the best thing anyone has ever done. Every joke is the funniest, every look is the sexiest, every story he tells is the most interesting and insightful and makes me like him even more than I did before he started. How did I get here so quickly?

He smiles at me. "Agreed?"

I nod. "Agreed."

"Make your plans and know that I'm behind you, supporting you every step of the way."

He releases me and slaps me on the ass. I squeal as he turns on the shower, a grin on his face almost as big as mine.

"Everything okay?" Tommy asks as I go back into the bedroom and approach the phone.

"Fine." I catch sight of my rosy cheeks in the small on-screen window at the left of my screen. "So tell me what you think the best response is and why."

"A whirlwind engagement," Felicity says. "It consigns Matt and stories about him to history and shows you've moved on. Together with the new album, the narrative is going to be all about your new direction. Your new life."

"I like it," I reply. Not because my bruised ego needs to respond to Matt dating his co-worker so publicly, but because it's how I feel—hopeful about the future. Whatever is going on between Beau and me is ours, private, and doesn't have anything to do with what we'll say publicly. "Let's do it," I say.

"I want to warn you that doing this might..."

"Be open with me, Felicity. We agreed you'd tell me everything."

"We did. There's just something in my gut that tells me Matt will use this as an opportunity to spin his victim narra-tive. He might get some publications interested in his response and he might hit out—claim that you were dating Beau before you guys split, or that you had affairs or were a nightmare to live with, or—"

"I get it," I reply.

"Or," Tommy says. "He might come out and say he doesn't believe the two of you are actually dating. He could make some kind of commentary about you saving face by dating again and getting engaged."

I nod. "That sounds plausible. But I've stopped guessing what goes on in Matt's head. I'm thinking about what's best for me now. I want as many people to hear this new music as possible and...Beau's okay with this, so fake engagement it is."

Felicity smiles. "Good decision. And for what it's worth, that man in the bathroom seems like the real deal to me."

"Speaking of," Tommy says. "You should know that he never signed the contract. Just the NDA."

I frown. "Is that a problem?"

"It just means we've not paid him a penny. And he's not been obligated to spend any time with you."

What Tommy's saying aligns perfectly with what Beau has said and what I'm feeling. What's happening between us is between us. And it's real.

"Also," Tommy says, raising his voice. "He seems hot as holy hell."

"I hope you're talking about me, Tommy," Beau calls from the bathroom.

The shower is still running and I can't help but imagine a naked, hard-bodied Beau wet from head to toe.

"If there's nothing else, you both should go to bed," I say.

"And you look like you need a shower," Tommy says.

I laugh, press cancel and pad into the bathroom.

"Want some company?" I ask.

"If it's you, then always," he replies as I strip off my clothes.

TWENTY-SIX

Beau

I take a seat in the wingback chair in Nathan's office and glance around. "There's an awful lot of tartan in here," I say. "I'm half-tempted to do a Scottish jig."

"Don't let me stop you," Nathan says as he sits in the chair opposite, which is also a navy and dark green check.

He's holding the papers I gave him. "Everyone Adventures" is written in large, bold font on the front, and I hope it will pass for a business plan.

I put my hands on the arms of the chair and lean forward as if I'm about to stand and summon the pipers, then sit back as I realize that me trying to do some Scottish dancing is not going to make anyone laugh. "I think it might turn awkward if I start dancing and you're sitting there like you've got a pocket of dollar bills."

Nathan just shakes his head. "What goes on in that head of yours?"

"Well, that's what we're here to talk about, isn't it?"

"Tell me."

I nod toward the business plan. "I've put it all in there."

"Right, but tell me about it. If I was an investor, I'd want to hear the founder's passion in their own words."

"But you're not going to be an investor."

Nathan doesn't respond. I roll my eyes. There's no point in an argument about roles when all I'm looking for is advice. Direction. I don't know what happens next.

"Well, it's something I've been thinking about for a while. I know how lucky I am to go off on the trips I do. Lucky because I have the money, but also because I'm able-bodied." I roll my shoulder back, the one that was dislocated. "You know I was more than lucky with the burns."

He nods.

"If Mum hadn't been there or hadn't been a doctor, I would have died or at least have had a very serious and permanent disability."

"You've got nine lives," he said.

"Seven," I mumble. "The idea is to provide trips to people who haven't been as fortunate as me. They still want to see the world, but it's more difficult for them because of their disability."

"Is it a charity or a business?" he asks.

I think about his question. "Now that you ask, I don't know. In my head, I've always thought about it being a travel business—I didn't consider that it could be a charity. I suppose that adds another element—all the fundraising and..." I exhale. It all seems so complicated.

"And who would run it? You?" Nathan asks.

"Who else?"

"Someone you pay?"

I'd never thought about not running the business myself. "You mean I'd hire someone to run my business?"

"Yeah. Think of it like you're a private equity fund that

only invests in one business. I know people, if that's the route you want to go down."

"And what would be my role then?"

"Whatever you want it to be. You could still be involved with the day-to-day running of the place or be the medical director or...you could just continue life as it is now."

All this time I've put off doing anything with Everyone Adventures because I didn't think I could continue my life as it is now if I took it on. Now, continuing with business as usual doesn't feel as appealing as I expected. It's all the evidence I need to know that my future is going to look very different from my past. "Right. So it's just like if I owned a gym or something."

"Exactly. Do you think you'd want to run it yourself?"

"I don't know. I don't see myself as a businessman. I'm a doctor."

"Right. Would you fund it yourself or get third-party funding?" he asks.

"I'm not sure." All these questions. Yes, I put together a business plan, but everything is in the abstract. There's still a huge element of *if*, but Nathan is talking in *when*.

Nathan starts to flip through the pages. "My gut tells me that your biggest clients will be charities, even if you're not one yourself. That might cap potential profits."

I never planned to get into this business for the profit.

"Makes sense," I reply.

Nathan fixes me with a look. "The other thing to do is raise or donate or raise *and* donate money to enable kids to go on these holidays with other companies. I did a bit of desktop research, and there are other companies around that do this kind of thing. I get you're passionate about these kids getting an opportunity to do the things other able-bodied kids get to do, but you don't need to reinvent the wheel. It's a lot easier to donate some money to charity or even direct to individual families, than it is to set up a business, make sure it's run well and turn a profit."

He's right. When I first had the idea, years ago, nothing like Everyone Adventures existed. But now? There are definitely companies that do pretty much the same thing I imagine Everyone Adventures would do.

"You need to ask yourself what Everyone Adventures would do differently. How would it stand out? Would it go to different places? Offer something different or something more expensive or less? If it's just the same, it's less compelling. Not just to investors, but to customers."

I don't really have anything to say. I've been so focused on the idea of getting kids to see the world, the intricacies of running a business were never my focus.

"You could also do both. Hire an assistant or someone with experience in the charity sector and have them research ways you can make your donations as effective as possible. Or have them research families that would particularly benefit. Then you know your money is doing what you want it to do. After you've gathered more data, you can decide whether or not it makes sense to set up your own company."

No wonder Nathan is so successful. I'd like to consider myself fairly clever, but he's thought of things I haven't even considered.

"I really like that idea," I reply. "I'm getting to make a difference immediately and at the same time, gathering data to help any future business I might create."

"Exactly."

"You're clever," I say, not shocked, but impressed. I knew Nathan was successful, but now I know why.

Nathan laughs. "I know. Now I've figured out your life for you, let's go and get a glass of wine."

We stand and head out of the study. In many ways, Nathan's helped me put the puzzle pieces into place. I don't think I'm at the point where I want to start my own business, even if I was to pay someone else to run it.

I can use my money to help kids see the world. I can start doing it quickly and have an immediate impact. That feels good, but in some ways puts me back to square one. This won't quench the thirst I have to change *something* about my life. I'm still at a crossroads; I don't want to go backward and keep doing what I have been for the last decade, but I can't see a clear path forward, either.

The question remains: what's next for me?

TWENTY-SEVEN

Vivian

There are about three cars ahead of us for the red-carpet premier of the latest action movie starring...I can't quite remember who. But tonight isn't about the film, it's about starting the publicity tour for the new album that's not even completed yet.

"I could have come on my own tonight to take the pressure off," I say to Beau as I glance out the dark-tinted window.

"There's no pressure if we don't let ourselves feel it," he replies. "Anyway, it will be fun. We're all prepared and now we get to have our own cinema experience and watch the Reese Witherspoon film without an audience." He'd surprised me and arranged for a private screening of the new romcom on Netflix that I'd been desperate to see. It's so thoughtful of him. Caring. Kind. He pats the backpack on the seat beside us. "Your security guy is okay to carry it?" he asks.

"He said so."

"As soon as we're inside, he can pass it to me."

I nod and slide my hand into his. I've never skipped out of a movie premiere before. It was the only time Matt and I ever went to the movies, so we'd accepted every invitation we got, no matter the film. I always liked attending because it was a way of going to the movies without all the attention being on me, but looking back, I wonder if Matt enjoyed walking the red carpet. Maybe he even resented walking two steps behind me the whole way down.

The car stops and I wait for the door to open. Beau will get out first, so every picture of me doesn't have his face at my ass level.

"You okay?" I ask.

"I'm fine." He laughs. "This is no big deal."

The flashes of the camera as he steps out light up the interior of the car, but they die down quickly. I shift to the other side of the car and ready myself for the exit. I'm wearing a two-piece skirt and bustier, so at least I don't have to worry about anyone getting a shot of my panties. I've learned my lesson.

I paste on a smile, and it's not as difficult as I expect it to be. I have Beau with me, which means I have a lot to smile about.

He takes my hand and I step out of the car, the exact same way Felicity taught me over ten years ago.

I try not to blink as the flashes go off—it's all too easy for the photographers to get a picture of me looking drunk if I react too much to the lights. As I stand, I lock eyes with Beau and my smile goes from fake to real.

He's here.

With me.

And I couldn't be happier about it.

"You look gorgeous," he says.

"It takes an army, as you've witnessed." I put my smile back in place.

"Shall we?" he says, and we head up toward the bank of photographers.

They're calling my name. Some of them are calling Beau's name, but when I glance up at him, he doesn't seem to have noticed.

"Vivian! Vivian!" one shouts. "It's Liz from NBC. Just a couple of questions." I head toward the familiar voice and find Liz in the crowd.

"You look gorgeous. Who are you wearing?"

"Alexander McQueen," I answer. It's not the Oscars, but who can resist a little dressing up for a red carpet?

"Are you moving to Britain to be with your fiancé?" she asks.

Moving to Britain? I guess I could do a Madonna and call London my home. I can't imagine Beau would want to move to America if we really got married. He'd be too far away from his family. "We're likely to spend time on both sides of the pond," I reply.

"How did you two meet?" she asks.

"In a coffee shop. I accidentally poured coffee all down his shirt." I look around for Beau and find him standing behind me, watching me, not trying to interject. Not looking bored or pissed off. He just seems happy to be here, by my side. "Nice to see you, Liz," I say before she can ask me another question. I reach for Beau's hand and head toward the entrance.

"I think they want you to pose." He nods toward the middle of the pack of photographers, where one of the stars of the movie is standing. His name was on the list Tommy sent me. It doesn't seem like he's brought a date. "I've been watching and that's what seems to be happening. But you probably know that already."

I grin up at him. He's entirely adorable. "You wanna come with me?"

"They don't want me. They want you. And rightly so. I can stand here and admire you while you get your picture taken. It's a win-win."

His confidence makes me want to strip naked and mount him right here on the red carpet. It feels so nice that I can just be here and do my job, unworried about my partner's emotional resilience. I've never felt so relaxed at an event like this.

After a couple more questions from reporters and a lot more pictures, we finally go inside the theater. There are lots of people milling around the lobby, waiting for the red carpet scene to end before they take their seats.

My security guard hands Beau his rucksack and Beau takes my hand. "You ready?"

"We didn't think this through," I say. "Our clothes are in one bag, but we're going to have to change in separate restrooms."

Beau laughs. "We'll find a disabled loo. Come on."

He seems to know the way and he leads us through the crowds as I keep my head down so I don't catch anyone's eye. Now is not the time to discuss my engagement, collaborations, or movie roles.

We go through a corridor and down a few steps before he stops. "Here," he says. He opens the door and I go in first.

"This isn't very romantic. Changing under strip lighting next to a toilet and a trash can."

"What are you talking about?" He's already shrugged off his jacket and is unbuttoning his shirt. "We're like

Bonnie and Clyde. Partners in crime—sneaking around, trying not to get caught. This is beyond romantic."

Somehow we manage to get changed, put our red-carpet outfits into a suit carrier, and head out of the loo. Jim, my security guy, is waiting for me when we emerge.

Wordlessly he leads us farther down the corridor, me in front and Beau trailing behind.

"I don't want any photographers following us," I say.

"I know. I'm keeping an eye out, but we're good so far."

I glance around to find Beau grinning like this is some kind of escape room and we're beating all the other teams.

We get to the exit and Jim makes us wait while he checks that the car's there—and paparazzi are not.

A couple of seconds after he disappears, he's back and encourages us out. I keep my head down as I head into the open door of the sedan. Beau jumps in behind me and slams the door.

"We did it," he says as if he's just landed from a skydive, or got to the summit of a mountain. "See that guy?" He nods at a photographer standing on the corner of the alley we're in. "I could see him skulking around, but he didn't see either of us." He grabs my hand and his pulse is hammering against my wrist as the car pulls out.

I can't help but wonder if trying to outwit the paparazzi is a bit like mushing huskies or navigating the Amazon for Beau.

If it is, I can't decide if that's a good thing or a bad thing. There's a ton of evidence that Beau is exactly who he says he is—exactly who I feel him to be in my gut. A guy who's into me because he likes me, not the fame, not the money. Not the accoutrements that come with both. The way he is with his family, the way he's thoughtful and never signed the contract... That's the Beau I know.

But maybe it's part of some elaborate ruse to trick me. Maybe my gut has the instincts of a toenail.

Could it be that Beau's here, next to me, because he enjoys the adrenaline high of the attention from the press? Or the novelty of being with someone famous?

Am I just a means to an end for him?

I'm probably just being paranoid because I haven't been in front of cameras and journalists for so long. But will the doubt ever go completely? Will I ever be able to trust anyone fully ever again? Even if I am paranoid, and even if Beau's heart is true and pure, would being with me, with all the corresponding fame and attention, change him like it seemed to change Matt?

Will being with Beau inevitably turn him into someone I can't be with at all?

TWENTY-EIGHT

Beau

Nathan, Jacob, Dax and I are gathered around Nathan's desk. It's not even seven, but somehow we're all available on a Saturday morning and have decided to do something together without leaving the city. Vivian is in the studio. Her producers only have a short window, so she's having to make the most of it. Madison's mum is coming over, Sutton is working and Dax is...single as ever.

"I've booked everything so we can decide." Nathan's two computer screens are each split into two, and an activity is pictured on each screen.

"That's walking over the O2 Arena?" Jacob asks, pointing at one of the screens. "Why would we do that?"

"Nice view?" Nathan suggests.

"The experience, I suppose," I reply.

"It looks tame," Dax says.

"It will suit you then," Nathan says.

Dax just rolls his eyes. Things rarely bother him. I guess

growing up with four older brothers and an older cousin means he's endured worse most of the time.

"What do you think?" Nathan asks, looking at me. "You've not walked across the O2 Arena."

"That's true. But it doesn't mean I want to."

Dax sniggers.

"I thought you might like it," Nathan says, and I feel bad because I think he genuinely thought it was a good idea. Maybe if I was in a different mood, I'd enjoy it.

"What about the ropes course in Alexandra Palace?" Jacobs asks. "Sutton said it's terrifying so...that sounds fun."

I pull my mouth into a grin because I want them to think I think all the options are a good idea. But I can't seem to muster any enthusiasm for them. It's kind of my brothers to try to find an adventure we can take together. It's not often four of us are off work and not in Norfolk, and I like the idea of spending time hanging out. I don't know if it's because the activities are on my doorstep, or because they all seem a little...well, to quote Dax, *tame*. Or maybe I'm just not in the mood. I'd rather have a game of tennis or just go for a walk on the heath.

"Climbing the rigging of the Cutty Sark. I've never even heard of that. Are you sure that's even a thing?" Dax asks.

"You're looking at the website publicizing it," Nathan says. "Of course it's a thing."

"Play that video," Dax says. He presses on the screen and the video comes to life. "Yes, I knew it." The screen shows images of fresh, smiling faces, harnessed with helmets, climbing up toward views of London. "Bloody kids," he says. "That kid is no older than twelve. If he can do it, where's the challenge for Beau? What about abseiling down the Orbit helter-skelter thing? It's two hundred and sixty-five feet. There's got to be some challenge in this for Beau. He's climbed Kilimanjaro for goodness sake."

"Yeah, but not in an afternoon with three layabout brothers in tow," I say. "Why don't we just go for a walk across the heath and find a pub? Chew the fat. Come home, order a takeaway. Job done."

A silence descends on the room.

I look around and try to figure out why everyone's so quiet.

"Who are you?" Dax asks eventually. "And what have you done with my brother?"

"What?" I ask, feeling a little defensive.

"You're always up for adventure," Jacob says.

"Not always. Some of the time I like to just have a nice quiet day."

"When?" asks Jacob.

"When I'm in London. I'm not charging around on my days off, trying to find adventure. I do that when I'm away."

"How's the husky mushing plan coming along?" Nathan asks, his eyes narrowed as if he's posed a trick question.

"What do you mean, how's it coming along?" Truth be told, I haven't thought about husky mushing in weeks.

"I mean, are you still planning on going?" Nathan asks.

"Yes, why wouldn't I be?" I haven't decided *not* to go, I just haven't put any definitive plans in place. When I do go, it will probably be for at least a month, maybe two. At the moment, I don't feel the need to be somewhere else. The part of me forever seeking out the new and unfamiliar is dormant inside my head, happily snoozing the days away.

Maybe it's Vivian.

Maybe it's thinking about Everyone Adventures, which,

despite my conversation with Nathan, I can't completely turn away from.

"Well, Vivian of course," Jacob says.

I shrug. "I've committed the next six weeks to her and then..."

"And then what?" Nathan asks. "You're going to end things between you and go off husky mushing?" He makes it sound like the stupidest thing he's ever heard.

"I don't know." Things with Vivian are good—better than good—but I've not let myself think about the future. Every time I do, the things Coral said to me, together with all the evidence from the last decade, send me hurtling back to the present. If I live in the now and don't think ahead at all, I'm happy.

"But that was before you met Vivian," Jacob says as if I'm being deliberately obtuse.

"Right...?" I say.

"But you're not faking it," Dax says. "I don't know why you're saying you're her fake fiancé when you're not faking it."

"We're not really engaged," I say. "We're just enjoying the moment. Neither of us is looking for anything serious."

"But you're with her. Like really *with* her," Jacob says. "I've seen you with plenty of other women before and it's obvious Vivian is different."

I really don't want to talk about this. I'm happy. In this moment. Today. That's all I want to think about.

They don't know about Coral. They didn't need to, so I never mentioned her. And after what happened, there's no way I'd give them ammunition like that to tease me for the rest of my life. "Vivian's different because she's American and she's...famous."

"That's not it," Dax says, and everyone turns to him.

That's the thing with Dax—he's the youngest, but he always gets our attention when he gives his opinion because he's usually right. "You like her."

"Never said I didn't like her," I snap.

Jacob pipes up to fill the awkward silence descending on the room. "I know where we need to go."

IT'S COLD. It's raining. And swimming in Hampstead ponds, in the freezing water, has nothing to recommend it in these conditions. Somehow Jacob convinced us that open-water swimming was what we needed. Luckily, Nathan only agreed on the promise that we'd go straight to the pub afterwards for a burger and a beer. And now we're here, around a pub table, at the good part.

"It would have been better with wetsuits," Dax says.

I reach across my chest to put my hand on my shoulder. The cold exacerbated the after-effects of the dislocation. "It still would have been cold," I reply, circling the joint.

"You need to feel the cold," Jacob says. "That's the point. It really helps the clarity of thought."

It didn't help me. My shoulder was fine before the swim, and my mind was too. I like Vivian, full stop. I like watching her play the piano and seeing the expression on her face as she sings about heartbreak and rebirth. I like watching the way she handles herself with other people— how she was delighted to peel apples and chat to my mum about Bach. I like how her breakup seems to have fueled something in her rather than made her bitter. I like her focus, the way she knows exactly what she's here on this earth to do.

And I like how she feels by my side, in my arms and underneath me.

But so what? We live in two different worlds and we were never meant to be any more than a fake relationship.

As long as I don't look ahead, everything's just fine.

The future seems full of obstacles. Our incompatible lifestyles. The fact we live three thousand miles away from each other.

And...the fact that I'm the warm-up guy. I'm not the guy who settles down.

"Can we order?" Nathan says. "Do you all know what you want? Or shall I just order burgers for everyone."

"Fine with me," I say and everyone else agrees. I don't know if it's because I'm so close to the open fire, or because I'm wearing too many layers, but it's like I can't fill my lungs enough. I circle a finger around the neck of my jumper, trying to loosen any restrictions and allow the air to flow more freely, but it doesn't do anything. I don't seem to be able to breath.

Nathan heads up to the bar to place our order and I take a sip of my pint, trying to distract myself from the way my trachea feels like it's closing in.

"How's work?" Jacob asks Dax. I'm relieved to be off the hook.

I don't want to think about anything other than breathing.

"Good," replies Dax.

"Is that it?" Jacob asks.

"What do you want? Details?" Dax asks.

"No," I say. "Leave it, Jacob."

Dax and Jacob are clearly getting on each other's nerves, but I'm not sure why. The last thing we want is Dax to start talking about his research. The family is pleased he loves his job, we just don't need to know the latest ins and outs of whatever the hell he does on a day-to-day basis. No one does.

"What about you?" Jacob asks, looking at me. "Are you clear-headed now? The cold really helps, doesn't it?"

"I'm going to be cold for the rest of my life," I manage to get out, then stare at my pint, hoping the conversation will move past me.

"The fire will help," Nathan says as he returns from the bar.

"October isn't a good time to go swimming outside," I say. "And no, it hasn't helped." I enjoyed it the first time I'd gone with Jacob, but today felt like too much. My shoulder is really irritating me. And all these layers are almost suffocating. Maybe I need to walk it off.

"Let's break this down," Dax says. "We can do it logically."

"Of course. Logically," Nathan mutters before he takes a sip of his beer.

"First, do you enjoy spending time with Vivian?"

We aren't still talking about this, are we? "I'm not up for discussion. Change the subject."

Suppressed laughter ripples around the table. "Come on, it's not often that so many of us are together without Dad barking at us, or our wives and girlfriends being the center of our attention," Jacob says. "We can help you work through this."

"Through what?" I ask. "There's nothing to work through."

"What happens when she goes back to the States?" Jacob asks. "Sutton tells me she has a tour next year. Are you going with her?"

I half-choke on the beer I've just swallowed. I hammer

my fist on my chest. "I'm not looking at the end of the week, let alone next year."

"So, you're going to end things?" Dax asks.

It's like my stomach turns to sludge at the thought. Once again, I can't catch a breath.

"Or will you give up your life here and head to New York?"

"Nah, he won't do that," Nathan says. "He likes London too much."

I like *her*. I never said I would move to America. My life is here, in London. Why would they even think that?

Does Vivian think that?

"We haven't known each other that long."

"Right," Jacob says. "But when you know, you know. When you're willing to risk everything to be with her, you know it's right."

Why's he talking about risking everything? I just told him I'm not thinking beyond the end of the week and neither is Vivian.

"I have nothing to risk," I say. "We're not like you and Sutton. I'm not putting my career on the line. It's good between us, mate, but it doesn't have to be all or nothing."

"Okay, so her publicity tour is over and you're off the hook. She flies back to New York, you go husky mushing and that's it? She's just another woman in another port?" Nathan says.

It's like someone is rooting around my stomach, trying to pull out the sludge with a rake. I might be coming down with flu or a gastro thing, because I feel awful.

"Maybe," I say and stare into my pint. What's between me and Vivian doesn't feel like just another hook-up, but I'm not sure I'm meant to be with anyone for real. As Coral so cuttingly observed, I'm not that guy.

"It will be fine," Jacob says, clapping me on the back. "You're going to love being in a couple. Having someone to hang with all the time, someone who knows exactly what you're thinking all the time..."

He's grinning, but what he's saying is low-key creepy.

"You're going to have to learn to compromise, but that's life," Jacobs says.

Except it hasn't been *my* life. I've had my life exactly how I've wanted it for years now. I don't do anything I don't want to do. And I don't go anywhere I don't want to go.

"You can't just run off for a couple of months when you've got a wife," Jacob says. "Or a kid. It doesn't work that way."

Kid? What's he talking about kids for? I've known Vivian ten minutes. My brothers need to calm down.

"Don't frighten him," Nathan says. "Being in a couple. Being married. It's good. Better than I could have ever expected. It's the big stuff—I love her and want to spend my life with her. But it's the small stuff too, like how she always makes me chicken soup when I have a cold and she's the first person I want to go to with good news or bad. But...it's a two-way street. She's going to be developing all these feelings too. You need to get on the same page. Don't mess her around if you're not going to follow through."

My leg is bouncing under the table. I can almost feel my amygdala firing in my brain and I'm pretty sure I'm going to throw up. I'm not quite sure why they're getting to me. I can usually shrug off their jibes and the banter.

Maybe it's the thought of settling down.

Maybe it's the thought of hurting Vivian.

They all need to stop.

Vivian and I aren't serious. We're not going to be serious.

She knows that. I know that. Right?

I need to leave before I say something I regret.

I drain the rest of my pint and set it down on the table. "I'm out of here."

I don't want to talk to them anymore.

Come to think of it, I'm not sure what I want at all. My first instinct is to run to Vivian. But why? We're not a couple. Yes, we got physical. Yes, I like her. But it's not what my brothers think. We're not about to get married.

I need some space.

From everyone.

TWENTY-NINE

Beau

I stumble out of the pub, desperate to get some air, clawing at my collar because I can't breathe properly.

"Beau," a familiar female voice says. "It *is* you!"

I look up just as Coral slings her arms around me. *Of all the people to show up...* What's she doing here? I step back, still desperate for some space. "Hi?" I say tentatively.

She's staring at me with a wide grin, like I'm all her dreams come true. "I can't believe I ran into you. I've been in London three days."

"Right." I'm a little shell-shocked and still figuring out what's happening.

"It's fate," she says, putting her hand on my arm. "You want to come in for a drink? I'm meeting a friend, but I'd love you to stay. We can go back to yours after, if you like?"

I shake my head, wondering if she missed the part where I asked her to move in with me, she laughed, and then I was medevacked off a mountain. She never even checked in with me to see if I survived the fall, let alone suffered an injury. "I'm just leaving," I say.

She doesn't acknowledge my suggestion and instead holds up her hands, palms facing away. I'm not quite sure how to read the gesture. Is she...playing peekaboo with me? "I'm not engaged anymore!" she says, grinning, and lowers her hands. "I don't know what I was thinking really. People like us—we're not mean to be in relationships."

Anxiety booms in my chest. What is she talking about? People like who?

"I thought I would try it. He was rich as all holy hell. And good-looking. It's just not the way I'm wired." She smiles at me. "I know you're exactly the same way. I guess that's why it kinda shocked me when you said that thing in France. We're both cut from the same cloth."

"In France...where I fell off a mountain."

A look of shock passes over her face. "Oh god, yes, I forgot. You okay?"

Coral and I never did much talking, but I never realized how bloody unlikeable she was.

"I hope you didn't injure that dick of yours. That thing does good work. Speaking of, let me take your number. I have a new phone and lost all my contacts."

My stomach churns. Coral hasn't even paused to hear if I'm okay or not. Was she always like this?

She pulls out her phone and pauses, waiting for me to recite my number.

"How did you and your fiancé break up?" I ask. Had he seen through her?

She winces. "I stayed out late one night." She shrugs, and I take it as an admission that she'd been unfaithful. "I thought he was away for the night. It's for the best. Yes, I've hurt him now, but we'd only been together six months. Can you imagine if we were six years down the line or we'd had kids or—" She shakes her head. "Better to rip the plaster off now. He's hurting today, but I've spared him long-term pain. That's the way I see it."

"So you cheated on him, but really...you did him a favor?" I try and clarify.

"Exactly. It's good that he caught me. He never had a clue about you and me." She laughs. "Was happy for me to go away with a girlfriend skiing." She sighs. "Honestly, I think it was a huge red flag. If he'd been more attentive— cared more—he would have never let me go skiing. Even if I had been going away with a girlfriend, the après ski in these places—he knows what it's like. It's like he wanted to turn a blind eye to it."

"So, it's his fault you cheated? Because he let you go skiing? Or was away for the night?"

"Not his fault exactly. It's nobody's *fault*. Assigning blame is so..." She gestures vaguely at nothing in particular.

I narrow my eyes, because from where I'm standing, it seems pretty clear that blame is absolutely warranted. The fault in this situation rests with one person and one person only, despite her refusal to admit it.

She sees the expression on my face and lets out a huff. "I mean, I can't help it. You get it, don't you?" She reaches out for me, but I take a step back and she pouts. "You're not still holding a grudge, are you? We need to stick together, people like you and me. We're wanderers. We're not meant for monogamy—in partners, in jobs, in life. And if we forget who we are, we end up hurting people."

Anxiety spreads through me. The veins in my neck throb.

"We are not the same." She's a monster. I don't know

how I missed it for as long as I did. Maybe she put on a good act.

She laughs. "Of course we are! 'Not the marrying kind'—that's how they would have said it in the olden days. The sooner we accept it and stick together, the better it is for the others—the ones who *are* the marrying kind." She smiles. "That way, no one gets hurt. I've learned my lesson. No more engagements. No more trying to settle down because I think this one is The One—none of them are The One. There is no *one* for people like us. I've accepted that now." She smiles again. "I'm gasping for a glass of wine. Hit me up on Insta if you want to hook up. No more offering me a key though." She cackles, pats me on the arm and heads into the pub, leaving me reeling.

I walk briskly toward Nathan's house. The last thing I want is Coral bringing her wine outside to continue our conversation. I never want to see that woman again. I don't know what I was thinking when I decided the two of us were compatible. We're not. We're very different people. For a start, I've never cheated on anyone. But then again, there haven't been many people to cheat on. Almost all my relationships have been casual. That's probably why hearing my brothers talking about Vivian and me as if we're really engaged and about to embark on a life together was so uncomfortable.

A voice in the back of my head tells me my discomfort with my brothers—and Coral—doesn't have anything to do with the newness of my relationship with Vivian. I know I'm not casually cruel like Coral, but part of me wonders if I'm built for monogamy the way my brothers are. Can I really do what they do and be okay with a more traditional way of life?

I've deliberately not thought too far ahead when it

comes to Vivian. I haven't had to, since our relationship has always carried an expiration date. Except, if what we have isn't a fake relationship...where does that leave us? What are her expectations?

"Fuck," I scream out. Why did I take her to Norfolk to meet my family? Surely that built expectations—ones I'm not sure I can meet. Am I being casual with Vivian's heart in the same way Coral was with her ex-fiancé's?

Nausea rises in my stomach. Coral and I aren't the same.

Are we?

I like Vivian far too much to hurt her. Especially after everything Matt did. How could anyone endure two betrayals? The deeper Vivian and I get, the more I run the risk of doing the exact thing I set out not to do: break her heart.

THIRTY

Vivian

Even though I've only known him a few weeks, waking up without Beau feels wrong. The bed feels far too big. I was working late last night and he had to be up early this morning. It didn't make sense for him to stay over. At least that's what I told myself when Beau replied to my text saying he was going to stay at Nathan and Madison's after spending the day with his brothers.

I get it. And actually, it's helped me get a little perspective. I was just being paranoid that Beau was getting off on the thrill of being recognized. I know he's not that guy. I can't let Matt's betrayal poison my relationship with Beau. I won't let Matt destroy any more than he already has.

It's insane, because I'm just out of the only relationship I've ever had in my life, but I'm struggling to remember the details of how Matt and I were when we were together. It's like we ended years ago. Probably because my mind is too full of Beau. I think I'm falling for him. No, that's not true, I *know* I'm falling for him, and I'm equal parts excited and terrified.

My phone starts to beep again and I see Tommy calling. I accept the call, but before we can exchange hellos, he says, "Let me get Felicity."

I sigh. What has Matt done now? I'm not sure I care.

When all three of us are on video chat, Tommy goes first. "You know we are here to protect you—your career and reputation, but also your heart."

Felicity interrupts. "*The Daily Mail* has a story running today."

I groan. "I don't care what Matt said. Honestly, I think I'm past the point of hurting when it comes to him. I'm numb to it."

"This isn't about Matt. It's about Beau. Or it might be."

I freeze and grip the phone a little tighter. "What?"

"This is going to be rough, darling, but you said you didn't want me to keep anything from you." I'm aware that Felicity is speaking and I know I want to hear what she's going to say, I just don't know if I can focus on the words coming out of her mouth.

"The source of the article talks about how you and Beau are on the rocks because you're consumed with...*writing new material because you're dumping the old album.*"

I gasp. No one knows I'm trashing the old album. Only me, Tommy, Felicity, my producers and...Beau. I haven't even told the label yet. I was waiting until I had the songs completed and could present them with a fait accompli.

Still, this doesn't mean Beau is the source of the leak. It just means Beau *could* be the source. A swell of doubt rises up in me and I realize I haven't felt like that before about Beau. He doesn't deserve my doubt. He's a good guy.

Maybe it's always going to be like this now.

I'm never going to be able to fully trust anyone again.

"Apparently, the two of you are struggling because you're going to be on tour next year and he has a life in London."

"That's just tabloids spinning something out of nothing. They could have pulled that out of thin air." I push the covers back and stand.

"Do you think Beau leaked about the album?" Felicity asks. "Who else knows about the new material? Have you told anyone?"

"It could have been a guess." I push my fingers into my hair. "It could have been..." There's no way it came from Bobby or Judo. I'm using my rented house as the studio, so it's not like someone's spotted me coming and going from Abbey Road or another well-known studio. "There's no way it was Beau. He wouldn't know how to speak to the press."

"People learn fast," Tommy says. "I'm sure he knows people who know people."

"We've kept it so quiet, I'm failing to see another explanation," Felicity says.

But there has to be one. I believe in him. And I believe in how he feels about me. How we feel about each other. "Things have changed over the last few weeks. I really don't think he would have done this."

"You know what it's like," Tommy says. "Some people love the attention."

I'm not sure Beau is someone who loves attention, but he likes an adrenaline buzz, there's no doubt about that. Or did he say it was serotonin? Maybe my instincts when we were at the movie premier were right and he's trying to get a quick fix...

No, it can't be. Not Beau, surely.

"I'll talk to him. Do what you need to control this. Shut it down."

"You don't want us to announce a split?" Tommy asks.

"We only just got engaged. You think a split now is a good idea?" I ask.

"No," says Felicity. "But at the same time, I want to protect you. I think we can maintain that you're still together. You can still gush about him in interviews, still wear your ring, but we can wrap things with Beau so you don't have to see him again. You don't ever need to be seen together again. Then we can quietly announce the split once the album is out. We'll pick a day when there's something else going on and we can bury it."

She has this all planned out. Felicity is certain the leak came from Beau. She's a professional who's seen this kind of thing a thousand times before.

I vowed I wasn't going to be taken for a fool again—that I'd never be blind to another man's need for fame and attention. Although I don't think Beau is capable of doing what Matt did, I didn't think Matt—a man I'd known half my life —was capable of betraying either.

I can't trust myself. Matt's proof of that.

"I don't understand," I say. "If Beau was only required for like two events, why was the contract until the end of the promotional tour?"

"It would be better if you'd done more appearances together, but I'm determined not to let you spend time with men who can't be trusted if I can help it. We can just say he's decided he doesn't want to be in the spotlight. He's too busy saving lives, yada, yada, yada. It's not as clean as it would be if you were still appearing together, but we can have him do a couple of shots going into hotels where you are and leak them to the tabloids. I can manage the whole thing."

"I want to speak to him," I say. Even though Tommy and Felicity are protecting me, something about this doesn't sit right. Beau isn't Matt.

"We need to change phone numbers, move you to a different hotel," Tommy says. "Maybe Paris—"

"No, Tommy darling, Paris won't work. She has to be in London to maintain the pretense of her still being with Beau. If she's in Paris, our plan falls apart."

"I want to speak to him," I repeat. "I just don't think he would have done something like this..." I want to judge his reaction for myself when I ask him.

Felicity's lips are pulled into a straight, disapproving line. "Darling," she admonished. "It will only add to your...woes."

"Maybe Betty could be there," Tommy says. "She could give you an outsider's perspective on the entire thing and if things get heated, she can—"

"They won't get heated," I say. I might not trust myself to be fully sure whether Beau would leak stories about me to the press, but I'm absolutely sure he won't lose his temper.

"I'm just saying, it doesn't hurt to have a third party in the room," Tommy says.

Tommy doesn't trust my judgment of Beau either. But who can blame him? I get it. He's trying to protect me—and maybe to some degree, himself. We were all fooled by Matt.

I shake my head. "I'll figure it out. On my own. I'll let you know when it's done."

THIRTY-ONE

Beau

I know I'm about to do the right thing, but there's a heaviness in my limbs that says otherwise. Maybe it's the half-truths I'm about to tell Vivian. Maybe it's because I like her. Whatever it is, it doesn't change anything.

I ignore the security guard at the hotel room door and knock.

I brace myself to see her smile. I know how hard-earned each of her smiles is, making each one more valuable. And all the more painful that I'm going to put a stop to it.

She opens the door, but a smile isn't what I'm greeted with. It's as if I've already told her I'll be flying to Finland tomorrow. Her gaze hits my shoes

I narrow my eyes. "You okay?" I shouldn't ask. It's none of my business, except I still want to know every thought in her head.

"Come in." She turns and heads into the suite. "We need to talk."

Does she somehow know I've come here to end things between us? She couldn't.

She heads over to the living room and sits in one of the chairs in front of the window, rather than the sofa where we normally sit.

Something's really wrong, but it can't be my news. There's no way she can know because I've not told anyone other than Dax.

"What is it?" I ask, taking a seat.

"The fact that I'm recording new music for the album has gotten into the press." She looks me dead in the eye.

"Shit. You wanted to keep that to yourself, right?" She can't catch a break. Every move of hers is documented. I try to think if there's anything I can do, but the horse has bolted. It's out there.

"My label doesn't even know. I had to have a call with them today to explain myself. It wasn't pretty, and I've been so distracted with that and the leaks that I haven't done anything in the studio."

God, I hate that she had such a shitty day. When did that happen? When did I start to hate when a woman I was dating was having a hard time? It's not like I ever enjoyed someone having a bad day, but it's almost as if Vivian hurting, hurts me too. Like I've taken on her pain or something.

Thank god I'm getting out of this mess. I don't want to be doing the same for her. I'm the good-time guy. I want to be living life. Making the most out of every day.

My shoulder starts to twinge again and I circle it, trying to ease the pain. "What does Tommy say?"

She holds my gaze again. "Tommy thinks you're responsible for the leak."

That irritates me. Tommy doesn't know me that well, but Vivian does. I lean my head to the right and continue to circle my shoulder. Why would she even entertain the idea? "Why would he think that?"

She sighs. "Because no one else knows, Beau. Just you, me, Felicity, Tommy and my producers. I've kept this such a secret because there's so much at stake."

"I know...I mean...who does Tommy think I've told? I wouldn't even know how to leak something to the press. It's not like I've got a number in my phone or something."

"But Nathan—he has a PR team, right?"

Now I'm pissed off. "Vivian," I say, my voice thick with irritation. "You know I didn't leak anything." I understand that Matt fucked her over. It doesn't mean I will.

"Maybe you mentioned it to Nathan or Madison...the journalist."

"She's not *that* kind of journalist—"

"But her mother—"

"How the fuck do you know that? Have you been—?"

"She told me, Beau. In Norfolk."

"That's right. Norfolk. Where you stayed with my family and they treated you like you were one of us. No way have I or any member of my family, including Madison, betrayed you and gone to the press."

I wait for her to respond, but she just stays quiet and presses the palms of her hands into her eyes, like she's trying to reset.

"It doesn't matter," she says. "It doesn't—"

"It matters to me," I say. "You can't accuse me of betraying you like that and then tell me it doesn't matter."

But does it matter? I'll never see Vivian again after today.

"Forget that—you're right. It doesn't matter." I stand. "This got more complicated than it should have," I say.

I look up from the floor to find her staring past me.

"I have an opportunity for a week off from work and I've decided to go to Finland." I pause. "I'm going to take it. It's a win-win. I won't be around to hear any insider information, so next time it happens, you'll know it definitely wasn't me."

"I didn't say I thought it was you."

She didn't say she didn't think it was me, either.

It doesn't matter either way. After today, I can get on with my life. It's not like the last-minute husky mushing week is the most exciting thing I'd ever done. But I haven't experienced it before and ironically, I've always found something comforting in the unfamiliar. In the new. I need to be making the most out of life rather than arguing in hotel rooms about things I haven't done.

"So you're leaving. Like, that's it?" She frowns. Perhaps she was expecting me to beg her forgiveness or confess.

"Not because you're accusing me of leaking stories or whatever, but...I don't want to pass up this opportunity to go to Finland."

"Right," she says. "What about Everyone Adventures?"

I shrug. The business plan is finished. But now I'm not sure that's what I'm looking for either.

She lets out a half-laugh. "Right. Running away from that too. Makes sense."

I push my hands through my hair, trying to ignore the ache in my shoulder. "I'm not running away, Vivian. I'm running toward something. Life. Adventure. A good time."

She nods. "Keep telling yourself that. So you want to be done with our arrangement. How convenient."

"You haven't told me of any events that you need more for, but if you want..." I haven't really thought about her end of things—managing the PR fall out.

"It's fine," she snaps. "If you don't mind, we'll hold off

announcing the split until after the publicity tour. We don't need to be seen together again."

My stomach twists itself into a knot. Even though I know it's the right thing to do, the idea of not seeing her again still feels shitty, like a ten-ton weight has attached itself to my insides. "I didn't leak anything. My brothers. Madison. They didn't either."

"I believe you," she says.

Her statement takes me aback a little.

"Right. Good." I'm not sure if she's telling the truth or not, but it doesn't matter. I know the truth.

She sighs. "I should never have let things cross a line between us."

Her words hit me in the sternum so hard I actually cough. "Right," I manage to say. I can't help but wonder if she regrets the time we had together. I hope not. Because even though this is awkward and uncomfortable, I don't wish I hadn't met her.

"I had a blast with you," I say and mean it. I just don't want to create expectations in her. In the people around us. In myself. I don't want her to think I'm going to change the way I live my life. Last time I even thought about a change, I got a dislocated shoulder.

She nods, but folds her arms in front of her like she's trying to shield herself from something.

There's nothing more to say.

"Have a good life," I say and head to the door.

I mean it. I want her to heal from her shitty ex-boyfriend and have exactly the life she deserves—one filled with love and laughter and friends and family. One where she writes the songs she loves and plays them when and how she wants, on her terms. I want her to have the life she's always dreamed of.

I just won't be a part of it, and I know that's how it's meant to be.

The freedom and relief I expected to feel in this moment never materializes as the hotel room door shuts behind me with a soft click.

THIRTY-TWO

Vivian

I've forgotten which day it is. All I know is that the hotel I'm sleeping in now isn't the same place Beau and I played Twister. It's not the same place he picked me up for our first date. I'm grateful, but I'm also sad.

I look out onto the London skyline. There's an expensive gold compass on the coffee table that tells me I'm looking west. I wonder if somewhere down there, Beau's grabbing coffee and flirting with a stranger in the line. Or maybe he's in Finland. When did he say he was going?

The way I miss him cuts so deep that I'm trying to stop the blood gushing from the wound, yet no one seems to notice. The only thing that's been resolved over the last few days, since Beau left, is that any doubt I had about him leaking the stories has completely disappeared. Of course he didn't.

I wonder if he misses me? It's unlikely. He was always going to run.

Tommy and Felicity are in fight mode. Tommy seems to

have won over the record company after sending them six of the completed songs. The only problem is, I don't know if I can finish the rest of them. I need at least another four and I don't have the energy to shower, let alone go to the studio.

"Listen," Tommy says from where he's talking to me on my laptop. "I can bring in an uncredited writer. No one needs to know." He speaks to someone off camera. "Okay good, and you've packed me?"

I lean forward and pour some of the water on the table into a glass. Is Betty here? I can't even remember.

"I'm taking an overnight flight to London," Tommy says.

Jesus. He must be worried.

"We've gotta get you back into the studio."

"You don't need to come here," I say. "I'll try and go in tomorrow."

"Who?" Tommy calls to someone off camera. "Okay, get her patched in here. Felicity is on the line. It's urgent, apparently."

I zone out while people start doing various things that don't involve me and eventually, I'm cut off. Thank god. Maybe I can get some sleep. Or something. I spot my guitar in the corner of the room, but before I can grab it, Tommy's calling me back. It's not worth ignoring him. The mood he's in, he'll have a thousand hotel staff ramming my hotel door down to get me to answer the phone.

"We're back," Tommy says, as he and Felicity appear on the screen in front of me.

"Good news," Felicity says. "I'm not even kidding when I say I've had to bribe a few people, but I've found out a little more about the leak. It wasn't Beau."

"That's great news," Tommy interrupts.

She's not telling me anything I didn't already know.

"Vivian?" Felicity asks. "Have you frozen? Did you hear me?"

"I know it wasn't Beau," I say.

"Right," she says. "But I'm confirming that it wasn't him or a member of his team. It was a team member on Judo's side."

"I knew I liked him. So, do you want me to call Beau for you?" Tommy asks.

"And say what?" I ask.

"I don't know, we could start by saying we know it wasn't him who leaked the info."

"He told me it wasn't him."

"I know, but now we have proof," Tommy says. "I'm sure he'll understand, given your history."

I shrug. "It doesn't matter. I'll try and get in the studio tomorrow to stop the label freaking out. Can you tell Bobby and Judo I'm sorry for being out of it for a few days?"

"Wait," Tommy says, "I don't get it. You should be delighted that Beau wasn't the source of the leak?"

"Because it doesn't change anything. I knew in my heart of hearts it wasn't him, but there was still doubt. There will *always* be doubt because of Matt." The innocent part of me who could assume people were the good guys until I was proven wrong has been removed. Permanently. And that's what I hate Matt for the most. He's turned me into a cynic.

I don't want Tommy and Felicity to think badly of Beau, so I haven't told them he would have left eventually anyway. Beau's not a bad guy, but he's a man who runs— from a career, from his business idea, from relationships. He thinks he's chasing life, but he's running away from it. There's no changing that.

"Oh, darling," Felicity says. "It's only been a few

months since you found out about Matt. It's bound to take a while to heal. You just need to give it time."

"Felicity's right," Tommy says. "It will be easier with the next boyfriend. We all need a little palate cleanser between boys, isn't that right, Felicity? Beau was just your between-relationships relationship."

Tommy is wrong, but I'm not going to correct him. In some ways, even though it was short-lived, being with Beau was much more of a real relationship than Matt and I had been. My eyes were open to the world when I was with Beau in a way they hadn't been with Matt. I got to see the real man in Beau—not the fake one Matt showed me.

But Beau's gone. Run away. Just like he always does. Except, I can't help but wonder whether things would be different if I hadn't questioned him. If the doubts I had about him and his ability to betray me hadn't existed—maybe I could have convinced him to stay.

THIRTY-THREE

Beau

From my cramped plane seat, I glance across at Dax, whose nose is buried in some academic journal or other.

I would have come to Finland on my own. I know he didn't want to come, but when he offered, I didn't say no. Usually I'd have no problem traveling alone. But at the moment, I don't feel myself. It's like I'm trying to walk on a broken ankle. It fucking hurts, and I'm limping.

"You're a good brother," I say.

He doesn't look up. "I know."

He's a man of few words, but when he speaks, it counts.

I chuckle and turn back to my phone, scrolling through the messages between Vivian and me. Who the hell am I? I chose to leave. Flying to Finland is the right thing to do. I'm hoping that the trip will help me stop me thinking about her. Maybe being cold and, most importantly, away from London will do the trick.

"You want to talk about it?" he asks, his focus still on the magazine in his hand.

"Talk about what?" Dax rarely talks about anything.

"You? This trip? Why we're here?"

"I thought I told you," I say. "We're getting picked up at the airport and taken straight to the camp. It's a bit remote, but I've checked and there's electricity. But..." I haven't shared just how remote the lodge is. "No running water."

"What about WiFi?" he asks.

"There's no running water," I say. "I think I can say with authority, WiFi isn't on the list of amenities being offered."

He sighs a deep sigh and sets down the journal. "Fuck, Beau. Why did you, of all people, have to go and get your heart broken?"

I frown. "What are you talking about? I haven't got a broken heart." Did he mishear me when I explained *I'd* ended things with Vivian?

Yes, of course I liked her, but ending things was the right thing to do. Our relationship was supposed to be easy, fun, flirtatious—but it had started to shift. Better to cut things off now, before either of us can get hurt.

Being away from Vivian might not feel good in the short term, but it was the right decision for the long term. Now I feel a weight on my chest and my mind is full of Vivian, but these things will pass. Soon I'll start to feel better.

"Oh, okay. She seemed nice though. Not someone who was likely to overreact."

"From the king of underreactors, that's praise indeed." I go back to scrolling the messages she left me over the weeks we were together.

"She's going off on tour. Is that why you split?"

"No, I told you, things were getting..." Not serious exactly, but...was *deep* the right word? "I didn't want to create any expectations in her. You know what I'm like—I'm never in one place long."

"She didn't want you to come to Finland?" he asks.

"No, it's not that."

"She didn't want to join you traveling more generally?"

"I never asked her." Probably because traveling hasn't been front of mind since I met her. I've been focused on my business plan and spending time with Vivian.

"Then I don't understand why you broke up."

I roll my eyes. "You wouldn't." Dax doesn't subscribe to emotions.

"I'd understand if it were rational. You're saying you broke up *in case* she started to like you?"

That wasn't *exactly* how I'd put it, but...

"It sounds like you got a little uncomfortable and took off."

"Great chat, mate. Go back to your journal."

He shrugs and opens the article he was reading before we started to talk. "Only trying to help."

"What will help is a little distance between me and London, and getting back to the old me."

I don't feel great at the moment. The heaviness is still there. I think about Vivian all the time. It all feels so alien and uncomfortable. I want this trip to fill the spaces in my life that she occupied. I'm not sure how those spaces were created so quickly, but now they're echoing chambers of loneliness. I hate feeling like this.

I need some dopamine flooding my nervous system, adrenaline and serotonin chasing each other through my veins.

"I hate to tell you..." Dax says.

"Then don't," I snap. I check the time on my watch. It feels like we've been on this plane for nine hours.

"We can't go backwards. This trip might help, but it won't take you back in time to before you met her." He winces. "Rovelli might say different, but as far as you're concerned, you're not going to be able to be the old you."

"You're meant to be being supportive," I say.

"I am, but you know it as well as I do. You're not the same man you were when you took your last trip. You've spent your entire life searching for the meaning of life through some adventure or experience that would get you to the edge of your consciousness or something."

"No, I've spent my entire life trying to get the most out of it. Trying to experience all there is that life has to offer because I know how short life can be." I'd been lucky with my burns and I'd been lucky with the dislocated shoulder. I don't want to waste the chances I've been given.

"Exactly. You've been looking for things here and there and by doing this and that. What you've really been searching for is depth of connection."

He's silenced me.

"You have it with us—your family. But you were searching for something outside that. And it wasn't boomeranging off of Uluru or whatever the fuck kind of ridiculous thing you've spent years doing. You were searching for a connection with the world that would make you feel worthy of being here. What you failed to realize is you're never going to find that out there—certainly not with a load of old barky dogs where there's no fucking running water. I'm not going to forget this for a while, by the way." He shoots me a look to let me know he's serious and then continues, "You're going to find it when you meet someone who makes you feel like a king."

I let that sink in.

Is he right? Have I been making the most out of life or

searching for something that's missing? Is that why when I met Vivian, the desire for thrill-seeking and adventure slowly began to seep away?

"Not possible. Otherwise, why am I on this plane?" I let out a dry laugh. "If she's what I want, I would never have broken up with her."

Dax just shakes his head like I'm the one who's completely delusional. "You're scared. You're running."

Running? Was that what Vivian had said I was doing in our last conversation? But what I am running from? It doesn't make sense.

"Are you really the only one who can't see it?" Dax continues. "Maybe you want to get the most out of life, but what that's led to is a man who can't commit to a job, a woman, even a hobby. You're everywhere all the time so you don't have to be in the right now."

Is he right? Am I...a commitment-phobe? I'd tried to commit to Coral, hadn't I? Where had that got me other than free-falling down a mountain?

"Done anything about that travel business for the disabled that you've been talking about for years?" Dax asks in an accusatory tone.

"Yeah, actually." I can disprove his theory if he's going to talk about my business idea. "I've worked up a business plan. It looks great."

"And what? It's sitting on your computer waiting for...?"

It's like he's hooked an anvil on my insides.

Running away.

Vivian's accusation echoes in my head. Does everyone in my life know something about me I don't? And if so... what does that say about the kind of man I've become?

THIRTY-FOUR

Vivian

Back in the hotel suite, Tommy and Betty are flitting around me like overexcited butterflies. Live TV will do that to people, even if it's not actually them on TV. But the people who work behind the scenes in those shows are so fully charged that it can be infectious. I head to my bedroom to give the pair of them some time to calm down, and me a few minutes to decompress by myself. "Just going to change," I say.

"Need a hand?" Betty asks.

"No thanks." I'm wearing jeans and a shirt. I figure I can manage it myself. I undress and put on my peach cashmere loungewear. That's always what I'm most comfortable in. I scoop my hair up and manage to get it in a band without too much effort. It's grown. Back in London, it was difficult to get under a cap. I know it's stupid because they don't even have the *Today Show* in the UK, but as I was being interviewed and they were playing a clip from my video, I wondered whether Beau was watching.

I haven't seen or heard from him in weeks.

I close my eyes and take a deep breath, hoping to banish thoughts about him with a fresh injection of oxygen. Of course it doesn't work. It never does. I glance at the ring of gold willow leaf, wrapped around my left ring finger. I'm wearing it because I'm keeping up pretenses of being engaged to Beau. But even if I wasn't on a publicity tour, coming face-to-face with people asking about my personal life, I don't know if I'd want to take it off. I twist the metal around my finger once, then twice, then set about taking off my makeup.

Being back in New York feels strange. I know I'm familiar with the lumpy roads and the constant beeping of horns, but it feels like I left this place a long time ago. It doesn't feel like home anymore.

I've got nothing in the schedule now until lunchtime tomorrow. I have a melody in my head that I want to play around with and then I just want to go to bed with some popcorn and a movie.

Betty's hovering by my door when I come out of my room. "It was so good. You came across so excited about the new album, it was palpable. And they didn't even mention... you know," Betty says as I come out of my bedroom. I've just finished the first day's publicity. I smile at her. She's being kind, but I don't really have the energy to get into it. "Do you want me to run over to your apartment and pick up some stuff for you?"

"Uhhh..." I think about it. "Like what were you thinking?" There was no way I could go back to my apartment without getting papped, but that's not why I don't want to go back. I want to keep moving forward, and the apartment feels like part of my past.

"I don't know. You've been separated from your things

for so long now, I thought there might be bits you were missing. I can go and get them for you. Photographs. Trinkets. Clothes even."

The only photographs in the apartment are ones of me and Matt and I'm one hundred percent sure that I don't want those back. "Not today, but I'll have a think about it. Thanks, Betty. That's a thoughtful offer."

The phone to the suite starts to ring and before I can reach it, Tommy grabs it.

His face turns bright red as he listens to the person on the end of the phone. "Absolutely fucking not. Are you kidding me?" he yells. "Tell him to wait there. I'll be down in a minute." He slams the receiver down.

"You okay?" I ask.

"Fucking Matt is downstairs, the little shitbag. No doubt, coming to beg for attention or a snippet he can sell to the press. Can you believe it?"

It's almost like the air in the hotel suite has been sucked out, and I grab the back of a nearby chair to keep my balance.

Matt? We're in a city of eight million people. Why does the one person I don't want to see have to turn up on my doorstep?

"What's Matt doing here?" I ask. "How does he know where we are?" I glance at Betty and Tommy. Betty shrugs her shoulders and Tommy is thrusting his arms back into the jacket he just took off.

"Wait, Tommy. I want to know what he's doing here." Why would he think he can just turn up here? Why does he want to see me?

"I'll ask him. Just before I punch him in the face."

I roll my eyes. I'm pretty sure Tommy's never thrown a

punch in his life and if he did, I doubt it would have the desired effect.

I stalk over to the phone and dial reception.

"What are you doing?" Tommy asks.

"I'm sending him up."

"What?" Tommy and Betty say in unison.

"I want to see what he's got to say for himself. I want to know why he's here and how he found me. Is he stalking me? Do I need to call the police? That kind of thing."

"He's a monster," Betty says.

"No telling what he's here for," Tommy says. "You've got to think of your safety."

"Right. And I have a security guy on the door. He can step into the suite while Matt's here. Plus, you and Betty will be here."

I tell reception to send him up and then I pop my head out of the door of the suite and ask my security guy to escort Matt into the suite when he appears and stay for the duration of his short visit.

"He doesn't deserve five minutes of your time," Tommy says.

"If you don't want to see him, I understand that," I say. "You can go into the study or you can leave. Same goes for you, Betty. But I'm doing this for me. Not him. I'm very aware he doesn't deserve anything from me."

Tommy sulks but takes a seat on the sofa. I sit in the chair at the head of the dining table.

Betty glances between me and Tommy, and then heads toward Tommy.

"Betty, can you arrange to move me to the Mandarin Oriental after this? I heard the Oriental Suite has a gold leaf ceiling. I'd like to try that." I sound calm, and my breathing is normal, but I'm about to come face-to-face with the man who slept in my bed for twelve years and betrayed me. I should feel murderous.

The door to the suite opens and a familiar figure appears. He looks just as handsome as he ever did. He's wearing his favorite blue suit—one I never particularly liked because of the sheen of the material. When he sees me, he breaks into a smile.

"Vivvy," he says and bounds toward me like I'm his favorite person in the world. I used to love it when he greeted me like this, used to love feeling so loved by him. Now I see it for what it is—an act.

I don't say anything and I do my best not to flinch when he presses a kiss to my cheek.

He turns and sees Tommy and Betty. "Hey guys," he says with a wave.

It will irritate Matt that I haven't asked Tommy and Betty to leave us in private. He always used to complain that we never had any private space. Had he meant it or was he just playing a part? Looking back, it's difficult to know what was authentically Matt. Maybe Matt was just authentically a dick.

"It's so good to see you, Vivvy. Your hair got long." His gaze snags on the ring on my left ring finger but he doesn't say anything. "You look good though. I always liked you without makeup."

"What is it that you want, Matt?"

His face turns serious and he pulls out a chair and takes a seat. "I came to apologize." He reaches for my hand and I pull it away, folding my hands on my lap. "I was getting hounded by this tabloid and I just thought I'd control the narrative better if I gave them something."

It takes all my willpower not to laugh. Control the narrative? What's he talking about? "That's something

Felicity deals with," I say, trying to sound as emotionless as possible.

"You're right," he says, and if I didn't know him, I'd say he sounded contrite.

"Why have you left it so long before saying this?"

"I didn't know where you'd gone," he says.

"I was at the apartment for months after I found out what had been happening. You lived there for three years, Matt. Did you forget the address or something?"

"I was trying to give you your space. That's all. I didn't expect you to change your cell number and just disappear. I thought...we'd take a little time apart and you'd...we'd come around."

"You mean you thought I'd change my mind about wanting you gone? I still haven't, for the record."

Betty titters in the background and Matt's jaw twitches.

"I thought we both needed time to cool off."

"Why would you need time to cool off? It wasn't me who sold stories about you to the press."

"No, Vivian, but you did put me in the position where I could."

I let out a half-laugh. "Oh, so it's my fault because I became famous."

He lifts up his shoulders as if to say, *well, yeah.*

"How's Amanda?" I ask.

He waves his hand in the air. "That was nothing. I just needed the tabloids to realize I'd moved on so they could stop following me."

"So you weren't sleeping with her?" I ask.

"Were you sleeping with this British guy the tabloids were full of?"

"The guy I met after I split up with you? You worked

with Amanda for months before. I always suspected you were cheating on me with her."

He wrinkles his nose. "There wasn't really a crossover."

"Matt, seriously, what do you want? Betty and Tommy and I are due to go through some things for tomorrow. I'm keeping them waiting."

"They're on your payroll. They'll cope." Then he raises his voice. "Love you, Tommy."

Was he always this much of an asshole?

"I just want you to know I'm sorry. And I know this British guy is just a fling or a publicity stunt or something. Nothing can compare to the twelve years we had together. Nothing. I don't want to walk away from that and I don't think you do either."

"You want me back?" I sound incredulous, so I soften it. "I just want to be clear that that's what you're saying."

"Yes, of course I want you back. I want our life together back. We were good together, Vivvy. You know it. Yes, we had a little bump in the road back there, but that's life. We're over that now. We just need to get back on track. If you like, I'll quit the office job and come out on the road with you while you do the tour."

He'd been adamant about wanting to leave my payroll and go back to working in a firm. I guess the grass wasn't necessarily greener, and collecting a salary while contributing absolutely nothing was a better life.

"You just want to turn the clock back?" I ask. "Pretend you didn't betray me, leak personal messages from me, sell private photographs of me and give interview after interview? And then there's the cheating..."

"Vivvy, we both cheated. Come on now."

"No, I never cheated on you. I started dating Beau after we broke up."

He rolls his eyes. "Seems like you moved on pretty quick. You think you'd give it a while. We were together a long time. A little respect would have been nice."

Out of the corner of my eye, I see Tommy stand and Betty pull him back down again. I can tell he's just itching to escort Matt out. But I won't give Matt the satisfaction.

"Do you hear the hypocrisy of what you're saying?" I ask.

"I'm not being a hypocrite. Okay technically, we were still together when Amanda and I started sleeping together, but things had gotten stale between us, you've got to admit that. We needed to shake things up. Just because we were technically broken up when you started dating this British dude."

He pauses, which gives me a moment to realize how ludicrous this situation is, and how few feelings I have in this moment. I'm not even as angry as Tommy is. Even though I spent twelve years of my life sharing everything with Matt, growing up with him, I feel so little for him. It's like I barely know him.

"Have you actually slept with him?" Matt asks. "Or was it all a publicity thing? Am I still the only one you've been with?" He looks at me under his eyelashes like he always did when he suggested we have sex.

My stomach churns.

"It's none of your business," I reply. "You know what's in the public eye and that's all you need to know."

A huge rush of need surges inside me. But it's not for Matt. It's for Beau. I miss him. I wonder if he's back from Finland. Does he ever think of me?

"Vivian?" Matt says.

"What?" I completely zoned out for a second there.

"Shall we have dinner? Tonight? We can talk about getting back on track."

"No, Matt. We won't have dinner tonight. Or any night. And there will be no getting back on track."

He sits back in his chair. "What? I've apologized."

"And I listened. But it doesn't change anything."

"You're trying to tell me that just because you're with some guy you've known for five minutes, we're over?"

"No, I'm saying, it wouldn't matter whether I was with Beau or not, we're over. You're not the man I thought you were, and you're not a man I wish to spend any time with. Now if there's nothing else, I'd like you to leave."

"So you just want to walk away?" he says. "That's it? Twelve years down the drain."

I realize that even if Matt hadn't been selling stories to the press, we should have split up a long time ago. Perhaps it was just because we were so used to each other, but his mannerisms, the way he treats people, the arrogance with which he waltzed in here and expected to win me back with a half-assed apology—the man didn't even bring me a coffee for crying out loud. I've known all these things about Matt for a long time, but I'd minimized them, tried to make excuses for his behavior. Now I see those excuses for what they were: willful ignorance of his true character. Selling stories to the paps was just an extension of who he is—who he's been all along—and I don't want any part of any of it.

"I should have walked away a long time ago." I glance over at the security guard and give him a nod. "Security will see you out."

I stand and Matt does too. "Are you serious right now? You're just walking away from a future together?"

"I'm not walking, I'm running," I say, and head toward

the sofas where Tommy and Betty are sitting, their mouths
slightly agape.

Matt shrugs off the security guard's hold on his upper
arm and steps toward me. That's all it takes for the guard to
take both Matt's arms, twist them behind his back and
march him out of the suite, with cries of "Get the fuck off
me! I'm going to call the fucking police," echoing behind
him as he's escorted out.

The door closes and Tommy and Betty jump to their
feet.

"Are you okay?" Tommy asks. "You handled that like a
champ. That guy is a nutjob."

"Yeah, he thought you were just going to accept his
apology and go back to business as usual," Betty said.

"It was weirdly good to see him," I say.

"What?" Tommy asks.

Betty nods. "Closure."

"Yeah," I say. "Maybe it's closure. But it's like I finally
saw the Matt I should have seen a long time ago. The man
as he really was, without all the history between us and
without the concerns I had that I wouldn't ever find anyone
to trust again if he left. I know it's only been a few months,
but a lot has happened since then. I've grown up."

"You thinking about Beau?" Betty asks.

"Always," I say. "But we've just got to move forward."

"You should put that in a song," Betty says. "I know you
didn't want to do it with Matt and I totally get that. But
even if you don't ever make what you write public, I think it
would be good for you to figure out your feelings by playing
some music."

The melody on a loop in my brain surges to the fore-
front. "Can you make sure the Oriental suite has a baby
grand?"

Betty breaks into a grin. "Of course. It's already booked. I'll get you packed and out of here in a couple of hours."

"I'm ready," I say.

And I am. For moving to a new hotel suite, sifting through my feelings for Beau, and to writing music about the most beautiful man I've ever met.

THIRTY-FIVE

Vivian

I don't often meet Tommy at his office, but given Felicity is coming too, it made sense.

I'm not late, but both Felicity and Tommy greet Betty and me as the elevator doors open.

"Thanks so much for coming," Tommy says as we trade kisses on both cheeks. "We've got people lined up on video conference if we need them as we work through the agenda."

There's lots to discuss today. The reception to the album, the publicity tour, album sales, buzz for the tour, scope of the tour and tour dates. It's going to be a long afternoon.

"What can we get you? Coffee?" Melanie, Tommy's assistant, asks.

I lift up the bottle of sparkling water I brought with me. I can't remember the last time I had a coffee. Probably the one Beau gave me. Over the last few weeks, I've lost my taste for it. No doubt because every time I look at a flat white, all I can think about is Beau.

"Okay," Tommy says as we all take our seats around the polished walnut table. Tommy's office is in One Vanderbilt, with three-hundred-degree views of New York. It's light and bright and optimistic—perfectly suited to the man himself.

Melanie and Felicity's assistant, Peter, are also in the room, and we all take seats around the board table, a screen at the opposite end.

"First thing's first," Tommy says. "What a phenomenal publicity tour. Congrats on getting such great placements, Felicity, but super amazing, Vivian. You handled it all like the true professional you are. You're so fucking likeable. If only people knew you're exactly the same way in real life." Everyone laughs, and I wish we could skip the bit where they all try to make me feel like a queen and just get down to business. Of course, I don't say anything.

"I think you've got *Saturday Night Live* coming up, but apart from that, there's nothing until the next single is released."

"That's right," Felicity confirms.

"Before we talk about the tour, I wanted to say that I've been writing recently. In fact, I haven't stopped writing since the album wrapped. Some of these songs—they're good. I don't want to wait two years for people to hear them."

"You want to put them on a deluxe version of *The London Album?*" Tommy suggests. "The label would love it."

"Yeah, I imagine the label would love it," I reply. "But I'm thinking something a little less formal."

Tommy looks at me like he's expecting me to say more, but I don't have more to add.

"Do you mean you want to release another album? Like an EP, within a year or something?" Tommy asks.

I shake my head. "I thought that maybe I'd just stick them up on YouTube or Spotify or something."

"Behind a paywall?" Tommy said. "Can we do that, Felicity?"

"No, not behind a paywall. Kind of like bonus content. A thank-you to my fans? I don't know. Is there a creative way we can get them out there without involving the label?"

"How many songs are we talking about?" Tommy asks.

It feels like I'm in a room where everyone is willing to listen, but I just can't find my words. Maybe it's because I'm not quite sure what it is I want to do with this new music, but it's just so important, so raw for me right now, that I don't want to forget about it. "Let's leave it for now. I need to get my thoughts together. Let's talk about the tour and come back to it."

"If you're sure?" Tommy says. I nod and he flicks through a notepad in front of him. "So, you deftly fielded questions left and right about the tour in your interviews. I know we have placeholder dates in New York, Dallas, LA, Toronto and London, but we really need to fill in the gaps and confirm dates with venues and start putting a crew together. First, I suppose we need to understand what your vision is for this tour. Do you have anything in mind other than it being focused on this album?"

I think back to the conversation I had with Beau not long after we first met, when I told him how my real love is writing. How although I love performing, I don't like touring.

"And...the placeholder dates you're talking about—the

ones we've already sold tickets to—remind we why we did that?"

"To lock the venues off. Selling out the dates we did meant we could put a hold on the other dates we wanted. We also wanted people to know you'd be touring. It helps create excitement and buzz." He pauses and when I don't say anything, he says, "You want me to get the promoters on the line? They can talk it through with you in more detail if you like?"

I shake my head. "So we're not committed to any dates, other than the ones you just described—the five we've already sold tickets for."

"Right. We haven't really looked at Europe outside of London, or Asia. We were right in the middle of those discussions when all the stuff with Matt..." He trails off.

"Yup. So we don't lose any money if we don't want to do any more dates than the five we've already booked."

"We're not forfeiting a deposit or anything like that, but at the same time, you're going to be rehearsing and employing staff and crew and you're not going to make any money if you *only* do those dates. But that's not what you're saying, right?"

"I still want to perform the album," I say.

"Phew," Tommy says, grinning and dramatically wiping his brow.

"But I was thinking I don't really want to be on the road for a year doing a big stadium tour."

Tommy pulls in a breath and starts fiddling with his phone. "Just to remind you that Taylor's Eras tour is set to pull in one-point-four billion in gross receipts. That girl is a fucking baller."

"You'll get no argument from me on that," I say. "But I'm not in competition with Taylor."

"Erm, no," Tommy says. "But—"

"And I don't want to be on the road for a year and a half. What am I going to do with a billion dollars? I already have more money than I could ever want."

Everyone assumed I'd tour this album since I didn't tour my last one. People started making plans without really consulting me. I get it. I'm not blaming them. But it doesn't mean I'm going to go along with their plans.

"I was thinking of doing a limited number of smaller venues," I say. "The new album is more intimate than some of my other records, and I'd like to have more of a sense of how people are enjoying it." I'm not sure how this is going to go down with Tommy. He's ambitious for me, which is part of the reason he's such a great manager, but I'm not sure I want the same things he wants for me.

He narrows his eyes. "When you say smaller venues, what are you talking about? The Barclays Center or Radio City?"

I shrug. "Actually, I was thinking smaller."

"Smaller than Radio City? It's got a six-thousand-seat capacity. At the moment you're booked into the Met Life Stadium, which has a capacity of eighty thousand."

"I'm not saying we cancel the venues we've already booked. We can do those. And then supplement with more intimate shows."

"Like where?" he asks.

I'm almost afraid to say. This has clearly come out of left field for Tommy, but for me it's been a long time coming. "I was thinking something like...Blue Note."

"The jazz club?" Felicity asks.

"You won't make any money," Tommy says. "That's got a three-hundred-seat capacity."

I pull in a breath. "Yeah. I think that sounds...right."

"Is it the touring you don't want to do? The traveling? We could look into a Vegas residency."

I shake my head. I can't think of anything worse than playing the same show to the same audience for weeks on end. That's definitely not what I want to do. "No, I don't want to do Vegas. And yes, the traveling is part of the reason I don't want to do a big tour. But it's more than that. I don't enjoy it. I don't like how it feels like my life is on hold for eighteen months. I can't ever write on tour because I'm so exhausted. And I'm not saying you can't connect to the audience—of course you do—but it's not like it used to be in the old days when I was just starting out."

"Darling, it's never going to be how it was in the old days," Felicity says.

"I know. But at the same time, I don't want to do a stadium tour just because that's what's expected of me, or because that will take my career to the next level, or because I want to set gross revenue records. I want to do the next thing because that's what will make me happy. I don't want to let you down, Tommy, and I love that you want everything for me, but I don't want the next big thing because it's bigger than the *last* big thing. I want what comes next to make me happy."

Beau is a perfect example of someone finding the balance between obligation and joy. He's a doctor, but he doesn't feel obligated to stand still and practice medicine how everyone else does. He does it his way. He puts his happiness first and doesn't let others' expectations dictate his life. It's inspiring.

He is inspiring.

Tommy takes a breath, and I brace myself for his reaction. Yes, he works for me, but he's been with me from the beginning and I don't want him to be disappointed. "I agree.

If a huge tour won't make you happy, don't do it. You don't have to tour this album at all if you don't want to."

It's as if the sun has broken into the office and I feel warmed from the inside out. "Thank you," I say.

"I'm here to support you," Tommy says.

"Good man," Felicity says.

"So let's figure out what *is* going to make you happy in this next stage of your career," Tommy says.

"I don't have any definitive answers or ideas of what I want," I say. "I just know what I don't want."

"Then we'd better figure it out," Tommy says. "Melanie, can you get a flip chart brought in, then you and Peter can leave us." Tommy and Felicity's assistants immediately jump to their feet and speed out as if they've been on standby and have just been switched on.

"Right," Tommy says. "What's going to make you happy?"

When he asks the question, the first image that comes to mind is Beau.

"Let's talk about the song I just wrote," I said. "It's called 'London Love Letter'."

THIRTY-SIX

Beau

Dad's clattering around in the kitchen, huffing and puffing as he rolls out pastry and finds a pie dish. I don't know if it was the drive or if I'm still suffering from Finnish jet lag, but I feel tired. Heavy. Like I can't be bothered to do anything. I just sit at the kitchen window, my focus flitting between a blustering father and the view out to the garden. The skies are gray. Exactly how my head feels.

"Get us some wine, will you," he says. "Malbec all round I think."

I lift myself up from my chair and then realize what he's said. "You're offering me your Argentinian Malbec? Without being forced?"

"Careful or I'll revoke the offer. As it's the two of us, I think I can spare some."

None of my brothers are coming up this weekend. It's just me and Mum and Dad, and Dog of course. I need the peace or the space or...something.

I grab a bottle of Dad's favorite and take it back to the table, along with two glasses and a bottle opener.

"I can't believe Vincent bought the vineyard. You think he makes money from that place?"

Dad laughs as he cuts the excess pastry from the pie dish. "Course not."

"Then why did he buy a vineyard? Was it just an ego thing?"

He glances over at me, a sorrowful look in his eye, then turns back to his half-made pie. "Vincent knows I love the wine there. It was an act of love. A need for him to belong."

Did I mishear him? "He wants to belong to Argentina? Or wine?" What did I miss? I pull the cork from the bottle and pour two glasses. I'll see if Mum wants a gin and tonic in a minute.

"No, to us. The Coves. You know when a cat catches a bird and brings the lifeless, feather-shedding thing into the house to show its owner?"

Are we still talking about wine?

"It's the same thing," Dad says. "The vineyard was a dead bird—although a lot more welcome. And expensive."

"I've lost you. You're saying Vincent was showing off his wealth to you?"

"No, he wanted to please me. I can't make him my son, but I try and treat him like one. I think he thinks it's conditional. Maybe that's changed now he has Kate. I hope so."

Fuck, Dad is right. It makes perfect sense. Vincent was trying to cement his place in the family, except it was completely unnecessary. He's always been one of us. "Have you ever said anything to him?"

"Actions speak louder than words, son. You should know that."

"So do you have all our foibles filed away in your head?"

"Yes," he growls. "That's our job—me and your mother. We're your parents."

Dad starts filling the pastry-lined dish with precooked apple filling.

"I've never bought you a vineyard," I say, my thoughts jumbled in my head.

"No," he replies. "I try not to hold it against you." He chuckles to himself, and I smile.

"So what do I do that gives away my deepest insecurity?" I ask.

Dad straightens and glances over at me. "You don't have a thing like Vincent does. But you try and fill a need in yourself by going off on all these trips. I thought you'd grow out of it, but doesn't look like that's going to happen anytime soon."

"I want to make the most of my life. What's the matter with that?"

"Absolutely nothing. Just as long as the price you pay isn't too high. Sometimes I wonder if never being in one place for long means you actually miss out on the things that would fill that gap."

I don't say that I've been having similar thoughts myself for a while now.

"Dax says I'm a commitment-phobe."

"How is Vivian?" he asks, and I can't help but laugh.

"Subtle, Dad. Very subtle."

"Wasn't trying to be," he says, laying the pastry lid on his pie. "I like her. Pretty girl, but also, not how you'd expect a pop star to be. She didn't put on airs and graces. And she seemed to like you an awful lot."

I smile as I remember her in Norfolk, how she'd been so worried she'd be recognized here. She probably also thought my family would be a little starstruck. It had been wonderful to watch as she realized neither of those things were going to happen and she could just be herself.

"She fitted in," he says, his words slicing into me like one of Mum's scalpels.

"I know," I say eventually. The heaviness I've carried since I walked away from Vivian hasn't left me. I think about her constantly. It's not getting easier; if anything, it's getting worse.

Dax was right. Vivian was right. I ran away from her when things started to get complicated.

"What happened between you?"

"I don't know," I say. "We come from such different worlds and I didn't want to hurt her. Maybe I am a commitment-phobe." I shrug. "A good-time guy. The warm-up guy so the girl's ready to marry the next bloke who comes along."

Dad narrows his eyes at me and then refocuses on the pie. "Don't believe much in labels. Life comes in seasons, phases. We all shift and change. Time stands still for no one. Maybe you have been a commitment-phobe. Doesn't mean that's your story forever."

I sigh. He makes things sound so simple. "I've always liked to travel and experience new things. The trip to Finland wasn't... I mean, it was okay. It just wasn't as exciting as I expected."

He binds the crust of the pie together with the prongs of a fork.

"You think I've run out of things to do?" I ask.

He scowls at the pie like it's wronged him, then paints the lid with egg wash. "Do I think you've run out of things to do on this planet of ten thousand cities, fifty seas and eight billion people? No. I think there are endless sights to see, rivers to cross and mountains to climb. But none of that will necessarily make you happy. Maybe it will. Or perhaps it did for a time and now you have to look elsewhere. Perhaps you're turning the page onto your next chapter. Maybe you need to think about your job and whether being a locum GP is your calling."

My calling? "You think I haven't found the right career?" I enjoy my job. I like helping people and I like the flexibility it gives me to do other things I enjoy.

"I didn't say that," he replies. "But it's important to keep asking yourself that question every couple of years. I had about five different careers during my working life because I shifted and changed as I reassessed things."

"And now you're an apple pie-maker extraordinaire."

"I don't think baking is my calling. But it makes my wife happy and that's a calling I'll have until the day I die."

I smile. They bicker at each other, but there's never been any doubt in my mind that my dad worships my mother, and my mother would walk over fire for my father.

"I've heard you talk about your disabled travel business over the years. Have you ever thought something like that might be your next chapter?"

"I have a business plan Nathan helped me with. I still like the idea."

"Has it occurred to you that the decisions you make today don't bind you for the rest of your life? I know you're used to these short-term trips, but every decision you make is temporary. You don't need to be so worried about making the wrong one."

Is that what I've been doing? Not wanting to make a decision that commits me for long periods of time? I guess that's another way of being commitment shy.

"Your mother and I make a conscious, ongoing decision to stay married."

"What do you mean? You're having marriage difficulties?"

"Absolutely not, but plenty of couples divorce and walk away from each other. Nothing is forever unless you choose it forever, and even then sometimes it's not. Say you start this travel company and you decide you don't like being in business. What's stopping you from going back to being a GP?"

I take a deep breath in. "Nothing." I've been thinking about being a GP a lot recently. I've even done a search for open positions back in the NHS. That's where I could make a real difference. Not on Welbeck Street, catering to wealthy customers, but ordinary working people who rely on free healthcare.

"Right. You end up in the wrong thing, you get out of it."

It sounds so simple, but I've never thought about it like that. All I could see with Everyone Adventures is how complicated it got and how out of my comfort zone I felt with it and...how much it would take me away from medicine, which is what I love to do.

"If you end up in the right thing, it might be better than you can imagine. Starting your own business might be the second-best thing you do. Marrying Vivian might be the best thing you do."

Marrying Vivian?

"Maybe," I say.

"Actions not words, my boy. Maybe you need to call Vivian and explore whether or not sharing some of your time on the planet with her is your next chapter."

There's no doubt I want Vivian, but that doesn't mean she wants me. I could reach out, see if all the bridges between us have been burned, but I saw Vivian post-breakup with Matt—she disappeared where no one could find her. Dad wants me to pick up the phone and simply call. She probably changed her number. I'm the last person she wants to hear from.

If Vivian says no to me, I won't end up with just a dislocated shoulder. I'm quite sure she has the power to paralyze me completely, right down to my soul.

THIRTY-SEVEN

Vivian

I peel open the box that's been delivered to the hotel under the name Adele Swift. I pull out the tripod and try and figure out why it's about half the size I'm expecting. I haven't got an answer from Tommy or Felicity on how I can share the new tracks I've written. Tommy is still thinking about ways of monetizing them. Occupational hazard, I guess.

Life feels like some weird limbo. I have nowhere to call home—I still haven't been back to the apartment Matt and I shared, and I'm still at the Mandarin Oriental in New York, despite feeling the pull of London.

I set the tripod down, adjusting the legs so the holder for my phone is about level with me when I sit on the piano stool. I glance out at the view. Maybe it would be a good backdrop. I planned to record myself singing the songs—one song in particular. After that, my plan runs out of road.

I ram my phone into the tripod and position it so the

piano is in between it and the window. I take a seat at the piano and place my fingers on the keys.

"London Bridge is falling down, falling down, falling down.

London Bridge is falling down, my fair lady."

I stop and check the recording. As I play it back, it's not even clear to me that I'm playing the piano. Having the light behind me doesn't work at all. I move the tripod and put it just in front of the window so I'm looking out onto the New York skyline.

I test it with the same song. It's much better but I decide it's even better to zoom in slightly. Eventually, I have the perfect placement of the phone. I press record and settle back behind the piano.

I start play the opening chords and say, "This is called 'London Love Letter'."

Woke up this morning, New York in my sights.

The world looks different, without you by my side.

Pictures on my phone, memories won't fade

Whispers of your voice, calling out my name.

It's sooner than expected, but better late than never.

The way I stumbled into you wasn't meant to last forever.

Now you're gone. And I'm here.

Sorry's too late. Goodbye's too much.

I lost your warmth. I miss your touch.

I can't think about tomorrow without you.

I keep going to the end even though I'm more emotional than makes sense. Writing this song, playing it over and over, it's never made me so full of...sadness.

I stand and turn off the phone and I realize what I'm going to do with the recording.

I'm going to put it on social media and see if he sees it.

I walked away from London as if I didn't care, and here I am writing love songs about a man I've known only a few weeks. The man I was actually engaged to doesn't even rent a room by the hour in my head.

Beau Cove is the love of my life, and it's taken three thousand miles, a love song and almost a month to make me sure of it. But other than write him a love song I don't know if he'll ever hear, I don't know how to win him back.

THIRTY-EIGHT

Beau

One of the benefits of being a locum is that you start each job with a clean sheet of paper, which is exactly how I like to leave my desk at the end of every day. I finish typing up the notes from my final patient when there's a knock at the door. The head of the practice, Charlie, pops his head into my consulting room.

"Have you got five minutes?" he asks.

"I have as long as you need." My only plan tonight is to walk back to Nathan and Madison's. It will take me a least an hour and I'm hoping by the end of it, I'll have some clarity about what's next for me. This job is up at the end of the week and I haven't booked to go husky mushing or anything else. I'll be unemployed without a plan.

"How was your day?" Charlie asks, plonking himself in the patient chair opposite my desk.

"Fine," I say, wanting him to get to the reason he's really here. "How can I help?"

"Well, we've really enjoyed having you in the practice,

and as you know, we have a huge demand for services. Patients have gone up by thirty percent since the start of Covid. We had a partners meeting last night and wondered if you'd like to join us on a more permanent basis?"

I smile. Charlie's a nice man and this would be a good gig for most doctors—it's central, the pay is good and the patients are nice. But, as Dad would say, this isn't my calling. "That's really nice of you," I reply.

He chuckles. "That's the politest no I've ever had."

"Sorry. I'm just—"

"Oh, are you still going to ride huskies?" he asks. I must have mentioned it in my interview.

"Something like that." Also known as *figure out my life and calling.*

"Fair enough." He slaps his hands down on the armrests of the chair and stands. "If you know of anyone who might want to join, let us know, would you?"

"Absolutely. It's a great place to work and my answer really isn't personal."

"Didn't take it that way. Hopefully our paths will cross again at some point." He heads out, and I sit back in my chair.

Saying no to him was so easy, it's the final evidence I need that being a locum GP is not what I want to do. It's not my calling.

I know what I want. I want to be an NHS GP, and I want to be with Vivian. I have a plan for one but not the other.

If only winning back the woman I love were as easy as figuring out my career.

I close down my computer and head out. Hopefully, an hour's walk across London will help me formulate a plan.

As I come out of the door onto Welbeck and head north

toward Euston Road, my phone buzzes in my pocket. For a split second, I think it's going to be Vivian, but when I pull it out, it's Madison. I ignore it and head up the road. It's cold and a coffee on the way home seems like a good idea, so I head to Coffee Confidential. I don't know if I'm deliberately torturing myself, but I find myself retracing the steps Vivian and I took when we were together. Last week, I had a cancellation just before lunch and so I took myself off to the National Gallery.

I've never been like this before. It's getting worse, not better. I'm constantly wondering what she might be doing or who she might be doing it with. I've deliberately not Googled her. If I saw her dating someone, I'm worried I'd spend endless nights obsessing about whether it was a genuine date or a new fake boyfriend in her life, and I can't bear the thought of either.

I should be focusing on my new career, making applications and networking, but all I can think about is her.

I arrive at the coffee shop and wait in line. I don't recognize any of the staff. I've not been in here since Vivian left, but now it's like I'm addicted to memories of her.

I order a flat white—more evidence that I'm a masochist. It's not something I'd ever drink, but there's a part of me that thinks I might feel closer to her if I drink her coffee order.

Who am I?

I collect the order and walk through the park, passing the skeleton sculpture and heading up toward the roses. We never came here at least—too many people—so there are fewer memories for me to worry about. Except I don't need to be where we were together to remember her. She lives in my brain. In my heart. In my soul.

"Fuck!" I shout out loud. I stop. "FUCK," I scream at

the top of my voice, like I'm trying to perform some kind of
self-exorcism.

I take a seat on the bench on the side of the path and
pull out my phone. Let's just rip the plaster off and see what
she's up to. I type her name into the search bar.

I scan my screen. There's a news story from yesterday,
but before I can read what it says, Madison's name
flashes up.

"Fuck off, Madison," I say. I don't mean it, I just need to
focus at the moment.

I cancel the call and click on the first headline.

Vivian Cross releases surprise new music.

I scan the article, but it doesn't say anything about
where she is or who she's with. At least it doesn't say
anything about her getting back together with her ex.

There's a still from a video in the article. She's sitting at
a grand piano in jeans and a white shirt. She looks incredible. But then she always does.

I continue to scan the article, which says Vivian's not
doing the world stadium tour, but instead will perform the
dates she's already announced and some smaller venues that
will be announced soon.

I wonder when she'll be back in London.

The article ends and I scroll back up to see if there's
anything I've missed. That's when I spot the title of the new
song she just released. "'London Love Letter'." I smile,
wondering if she mentions Regents Park or the National
Gallery. I press play.

And listen. And listen. And then I press play and listen
again.

My mind fogs over and I forget where I am. All I can
concentrate on is her voice.

And the music.

And those lyrics.

Those lyrics.

It's a love song to a lost lover—that much is obvious. Vivian told me that she can get inspiration from books and films, and not everything is personal. She split up with her boyfriend of over a decade just a few months ago.

This song *might* not be about me. It *might* not be about us. But I know it is.

The way I stumbled into you wasn't meant to last forever.

She's right. The way we met, our lives, the fact that we live an ocean apart—nothing makes sense. Except that in my mind, she and I together is the *only* thing that makes sense.

Halfway through my third listen, Madison calls me again. Instead of canceling the call, I accept it by accident.

"Madison, I'm on my way home. Can I speak to you when I get back?"

"Absolutely not. If you hang up, I will hunt you down and kill you."

Irritation prickles at the back of my neck. "What?"

"You need to put your phone on speaker and Google, 'London Love Letter Vivian Cross' right this second. I'll wait."

I sigh.

Thank fuck for Madison. I might not have seen this song if I'd decided to run home. She would have made sure I did.

"I've seen it," I say.

"What? When? Have you called her?"

"Just now. I mean, right this second. I was listening to it when you called."

"So call her."

"Madison, I'm not taking dating advice from my sister-in-law. I'm hanging up right now."

"Beau, call her or I will. And having your sister-in-law call the girl you're engaged to, to say you're sorry and you want her back, is way more embarrassing than me giving you dating advice."

"I'm hanging up," I say.

"Are you calling her?" she asks.

"You call her and I'll hunt *you* down and kill *you*."

"No you won't," she says with confidence.

I hang up. I don't want to fight about Vivian, because we're both on the same page.

I take a breath and press Vivian's name. I have no idea whether it will even connect.

But it does.

And then it goes straight to voicemail.

Fuck.

THIRTY-NINE

Vivian

I push through the door to Coffee Confidential and go straight to the counter. There's no line at all.

I take my sunglasses off. "A large Americano and a medium flat white, please." I smile at the cashier and a flicker of recognition passes over her face, but it's clear she can't place me.

I'm not particularly bothered about being recognized this time around in London. I'm not hiding from anything anymore.

I put a tip in the jar and wait at the collection station.

A flat white used to mean freedom to me. Now an Americano means I'm here to win over the love of my life.

I take my drinks and head out and straight into the waiting Range Rover. My driver knows where we're headed. I have a doctor's appointment.

When we arrive on Welbeck Street, I give my name to the receptionist and take a seat, trying not to spill either of the two coffees I'm holding. Betty made me an appointment when I figured I'd done enough waiting around and decided to take charge of my life.

I'm the only person in the bright waiting room and I check the clock. It's five minutes before my appointment is due. I wonder if he's realized it's me.

I soon get my answer when I hear doors slam, footsteps outside, and finally Beau appears in the doorway.

We lock eyes and I stand.

Without looking up, the receptionist says, "Adele Swift?"

"Thank you," I call and step toward Beau.

His mouth opens and closes a couple of times. I want to reach up and stroke his face, but I'm not sure if he's angry or frustrated or pleased to see me.

Silently, he leads me across the landing and into his office.

"Are you okay?" he asks as soon as the door is shut. "Are you in pain? Sick? How can I help?"

I take a seat opposite his desk and slide his Americano over to him. "I'm fine. I'm not here to see you in your professional capacity. I just wanted to see you as soon as I landed and I thought if I booked an appointment...we'd have some time to talk."

His gaze searches my face, asking me a thousand silent questions. "How are you?" he asks. "I've... I called you yesterday."

I nod. "I saw. I was on my way here, to London. I thought it might be better to have the opportunity to speak in person." I'm not sure what he wants to say, but if it's bad, I wanted a chance to win him over. That's best done face-to-face.

"Oh," he says. "You were coming here."

"To see you," I say.

"I'm in love with you," he says matter-of-factly. "That's why I called."

My heart lifts and twirls in my chest like a ballerina on pointe shoes.

"I'm in love with you too," I reply, trying to mimic his tone, but desperate to be touching him. Desperate for him to hold me.

He nods like I'm not telling him anything he doesn't already know. "But we have some stuff to figure out. Some things to say."

"Okay," I say, desperate to hear every word he has to say.

"First thing is, I'm sorry. For running. I shouldn't have done that. I think I've been running from things a lot, rushing from place to place, searching for...you."

"Me?" I ask.

"I don't want to do that anymore. I want us to run at life together."

I exhale. Is it possible that this beautiful, caring, joyful man in front of me wants to be better? For me?

"Okay," I say. "What else?"

"I've spent my life thinking I need to fill my days with all sorts of...things and experiences. Work. Sports. Doing. I've realized what I really want—what I need—is to be by your side. Since the accident, I've been so grateful to have survived that I've never wanted to take a moment for granted. But really, that's not what's important. I don't ever want to take *you* for granted. I want to be next to you, side by side, and I don't care if that means we're sitting in front of the TV or we're making apple pie together or I'm standing in the wings of Wembley Stadium, watching you perform."

My heart lifts in my chest, like it's grown wings and is desperate to fly over to Beau.

"I want that too," I say.

"And if you want to live in New York, that's where we'll live."

I shake my head. "I don't. I want to be by your side too, remember. And you belong here. With your family. In London. This is your home. New York is just somewhere I lived."

He sucks in a breath. "Okay. I like that. And when you're touring, I can take some time out of work and—"

"I don't want to tour."

"I thought that's what you were doing next year?"

"The plan's changed. I have a few dates I'll honor, but nothing that will keep me on the road for very long."

"What happened?" he asks.

"Being with you showed me that I haven't been making choices based on what will make me happy. I've been trying to please all these people in my life—mainly Matt. But Tommy and Felicity and the machinery around Vivian Cross...when I took a step back, I realized that for years before you, and for the weeks we've been apart, I haven't been happy. So I made some changes, particularly to the course of my career."

"How do you feel about that?" he asks.

"Happier."

He grins and it's infectious. "How's Tommy about that?"

"He's adjusting. It'll be tough for him, but he cares about me and I know he'll support me. It's not like I'm quitting writing or recording. I'm just Mariah Carey-ing the situation."

"Mariah what now?" he asks.

I laugh. "Never mind. I'm just not going to do much touring. It means I'll be poor."

"Well that's okay," Beau says. "I have plenty of money."

I laugh. He's always tried to convince me he's wealthy. Maybe he is. I just don't care. "And what about you? Are you going to get a permanent job as a doctor somewhere?"

He stands and rounds his desk, then pulls me up and into his arms. It feels so good to be near him like this. He smells so good, better than any man should, like the air after a thunderstorm. I snake my arms around his waist and look up at him.

"I was ready to ditch it all and come and live with you in New York. Now I have to rethink. Starting the business in London will be easier. I know more people here." He smiles and presses a kiss on my forehead. "There's something else," he says.

My eyes widen. What else is there? We figured out where we'll live and how we'll approach our careers from now on.

"I want to marry you," he says.

An embarrassed smile unfurls on my face. "You do?"

"Yeah, like as soon as possible. I don't want some fake engagement. I don't want to be your warm-up guy. I want to get to the main event as soon as possible. I want the real thing."

"Okay," I reply, nodding.

"I know I haven't hired out Wembley Stadium and proposed in front of the world."

"That's for sure," I say, laughing. "But I don't need that."

"I want it to be for us. Not the world."

"I want a nice wedding though," I say. "Doesn't have to be big, but I want my siblings and my parents and Tommy and Robbie and Felicity and Betty. And I want all your family there too."

He nods. "That sounds nice. But I don't want to wait. I've spent a huge chunk of this life not being married to you, and that feels wrong somehow. I need to spend the rest of my days being your husband."

My stomach swoops up, up, up. Beau Cove is going to be my husband.

EPILOGUE

Beau

A few days later

We walk into the lobby of the Dorchester and about twenty-five people do a double take.

Yes, ladies and gentleman, it's Vivian Cross, I think to myself. It makes me smile that she's not hiding anymore. Vivian isn't wearing a cap or sunglasses and instead of her athleisurewear, she's in jeans and a Taylor Swift t-shirt.

But I think it's the ring on her left ring finger that really makes her outfit.

She looks hot AF.

We have security with us—that's something I'm going to have to get used to, but I have no doubt I will. There's no other option. I want Vivian, and I want Vivian to be safe.

A young girl rushes up to us. "Vivian! Can I have a selfie?"

Vivian smiles and I take the girl's phone. I have a feeling I'm going to get used to a lot of different camera phones in the next few months.

"Smile!" I say and I press the shutter. "And again." I have a quick check and both photos are gorgeous. The first time I took the photos, Vivian asked me if I minded. How could I mind? People love Vivian, and I'm proud to take her photo along with her fans. She's amazing, and I'm so pleased it's not just me who sees it.

"Thank you so much," the girl says, not looking at me at all. Her attention is all focused on Vivian. A couple of other people have gathered and one of the two security guards with us has moved in closer to Vivian.

"I love your t-shirt," one of them says. "I love Taylor. But I love you more."

"I love Taylor too," Vivian replies. "She's such an inspiration to me."

"I love 'London Love Letter'," another girl says. "I think it's my favorite. Although I do like all your songs. Especially 'When the Weather Fades' and 'The Future's Here'."

I make a mental note to listen to more of Vivian's music. I've never heard of "The Future's Here", but it sounds like a good one.

"I can't wait for you to play Wembley," another one says. "You'll totally slay."

"Thanks girls," Vivian says. "I appreciate it."

"Oh, please can you sign my phone case?" one of them asks.

"Sure." Vivian pulls a Sharpie from her back pocket. Now I know why she put that there this morning. We've been stopped twice already today, and both times she's been asked for selfies, details about the album and her signature on random accessories.

"I like your necklace," the first girl who approached says. "Is that a leaf like the ring you wear?" Her fans seem to know everything about her, from the coffee she likes to drink to the mascara she uses.

"A sycamore seed." Vivian holds out the pendant for them to see. "It's pretty, right?"

My mum sent it from Norfolk. It's exactly the same as the one Vivian bought for her, Sutton, Madison and Kate. It arrived this morning—a welcome to the family, she said. Vivian cried.

"OMG," one of the girls gasps and I can't tell which one. "Do you have a new engagement ring?" Teenage heads swivel to me and then back to Vivian's left hand, which is holding her necklace.

I lock eyes with Vivian, and she's beaming.

"I do," Vivian says.

We're just back from buying the ring from a jeweler on Bond Street, a friend of Vincent's. As soon as Vivian saw it, she lit up and I knew it was the one. I decided at that moment, that I want to make Vivian light up as much as I can. That's what I'm here to do. As much as I hate to admit it, Dax was right—I've been searching for connection my entire life. And now I've found it.

"We love you, Beau!" The girl says, and Vivian moves toward me, bringing the crowd of teens with her.

"Gotta go, girls," Vivian says, and I scoop up her hand. "We have a wedding to plan!"

Vivian gives the signal to her security guy that she wants to move on—a quick touch of her earlobe—and he steps in and guides us away from the crowd and toward the lifts.

"Not just a wedding," I say as the lift doors close. "We've got a life to plan. We gotta decide where we're going to live."

"You need to decide what you're going to do for work."

That doesn't seem as daunting to me anymore. I'm no longer looking for a calling or a purpose, because I've found it. And I'm not looking to find the next adventure or experience. I don't need that anymore. I just need Vivian. She is— we are—the adventure of a lifetime.

"That's easy," I say. "I want to be a GP."

"But isn't that what you do already?" she asks.

"It is, but I'm going to set up my own NHS practice. I like the idea of making a difference to the people who need it most. And I like the idea of having my own thing. I'm going to bring in other partners to work with me and I'm not going to work full time—I'll still be able to travel with you for work."

"Now I'm not touring, I won't need to travel much."

"Well, that was easy," I say. "What about a place to live?" We exit the lifts and head toward her suite. The view of London always gets me. "As much as I'd like to live at the Dorchester, we should have a home. Don't you agree?"

She nods as she kicks off her shoes. "So long as we can get the Dorchester to give us a lifetime supply of their slippers, I don't mind where we live." She pushes her feet into the oversized slippers she left by the door this morning and heads toward me. "I was thinking we could live closer to your brothers? Unless you want to live in your flat?"

The way she says it, it's clear she doesn't want to live in my flat. She's never seen it, but I'm sure she's imagining the worst. I laugh from where I'm sitting on the sofa, looking out onto the city. I hold out my arms so she'll join me. "I've put the flat up for sale."

"When did you do that?"

I pause. "I probably should have talked to you about

that, huh? Being a couple is going to take a bit of getting used to. You might have to guide me through it."

"Being in a healthy relationship is going to take a bit of getting used to. You might have to guide me through it."

"We'll figure it out," I say.

"As long as we're together," she replies. "I probably should have told you that I've asked Betty to contact real estate people and figure out what's on the market."

"In North London?" I ask. She nods. "That's great!" I say.

"You're not mad?"

"No! Are you angry that I put my flat up for sale?"

"Not angry, but I'd like to make big decisions together."

"You're right." I pull her closer. "We can go and see my flat, and if you think we should keep it, we can pull it from the market. The agent says I should get north of six million for it, so I assumed we'd use that for a new place."

"Six million?" she says.

"What?"

"That's a lot of money," she says.

"I told you. I'm rich."

She laughs. "Fine. Sell your six-million-pound bachelor pad."

I pause. I think it's the best thing to do, but everything I have is *ours* now. I want her to be fully onboard. "Let's go and see it tomorrow. Then we can decide what to do next."

"I know what I want to do next," she says, gazing up at me.

"What?" I ask.

"Naked Clue," she says.

I tip my head back and laugh. "Well, that's something I haven't done before."

"Wanna know a secret?" she asks. "Miss Scarlett has a crush on Professor Plum."

"Do *you* want to know a secret?" I ask. "Professor Plum wants to spend the rest of his life playing naked *anything* with Miss Scarlett."

———————

WE'RE SITTING SEMI-NAKED, opposite each other at the dining table. The entire city stretches out below us.

"I feel like you cheated," I say, narrowing my eyes at Vivian. "I'm not sure I'd have agreed to Cluedo if I thought you'd still wear your underwear."

"I'm more disappointed that we can't really play with just the two of us."

"Twister it is!" I slap the table and stand.

I lay the mat out and Vivian grabs the wheel.

"You go first," she says, and spins the red pointer. "Left hand red."

I groan. It's as bad as it can be for a first go. The line of red dots is lined up on my right. I crouch down and place my hand on the red circle and reach out my right hand to grab the spinner. "Left hand red," I read out. "Is this thing broken?"

She smiles and crouches opposite, looking right at me. My gaze roams over her body—her lips, wide and soft, down to her breasts, which look incredible in her lace bra, even better that I can make out her nipples under the material. I'm not sure why I'm trying to mentally undress her when I saw her completely naked when we woke up this morning.

But I am.

She wiggles her left hand at me. "All yours, baby. All yours." She knows exactly what I'm thinking.

She takes the spinner from me. "Right foot yellow."

I shift awkwardly and get into position, then I spin for her. "Right hand green." She reaches across the mat so she's spreadeagled on her front.

I'm not sure that's technically within the rules, but I can work with it.

She takes the spinner.

"Right hand blue," she says.

"Now, that's better," I say, shifting my body so I'm facing the mat, my body hovering over hers. I lower myself and lick from the top of her arse, up her spine, until I get to her bra strap.

"You're cheating," she says.

"We're both cheating." I undo her bra with my teeth. "Right leg yellow," I say, even though I've not touched the spinner. She looks over her shoulder and then complies. "Left leg blue."

"It's not your turn!" she complains.

"Oh believe me," I say. "You'll get your turn."

She follows my instructions so she's in an awkward downward dog position, and I stand.

Because Twister's over.

I stand behind her and reach underneath, cupping her breasts, as I grind into her.

I strip out of my boxers and reach under the lace of her underwear.

She's slick with need for me and it makes me hungry.

I fall to my knees and pull her underwear to one side. I can't help but notice the darkened material where she's got them wet.

Just from a couple of moves of Twister.

"Games get you hot, I see," I say.

"You," she replies. "You get me hot."

I groan, flatten my tongue and press against her folds, pushing down to and against her clit. God, she's delicious from this angle.

Her knees buckle and I pause while she gets back into position. She wants more.

And so do I.

I plunge my tongue into her and she cries out. From here, I can use both my hands, one spanning her arse as my thumb replaces my tongue, the other stretched over her stomach as my thumb works her clit. My tongue fills the space in between, lapping up her wetness as if she's my last meal. Fingers replace thumbs and I go deeper and harder, and she bucks and moans and struggles to keep herself in place.

"Oh god. I'm—" Her knees collapse onto the mat, and I crouch behind her, my fingers pulling her orgasm from her, my arm around her waist keeping her from falling farther.

She shudders around my hand and collapses in my lap.

I'm so hard that just the pressure of her arse against my shaft might tip me over the edge. Carefully, I move, arranging her on all fours, taking her underwear off before I kneel behind her.

She's perfect.

"You ready?" I ask.

Her breathing hasn't quite recovered, but I can't hold back any longer. Thank god, she nods.

I hook my hands on her hips and slowly, so slowly, because anything else would be the end, I push into her.

"Fuck," I bite out. She always feels ten times better than I expect her to, and I always expect her to feel ten times better than I've ever felt before.

She's so fucking wet, her juice is running down her inner thigh.

Could she be any more delectable?

I run my hand up her leg to collect it and when I withdraw, I circle my cock, not that we need any more lubrication. I just want all of it. All of her.

I thrust in again, and the movement makes her breasts jolt and jerk underneath her and it's torture. I want them in my hands. In my mouth. I want her everywhere. All at once. All the time.

"You're so fucking sexy," I growl.

I piston my hips in and out of her and she whimpers underneath me. I'm not sure if it's the change of location, the Twister mat or the fact that it's been a whole eight hours since we last had sex, but I'm desperate for her.

"Beau," she calls out as I slam into her again.

"I'm so fucking hard, Vivian. Can you feel that? My balls are so fucking full."

She tightens around me and I groan. I'm not sure if she did it on purpose but it's beautiful torture.

I don't want to come before her. I'll try everything not to, but I'm holding on by a thread.

I hook my hand underneath her, pressing my palm wide, stretching from hip bone to hip bone. Her orgasm is going to be fast, but it's going to be good.

I press my hand harder against her and she screams, her legs start to shake and she falls forward so her head is resting on the ground.

Fuck.

Her entire body convulses in my hand and I don't know if it's the thought that I get to fuck this woman for the rest of my life or the fact that within a few weeks, I'm going to get to call her my wife, or even the sheer bliss that being with her brings me every day, but I can't wait a second longer.

I close my eyes, lights flare behind my lids, heat streaks from my chest and I explode into her.

Vivian

A Month Later

I'm sitting in my glam chair, facing a view of a snow-covered London. "Are we really getting married?" I ask Beau, who's standing behind me in a tux. I managed to get my way on that. I always want to climb Beau like a tree, but in a tux, he's six-star hot. Much better than those weird suits the British usually wear to their weddings.

"I'm pretty sure today's the day. It definitely said Christmas Eve on the invitations," he says, turning to me and lifting up either end of his bow tie. "I can't get it to look right."

"I'll do it," Tommy says, racing toward Beau. "I'm a pro."

"But can you tie a bow tie?" Beau asks, chuckling.

"It's a good thing I like you so much," Tommy says. "I don't think it's tradition on either side of the Atlantic for the Man of Honor to get into a fight with the groom."

Dax comes through the door of the hotel suite at the Dorchester, where we're getting married, looking immaculate as always.

"Who did your bow tie?" Beau asks.

He shoots Beau a look that says *you're an idiot.* "I did, of course."

Tommy does Beau's bow tie perfectly on the first try. "There," he says.

"Wow," Beau says. "Looks good. Where is everyone, Dax?"

"Waiting for you," he says. "Both of you."

"I'm nearly ready, right?" I ask the people flitting in front of me.

"Ten minutes," they chorus.

"Are you two supposed to be in the same room before the ceremony?" Dax says.

"Would never have taken you for a stickler for tradition."

"I guess whatever floats your boat."

"I'm excited to marry Beau," I say. "And I want to share that with him. I don't see why I shouldn't spend as much time as possible with my favorite human on my wedding day."

"When you put it like that," Dax says, "it's logical."

I laugh. "Exactly. And logic is the reason we're all here on Christmas Eve." It was the only date we could do this year that everyone we loved could make. I didn't want to spend another Christmas, or another New Year's, not being married to Beau.

"I'm excited for my first Cove Christmas," I say.

"It's going to be weird this year," Beau says. "All of us here and not in the kitchen peeling potatoes with Dad screaming at Dog."

"But at least you can spend it with Vivian's family?" Dax says.

My family are staying into the new year. Although they've all met Beau before, we haven't spent much time together.

"It's only for one year," I say. "Until they've finished the work on the house."

John was persuaded to build a larger house on the grounds of their current house, and the current house will serve as a guest house for extended family who need a little separation from the Cove chaos, like my parents. This year, we're all staying at the hotel, along with Madison's mom, Kate's granny, and various other family members and friends.

"And this year I get to celebrate Boxing Day," I say excitedly.

Beau smiles. "You need to manage your expectations on that front. Boxing Day isn't...well, what is it?" He turns to Dax.

"The day after Christmas Day?" Dax suggests.

"We usually just go for a walk and then eat leftovers. Play board games."

Beau and I share a look. Where would we be without board games?

"Sounds like my perfect day," I say.

"Apart from today, right?" Beau says, laughing.

I grin. "Well let's see. It's time for me to get into my dress."

Beau presses a kiss to my lips. "I'll see you down there. Ready for the beginning of the rest of our lives."

"Can't wait," I reply as my makeup artist reapplies my lipstick.

This morning has been chaotic and joyful and just about as perfect as a wedding morning could be. I have a feeling that's what life has in store for me from now on. A beautiful, joyful life with a fake fiancé I almost never met—and almost never married.

TO READ Dax's story read **Dr. Single Dad**

CLICK NOW!

Jacob and Sutton **Dr. Off Limits**

Zach and Ellie **Dr. Perfect**

Beau and Vivian **Dr. Fake Fiancé**

Nathan and Madison **Private Player**

FOR MORE OF **Beau and Vivian, sign up to my newsletter for BONUS scenes www.louisebay.-com/newsletter**

BOOKS BY LOUISE BAY

All books are stand alone

The Doctors Series

Dr. Off Limits

Dr. Perfect

Dr. CEO

Dr. Fake Fiancé

Dr. Single Dad

The Mister Series

Mr. Mayfair

Mr. Knightsbridge

Mr. Smithfield

Mr. Park Lane

Mr. Bloomsbury

Mr. Notting Hill

The Christmas Collection

14 Days of Christmas

The Player Series

International Player

Private Player

Dr. Off Limits

Standalones

Hollywood Scandal

Love Unexpected

Hopeful

The Empire State Series

The Gentleman Series

The Ruthless Gentleman

The Wrong Gentleman

The Royals Series

King of Wall Street

Park Avenue Prince

Duke of Manhattan

The British Knight

The Earl of London

The Nights Series

Indigo Nights

Promised Nights

Parisian Nights

Faithful

What kind of books do you like?

Friends to lovers

Mr. Mayfair

Promised Nights

International Player

Fake relationship (marriage of convenience)

Duke of Manhattan

Mr. Mayfair

Mr. Notting Hill

Enemies to Lovers

King of Wall Street

The British Knight

The Earl of London

Hollywood Scandal

Parisian Nights

14 Days of Christmas

Mr. Bloomsbury

Office Romance/ Workplace romance

Mr. Knightsbridge

King of Wall Street

The British Knight

The Ruthless Gentleman

Mr. Bloomsbury

Dr. Perfect

Dr. Off Limits

Dr. CEO

Second Chance

International Player

Hopeful

Best Friend's Brother

Promised Nights

Vacation/Holiday Romance

The Empire State Series

Indigo Nights

The Ruthless Gentleman

The Wrong Gentleman

Love Unexpected

14 Days of Christmas

Holiday/Christmas Romance

14 Days of Christmas

British Hero

Promised Nights (British heroine)

Indigo Nights (American heroine)

Hopeful (British heroine)

Duke of Manhattan (American heroine)

The British Knight (American heroine)

The Earl of London (British heroine)

The Wrong Gentleman (American heroine)

The Ruthless Gentleman (American heroine)

International Player (British heroine)

Mr. Mayfair (British heroine)

Mr. Knightsbridge (American heroine)

Mr. Smithfield (American heroine)

Private Player (British heroine)

Mr. Bloomsbury (American heroine)

14 Days of Christmas (British heroine)

Mr. Notting Hill (British heroine)

Dr. Off Limits (British heroine)

Dr. Perfect (British heroine)

Dr. Fake Fiancé (American heroine)

Dr. Single Dad (British heroine)

Single Dad

King of Wall Street

Mr. Smithfield

Sign up to the Louise Bay mailing list www.louisebay/newsletter

Read more at www.louisebay.com

Made in the USA
Las Vegas, NV
07 November 2023

80372700R00177